BN

The Power
of Dreams

Also by Rosie Harris

Turn of the Tide
Troubled Waters
Patsy of Paradise Place
One Step Forward
Looking for Love
Pins & Needles
Winnie of the Waterfront
At Sixes & Sevens
The Cobbler's Kids
Sunshine and Showers
Megan of Merseyside

Rosie Harris

The Power of Dreams

WILLIAM HEINEMANN : LONDON

First published in the United Kingdom in 2006 by William Heinemann

3 5 7 9 10 8 6 4 2

William Heinemann
The Random House Group Limited
20 Vauxhall Bridge Road, London, SW1V 2SA

Random House Australia (Pty) Limited
20 Alfred Street, Milsons Point, Sydney, New South Wales 2061, Australia

Random House New Zealand Limited
18 Poland Road, Glenfield
Auckland 10, New Zealand

Random House (Pty) Limited
Isle of Houghton, Corner of Boundary Road & Carse O'Gowrie
Houghton 2198, South Africa

Random House Publishers India Private Limited
301 World Trade Tower, Hotel Intercontinental Grand Complex
Barakhamba Lane, New Delhi 110 001, India

The Random House Group Limited Reg. No. 954009

www.randomhouse.co.uk

A CIP catalogue record for this book is
available from the British Library

Papers used by Random House
are natural, recyclable products made from wood grown in
sustainable forests. The manufacturing processes conform to
the environmental regulations of the country of origin

ISBN 9780434013449 (from Jan 2007)
ISBN 0 434 01344 7

Palimpsest Book Production Ltd, Grangemouth, Stirlingshire
Printed and bound in the United Kingdom by
Mackays of Chatham plc, Chatham, Kent

For Susie and Simon; Michele and Brad
with love

Acknowledgements

A big thank you to Georgina Hawtrey-Woore and the rest of the wonderfully supportive team at Heinemann/Arrow, and also to Caroline Sheldon of the Caroline Sheldon Literary Agency.

Chapter One

Cwmglo, September 1919

As an explosion shook the narrow, terraced house in Back Street, Cwmglo, sixteen-year-old Merrion Roberts clapped a hand over her mouth to muffle her scream. The baby in the home-made wooden cradle set beside the fire wakened and let out a thin, fretful cry, like the mewling of a frightened kitten.

Merrion picked up her baby sister, not yet a day old, and cradled the infant tenderly in her arms, crooning softly as she tried to rock her back to sleep.

The careworn woman dozing in the wooden armchair facing the fire, her feet resting on the polished steel fender, jerked awake. As her scant eyebrows knotted into a frown, her small brown eyes almost disappeared into her sagging, pudgy face.

'I thought I heard a crash,' she yawned, scratching between the rolls of fat around her waist. 'What happened? Have you dropped something, Merri?'

'Some plates fell off the dresser, Mam. They're all smashed to smithereens. I didn't touch them, though. The whole house shook . . .'

Their dark eyes met, an unspoken fear uniting them like a magnet.

'Frightened this poor little dab almost out of her life,' Merrion said softly, looking down at the squalling bundle in her arms, and rocking her to and fro even more energetically.

'You'd better give her here then, Merri, there's only one thing that'll quieten her down now,' Lora Roberts sighed.

'Shall I nip out and see if anyone knows what's happened?' Merrion asked as, very gently, she transferred the baby into her mother's arms. 'It must have been something at the pit – though it seemed almost like an earthquake!'

Lora Roberts nodded uneasily. Her squat, shapeless body sagged dejectedly as she unbuttoned the front of her dress, releasing one of her engorged breasts, and settled the baby to suckle on the distended nipple.

'Dada says the seam where they're working now runs right underneath this house . . .' Merrion's voice trailed off. Her expressive dark eyes widened in horror as her imagination painted a scene she daren't express in words.

'Oh, our Mam!' she gulped, pushing her dark hair behind her ears, and looking uncertain of what to do next. Her shabby grey serge dress, hiding her budding figure, added to her forlorn, dejected air. The one redeeming feature was the intelligence that shone from the big dark eyes that dominated her sombre oval face, framed by straight, brown hair.

2

'Well, don't stand there gawping! Go and see what's happening!' shrilled her mother.

The baby, frightened by the strident sound, and sensing the latent fear, released its hold on the breast and added its own pitiful little wail. Milk spurted in a bluish, white stream, spraying the front of the woman's dress and leaving a snail trail of damp patches.

'Duw! Now look what you've done,' she grumbled, with a look of reproach at Merrion.

Irritably, she pushed the baby's face back on to her breast, holding it firmly in place until the child was sucking once more. Rocking backwards and forwards, she stared fixedly into the fire, refusing to admit, even to herself, that the explosion must have come from the pit where her husband worked.

Through the open door she could hear raised voices, confused, anxious voices, as women gathered in the street outside, seeking news, and exchanging opinions about what had just happened.

All of the families living in Back Street, Cwmglo had a husband, or a child, or even both working at the colliery.

'It was the pit, our Mam!' Merrion hesitated in the doorway, her face ashen, her brown eyes wary. 'I'll go and see if I can find out what's happened, shall I? D'you want to come as well?'

'Don't talk so daft, girl! I'm in no fit state to go traipsing the streets, now am I?' her mother snapped petulantly. 'One day out of childbed

3

and you expect me to drag myself to the pit! Show some sense for once, can't you, Merri. Get a move on then, girl, if you're going. Find out what's happened and come straight back and let me know.'

'Are you sure that you'll be all right left here on your own? Shall I call our Madoc to come in? He's only playing outside in the road.'

The look of scorn on her mother's face cut short Merrion's words. She hesitated a moment longer, wondering if she ought to leave her mother alone. She'd not be gone long, she told herself. There'd be no need for her mam to even move out of her chair. She'd be back again in no time, probably before Mam had finished feeding the baby.

Snatching up the black shawl lying on the table, Merrion wrapped it round her thin shoulders and, without another word, left the house.

September sun dappled the rows of grimy back-to-back houses as she mingled with the women clustered in the roadway. Not only their house, but most of Back Street was right over the seam where her father's team worked, she reflected. The houses looked like a row of dominoes, the windows and doors shining spots against the soot-grimed fronts. If one fell down the rest would collapse like a pack of cards.

'Your dada's not at work, is he, cariad?'

'Indeed he is, Mrs Probert,' Merrion assured the middle-aged woman who was standing on her step a few doors away.

4

'Daro! I heard he'd stayed at home to look after your mam.'

'Only for one shift.'

'Duw!' Mrs Probert's face screwed up with sympathy. 'Your mam's sent you to get some news, has she, then?'

'Yes, she has. I'm going up to the pit now. Is anyone else going to come along?'

Merrion looked hopefully at the group of women. They were all older than her. Some of them carried babies, enveloped close to their bodies by a shawl or piece of blanket, while others had toddlers clutching at their skirts.

'Hang on a minute, Merri Roberts, and I'll come along with you,' one of the younger women offered. 'Let me find someone to keep an eye on my little Mostyn.'

Merrion sat on one of the narrow stone window ledges to wait. Ellyn Jones snatched up a very small child from where it was playing in a puddle in the roadway, and disappeared into one of the houses.

She liked Ellyn. She envied her, too. Ellyn was only nineteen, three years older than she was yet Ellyn had been married for over two years. Merrion sighed. It wasn't surprising really. Ellyn was so pretty: plump, with a round, merry face and curly brown hair. It was the sort of face and figure Merrion imagined her own mother must have had when she was their age. It wasn't fair, really, she thought, as she kicked at the wall with the heel of her boot. Both

Emlyn, who was fourteen, and Madoc, who was only five, took after their mam, so why did she have to be tall and skinny like their dada?

'Sounded pretty bad, didn't it?' Ellyn said worriedly when she rejoined Merrion. 'My Benji's down there. Another week and I'd have been back at work as well.'

'I thought you said that you were going to stay at home and look after Mostyn until it was time for him to go to school,' Merrion said in surprise.

'I was, but now Mostyn is almost two I can get him looked after easy enough and we need the money, see. We can't go on living with my mam much longer.'

'Why's that, then?'

'Packed in we are, like hens on a roost. Benji, me and little Mostyn have only got a curtained-off half of our Jinny's bedroom.'

'Number ten is coming empty.'

'Really! Old Granfer Thomas's not dead, is he?'

'No, but he's moving out. He's going to live with his son over at Govilion, so I've heard.'

'There's nice it would be!' she sighed. 'I only wish we could afford the rent of his place!'

'You could always let out a couple of rooms. Don't forget Betsy James is getting married next month to Harri Pickering and so they'll be wanting somewhere to live.'

'Even then I don't think we could afford it. Anyway, we'll see. Bad luck to make plans.

6

Fate always steps in and ruins them. Like this explosion that's happened today,' she added gloomily.

'There mightn't be anyone hurt,' Merrion said hopefully.

'Daro! There's daft you talk, girl. Have you ever known of an explosion when someone wasn't killed or maimed?'

Merrion didn't answer. Guilt drove every other thought from her mind. If her dada had been hurt in the explosion then it was all her fault. If he hadn't had to change shifts last night because Flossie Price had sent for him when Mam had started with the baby, he wouldn't be down there now.

She should have been there to help look after her mam when she went into labour. She'd known Mam was near her time because she'd been having twinges, and bad backache, for several days. She ought to have been there. Instead, she'd been with Roddi Jenkins and they'd been so engrossed in each other's company that they'd forgotten all about the time. They'd stayed kissing and cuddling until it was dark and the stars were out and the moon riding high. Then it had been guilt about her mam that had made her insist it was time for her to go home, even though Roddi wanted her to stay out a bit longer.

She was in love with Roddi. He was so good-looking, tall and broad, with dark red wavy hair, hazel eyes. He had a voice like honey that made her heart beat faster every time he spoke to her. He had a very determined square-jawed face and a strong character, too. He'd refused to go down the pit like his brothers. Instead he'd taken a job as a groom at Pennowen.

When they were on their own he talked to her about his longings and dreams for the future. Although Roddi loved animals, looking after them was not what he wanted to do for the rest of his life. One day, he avowed, a faraway look on his face, he intended to go to sea.

His hazel eyes mesmerised her, and whenever he confided in her she felt all shaky inside. When he took her in his arms and kissed her she could hear her own heart thudding. She tried not to dwell on what they did after that because she knew it was wrong. If her mam or dad ever found out they'd stop her from seeing Roddi again and that would break her heart.

Being married to Roddi had featured high in her dreams ever since she was ten years old and he had told her he was going to marry her when they were old enough. His talk about going to sea worried her greatly, though. She couldn't bear the thought of being parted from him for months at a time.

By the time she'd reached home Flossie Price was coming out of their house and she began to feel guilty. Flossie was enveloped in the striped apron that covered her from chin to

8

ankle which she always wore when she attended a birthing,

'Where've you been, girl? You must have known your mam was near her time,' Flossie had bawled at her.

'She isn't all on her own, is she?' Merrion had asked uneasily. 'Is my dada at work?'

'No! I sent your Uncle Huw to fetch your dada home. Your Madoc's a couple of doors up at Polly James's house. Polly said he can bed down with her young Darri tonight.'

'What's my mam got this time, then, Mrs Price?'

'It's a little girl, Merrion, and your mam's had a long hard time, so get along inside and see what you can do to help. Why you weren't here when she had it is beyond me. Disgraceful, I call it. Out with that Roddi Jenkins, I suppose, if I know anything at all about it.'

Merrion had tried to shut her ears to Flossie Price's tirade, but the words had stung. What was more, they'd gone on ringing in her head even after she fell asleep.

She'd had troubled dreams all night – or rather, nightmares. She'd been trying to drag a loaded coal truck up an incline, only it wouldn't budge. Then suddenly the truck had taken on a life of its own and come thundering after her. She'd had to run, and run, because she knew that if she stopped the clanking metal wheels would go right over her.

She'd been in a cold sweat when she'd

wakened, afraid that the horrible dream was some sort of warning; frightened out of her wits in case it meant Fate intended to punish her, and now there'd been an explosion in the pit where her dada was working.

'Sometimes I think those who are killed outright when there's a pit accident are the ones who are best off,' she burst out as they walked towards the pit, 'especially when it's a man with a family to support.'

'What on earth are you talking about, Merrion? I don't understand, whatever do you mean?' Ellyn gasped in a shocked voice.

'Well, if he's badly injured, then he might be laid up for months and not be able to work. Fancy having to pawn your belongings to pay the rent or having to rely on friends and neighbours for bread and handouts to feed you and your family,' she babbled.

'May God forgive you, Merrion Roberts! What terrible things you're coming out with and no mistake,' exclaimed Ellyn, the colour draining from her round cheeks.

'Well, it's the truth and all your protests won't make a scrap of difference,' Merrion declared, her chin up defiantly.

She knew she'd shocked Ellyn, she'd even frightened herself with her wild statement, but she wasn't going to admit it.

'If your da's one of those who's been injured then you'll just have to accept it, and learn to live with it, cariad,' Ellyn Jones said gently, her plump hand resting on Merrion's thin arm. 'And I'll have to do the same, see, if my Benji's been hurt.'

Merrion's mouth trembled. She shook off Ellyn's comforting hand and stared straight ahead, clenching her teeth together and blinking hard to stop herself crying.

Silently, she promised herself that if her dada was all right then she'd change her ways. No more gallivanting off to be with Roddi Jenkins! She'd spend every spare minute she had helping out at home to try and make things a bit easier for her mam. She'd even make sure that five-year-old Madoc was not only on time but clean and tidy when he went off to school each morning, and that he went to Sunday school each week.

They walked on towards the pithead in awkward silence. She wondered if Ellyn was still shocked by her outburst. She glanced at her sideways and saw that Ellyn was looking as prim, and starchy, as someone twice her age.

The houses seemed to march with them like one-legged soldiers. She counted the scrubbed front steps that gleamed like sentinels. There were one hundred of them in all. Her breath was coming more quickly by the time they reached the top and Ellyn Jones was puffing like a pit pony.

As they neared the pit entrance a number of other anxious women joined them from the houses they passed. In the fading light they

11

looked ghostly with their white pinnies over their dark dresses, and their woollen shawls around their shoulders.

Merrion answered their many questions about her mother and the new baby automatically, but the closer they came to the pit gates the more churned up her insides felt. If her dada had been injured then it was all her fault. He should have been the one to stay home with Mam and the new baby, and he would have done if she hadn't begged to be allowed to do so. It had been her way of trying to make up to her mam for not being there the night before and now look what had happened.

As they trudged up the deeply rutted track towards the long low building that served as an office, Merrion's heart sank even more. Lowering clouds had massed over the top of the mountain obscuring the patchy September sun, and turning the sky as grey as her mood.

Chapter Two

Men of all ages were gathered in the yard at the pithead. Shoulders hunched, their hands thrust deep into their trouser pockets, they shuffled their feet impatiently. Scarred, coal-streaked faces were set in grim lines and their dark, Celtic eyes had a worried, haunted look as they waited in silence for the inevitable words of doom.

'What happened, then? Does anyone know? We heard the explosion in Back Street,' Ellyn Jones commented.

'And felt it!' Merrion chipped in.

'There's been a cave-in. We're still waiting for news,' one of the men told them.

'Bad like, is it?' asked Ellyn anxiously, pulling her shawl tighter around her shoulders.

The man nodded, then he stared hard at Merrion, pushing back his greasy cap and scratching his head. 'You're Bryn Roberts's girl, aren't you?' He frowned. 'Still growing, I see. So tall now that for a moment I didn't recognise you! So how's your mam, then?'

'Fair to middling, Mr Pope. She had another babba, last night.'

'So your Uncle Huw told me. I understood

he came and told your dad that he was needed at home?'

'It was only for the one night – while Mam was having it. He came back to work this morning.'

'And you stayed home instead?' Gareth Pope asked.

'Yes, that's right.' Her voice dropped to a strained croak. 'My dada . . . have you seen him . . . or is he . . . ?'

'No need to start worrying,' Dai Williams, one of the older men, said quickly, patting Merrion's shoulder.

'A lot of them have stayed down to help with the rescue work, see,' one of the other men butted in, turning to his companions for confirmation.

'Do they know who's trapped, then? Have they given out any names?' Ellyn asked worriedly.

'Give them a chance, girl!'

'It's only just blown!' Dai Williams pointed out.

'Daro! The boss-men are still scurrying around the place like a bunch of scalded cats.'

'Half of them don't know if they're on their ass or their elbow and you ask if they've given out names?' Gareth Pope added scathingly.

'They won't know for certain who's trapped down there until they've moved some of the rubble,' Dai agreed, pushing back his cap and scratching his head.

'There's bound to be casualties, mun, it's a gallery roof that's caved in!' a burly chap added.

'Everything rocked in Back Street,' Merrion told them. 'It felt as if it was happening right under my feet. Dada said the seam where he's working runs beneath our house,' she gabbled on.

'Daro! I can see why your mam sent you down here,' one of the men commented sourly. He spat ferociously on to the ground and then rubbed the back of his hand across his mouth. 'A right little comforter you'd be to have around the place talking like that,' he muttered moving away, his mouth pursed up into a silent whistle.

'Dada wouldn't have come to work today if I hadn't stayed home to look after our mam,' Merrion muttered defensively.

'Come on now, look on the bright side, my little flower.' Dai Williams smiled reassuringly. 'It's much too soon for any of us to start worrying, see!' he added.

'I know.' Even as she spoke a shiver raised goosebumps all down her arms. Her guilt was now choking her. If anything had happened to her father then Mam was bound to say that it was all her fault. If she hadn't been so keen to stay at home then he would have done so, even though he hated anything domestic. She'd felt so scared, after her bad dream, that she'd jumped at the chance of a day off. Anyway, if she'd refused, Mam would only have started on at him.

15

'It's your babba, Bryn Roberts, as much as it's mine, remember,' she'd kept telling him all the time she was carrying. 'A little one needs a dada as well as a mammy.'

'I'll play my part, cariad,' he'd assured her. 'I'm still not too old to take it up over Coity or along the Canal bank same as I did the other three. Regular as clockwork I walked with them, so they could get a breath of fresh air in their lungs,' he'd added, puffing out his chest.

'Jawch! and then hang round the Navigation, or the Lamb and Flag, while you down pints of ale with your brother Huw and his cronies,' she'd retorted sharply.

'We were taking a breather, that's all.'

'Well, that might have been all right with Emlyn and Madoc, but it won't do if this one's a girl. I'm having no daughter of mine kicking her heels outside a public house and having her ears filled with the sort of ribald talk that goes on between men when they're supping beer.'

'Never did our Merrion much harm,' he'd responded.

'You've always treated her more like a boy than a girl,' she'd snapped back. 'You'd have let her stay on at school if you'd been let have your way even though we needed whatever pittance she could earn.'

'Well, that might have been so, but things are going to be much easier now. With both our Emlyn and Merrion working, and only young

16

Madoc to provide for then this one can go to school for as long as it likes providing it has the brains for it,' he'd promised.

Merrion's eyes misted as she thought of the way her dada always stuck up for her against Mam. He'd always been the one she ran to when she was in trouble, and he'd give her a quick hug, or a kiss, and make her feel better. Never to her mam, though. Mam seemed always to be busy with the others. And they'd been boys. Mam seemed to like boys the best.

Perhaps if she'd been pretty, with plump, rosy cheeks and curls down to her shoulders, her mother would have favoured her more. Instead, she'd always been as skinny as a rabbit with dead straight hair and eyes that were too big for her face.

And she'd been clumsy. Always bumping into things, tripping over and dropping things. Her mam said she was either careless or that she did it on purpose, but it only happened when her mam was shouting at her to do something. That was when she came over all clumsy, which only made her mam bawl at her all the louder.

If Dada was around he'd always put a stop to it.

'You'll make our Merrion into a bag of nerves by yelling at her so much,' he'd warn.

'If I don't shout then she takes no notice. Lost in one of her dreams most of the time. Or deaf!'

'Of course the girl's not deaf!'

'Then she's lazy! I've only one pair of hands and all of you to look after, so why can't she help out? It's time she learned that a home doesn't run itself. How on earth is she ever going to manage when she's married and with a family of her own to look after?'

'Lora! That'll do! Hold your tongue, woman, and stop taking your temper out on the child.'

Then, giving Merrion a quick hug, he'd whisper, 'Take no notice, cariad, it's just your mam's way.'

And now he was trapped. She was quite sure of that. He might never be able to stand up for her again; never have the chance to walk up over Coity or Blorenge with the new baby on his shoulder, like he'd carried the rest of them when they were small.

Who would take his place for this baby? she wondered.

It wouldn't be Emlyn, as he was rarely at home. And it couldn't be Madoc, since he was little more than a baby himself.

That left only her!

Minutes stretched like elastic into hours as they went on waiting. Her body was chilled through, her feet became numb, yet the flicker of hope refused to be douched.

Deep in her heart, and in her very bones, Merrion felt sure that her father was dead. Yet, as she stood there with the ever-growing crowd of miners and their families, she continued to hope.

18

Each time the cage came juddering up from the dark abyss, screeching to a stop as it reached ground level, her heart raced. As coal-grimed figures staggered out of it, coughing and spluttering and gasping for fresh air, she craned her neck to see over the heads of those in front of her, ears straining as names were called out in greeting.

But it was never Bryn Roberts.

Those survivors who could manage to stand upright, stumbled away on the arms of their friends or relatives, back to their homes. Benji Jones was amongst them and the radiant look of love and relief on Ellyn's face brought a lump to Merrion's throat.

Only after they'd washed away the grimy sweat would the men know the full extent of their cuts and injuries. And when these had been bathed and attended to, they would celebrate their safe deliverance and mourn for the workmates whom they knew would never come out alive.

Those who were badly injured, with broken bones and crushed limbs, were piled into an open cart and dispatched to hospital. Their mental anguish at knowing that one of their legs, or arms, would be amputated was far greater than any pain they would suffer at the surgeon's hands, since, for most of them, it meant the loss of their job in the pit.

Forty men were brought to the surface, yet still the name Bryn Roberts had not been called out. None of the survivors even worked along-side her dada.

The grinding cage groaned once more to the top. This time no one walked out when the gate opened. There were uneasy whispers as two bodies were lifted out and laid on the ground.

'Who is it, then?' Merrion asked fearfully of the woman who was standing at her side.

'Tomos Davies and Dic Panto.'

'Are you sure?' Merrion asked in a voice that shook.

'Yes, cariad.' The woman's tone softened. 'They both worked alongside your dad, didn't they?'

Merrion nodded, unable to speak.

She chewed on her lower lip, trying to concentrate every vestige of her thoughts on Tomos Davies. He was a giant of a man; six foot two in his socks, so it was said. He had shoulders broad enough to hold up a roof, her father claimed. This time they hadn't, though.

She rubbed the back of her hand across her eyes, then her attention became focused on an altercation near the cage. Llewellyn Morgan, the pit manager, a wiry looking man in his late forties, stood there facing the crowd and he was holding his arms wide, as if in despair.

He had only recently been put in charge, but his bowed shoulders and sallow complexion told their own story of the many years he'd spent working underground at the coal face.

'I can't do another bloody thing until one of

the owners gives the order,' he said, his voice as ominous as his deep-set dark eyes.

'Let some of us go down, then, and see if there is anything we can do,' offered one of the men.

'Out of the question! Far too dangerous, I tell you,' Llewellyn Morgan said angrily.

'For you, p'raps, y'lily-livered bugger.'

'Getting those two bodies out has almost cost Dan Davies his life,' Llewellyn Morgan retorted stubbornly. 'The fumes from the after-damp are overpowering . . .'

'Then the poor sods still trapped down there will be gassed, even if they're not injured, unless someone goes down and helps to free them,' Gareth Pope pointed out.

'It's not going down that's the problem, it's reaching them when you get there.'

'You mean because the cave-in has brought the roof down?'

'That's right!' Llewellyn Morgan nodded. 'There are any number of massive rocks and boulders blocking the way, see!'

'Give us some picks and shovels and we'll soon move a few boulders, boyo,' several of the men affirmed.

'Daro! It's not feasible, I keep telling you!' retorted Llewellyn Morgan heatedly.

'Well, we can't just leave them there!' Gareth Pope protested.

'How many are trapped?' Dai Williams asked quietly.

'My old man must be down there since you haven't brought him up,' a woman's voice shrilled out.

'Are you just going to leave him there, buried alive? You rotten swine!' yelled the woman next to her.

'Look now, Martha Watts, there's no call for abuse, that gets us nowhere,' snapped back Llewellyn Morgan. 'I've done everything that's humanly possible. No one is going to risk their lives by going down in that cage again until I get fresh orders,' he added stiffly. 'The owners have arrived and are assembled in the office, talking matters over right this very minute.'

'Talk! We don't want bloody talk, mun; we want action,' the men shouted angrily.

'All right, all right. I'm on my way in there now to hear their decision. A few more minutes . . .'

'Duw anwyl! Can't you get it into your thick skull, boyo, that every minute counts!'

'With all the fumes down there not even a canary will survive for very long!' Gareth Pope reminded him. 'We've got to do something and do it now. There's no time for chat, there're half a dozen or more men still trapped in that hell hole!'

'We can't stand by and let our mates die, trapped like bloody rats in a sewer!' agreed Dai Williams.

Llewellyn Morgan didn't answer. Hunching

22

his shoulders against the angry tirade he scurried back to the office, firmly shutting the door against the furious buzz of discontent in the yard.

Chapter Three

The mutterings grew louder. A thin drizzle of rain added to the misery of those waiting. The men turned up the collars of their threadbare jackets, wound their mufflers tighter around their throats, and pulled down the peaks of their caps to shield their faces. Women hitched their shawls higher around their shoulders, and hugged their bodies with their arms.

Merrion pushed straggles of wet hair back behind her ears and wondered what she ought to do. Mam must be out of her mind with worry by now, she thought uneasily. She'd been gone hours, and there was only young Madoc at home to fetch and carry for the baby. Yet how could she return home until she knew whether or not her dada was safe.

Her thoughts became jumbled as she tried to come to terms with what was happening. Supposing, just by chance, Dada hadn't been in that part of the pit where the explosion had taken place? He might already have gone on home, safe and sound.

There's daft you are, girl, she scolded herself. He'd still be hanging around here with the rest, anxious to do what he could to help those still trapped.

But then he'd want to let Mam know that he was safe. He'd know she'd be worried silly and he'd not want that in case it might curdle her milk and then the new babba would sicken.

If he'd gone home, though, then the moment Mam had said 'our Merri's gone to the pithead looking for you', he'd have come striding back to fetch her.

She chewed at her lower lip, wondering what to do for the best. She'd count to twenty and if Llewellyn Morgan hadn't come out of the office by then she'd run home and tell her mam that there was no news yet, and then come straight back.

When she reached twenty she still lingered. She'd wait a bit longer, she decided. She'd count up to twenty again. This time she'd do it very slowly and take a deep breath between each number. She'd reached fifteen when the office door opened and Llewellyn Morgan emerged.

A murmur ran through the waiting crowd as they waited anxiously for him to tell them what was happening.

'What are they planning on doing next, then, boyo?' Gareth Pope demanded.

'Sent you as a messenger to break the news to us, have they?' a voice sneered.

'Making you do their dirty work because they're afraid to show their faces, are they?'

Llewellyn Morgan held up his hand for

25

silence as cat-calls, boos and shouts filled the air. It was as if a signal had been sounded. One by one, men who were starting to drift away came back into the yard.

'If you're ready to listen, then the owners will explain the situation to you,' announced Llewellyn Morgan.

'We want some action, mun, not a load of bloody explanations,' someone shouted.

The cry was taken up, and angry voices and jeers filled the air as Llewellyn Morgan moved back towards the office again.

Before he reached the door it opened and an elderly black-suited man emerged.

'It's bloody Pennington himself!'

'Christ, it must be bad news!' Dai Williams exclaimed, loosening the scarf knotted around his neck.

'What's the bugger think he's doing? Why's he getting Llewellyn to move that cart?'

They watched in bewilderment as it was manhandled into place. Then the murmuring started up afresh as Llewellyn Morgan walked briskly towards them. Assertively, he began pushing those in front back until they were standing well clear of the cart.

Led by Pennington, two other well-dressed men clambered up on to the cart, arranging themselves on it as though it was a public platform. When Llewellyn Morgan joined them the mutterings from the crowd grew even more ominous.

Pennington surveyed the miners' coal-grimed, upturned faces disdainfully. It was almost as if he relished the fear he saw in their eyes.

'Men!' He held up a hand for silence. 'I've no need to go into details about what happened here today. We are as grieved as you are since it effects us all. We've done what we can to save as many lives as possible, but the following are still incarcerated.'

'Incarcerated! Darw! You mean they're bloody buried alive down there, don't you!'

'Dic Weeks; Llew Grant; Lewis Jenkins; Dai Davies; Elwyn Hughes; Bryn Roberts . . .'

Merrion felt as if the entire world was swaying, as if the sky and the ground were changing places and she was trying to balance between the two of them. She took a long, deep breath and screwed her eyes tight shut. Slowly she exhaled and opened her eyes again. The world had stopped spinning. A chorus of voices, demanding, threatening, cajoling, cursing, pounded in her ears.

'Duw anwyl!' What are you going to do about getting them out, then?'

'Let some of us get down there right now and see what we can do.'

'It's action we want not sodding speeches.'

Pennington ignored the outcry. 'The cave-in brought down the roof where these men were working,' Pennington continued, raising his voice slightly, 'so we propose to seal the gallery off. Is that clearly understood?'

27

Angry exclamations of disbelief swept through the crowd.

'Duw anwyl! You can't do that, mun! That's cold-blooded murder!'

'Some of those men trapped down there could still be alive!' Dai Williams muttered.

'You can't just leave them down there to die, you heartless buggers!'

'Entomb them without even giving any of us a chance to reach them?' Gareth Pope exclaimed in disbelief.

'Rescue is out of the question,' Pennington said pompously. 'We've already tested the air.'

'Don't talk so bloody daft, mun!'

'What is more to the point, the roof's collapsed! The explosion shifted the pit props that were holding it up!' he told them in a cold, dispassionate voice.

'There may still be pockets of fresh air beyond the boulders!' Dai Williams pointed out. There were murmurs of agreement. 'Possibly there's enough to keep them alive for hours . . . days even,' he went on.

The body of men surged forward. 'Play fair, mun! Give us the chance to try and dig them out,' Gareth Pope pleaded.

'It would take two weeks, or even more, to clear that collapsed gallery,' stated Pennington.

He paused dramatically, looking round slowly at the sea of faces and letting his words sink in. 'It would mean two weeks of work for which you would not receive a penny piece!

Remember, your earnings are based on the number of trucks of coal that pass the pithead weighbridge.'

He paused again and stared round at the shocked, unhappy faces.

'If we allowed you to clear the gallery some of you could be injured if there was another fall of rock and we can't risk any more lives. Furthermore, it would mean no coal coming to the surface – and that would mean no money for any of you!' he went on in a bland voice. 'So, in order that you may continue to earn your livelihood, we have decided to leave the bodies where they are. The collapsed section will be sealed off . . .'

Pennington got no further. The crowd seethed angrily. Fists were waved threateningly, shouts of fury filled the air. Those in front, nearest to the cart, surged forward, intent on reaching Pennington and the other owners. Llewellyn Morgan jumped down from the cart and tried to push them away, but he was thrust to one side.

Someone standing at the back of the crowd hurled a hefty lump of coal. A howl went up as it found its mark, landing in the middle of those standing on the cart. An indiscriminate barrage of shale and stones followed.

The affray became more violent by the minute. Men shouted abuse, women screamed as they were elbowed roughly out of the way. The cart was overturned. Fist fights broke out.

Miners and owners grappled with each other on the wet, slippery ground.

Merrion felt a hand grasp her arm, pulling her free of the mêlée. The next minute she found herself dragged across the yard, over bodies lying prone on the ground, until she was right away from the scuffle.

'Run for it, girl. Get back home as fast as you can,' Dai Williams yelled in her ear.

'But my dada . . . Whatever am I going to tell our mam?'

'Daro! There's nothing you need tell her . . . she's probably heard by now, so you'd best get back to her.'

'She'll blame me. He would have been safe at home if he'd had the day off and not me.'

And she was right. Lora Roberts would shout and yell and keep on reminding young Merrion of that, thought Dai Williams sadly.

'Daro! That's bad luck, girl.' He patted her shoulder clumsily. 'Don't worry, though, she'll understand,' he added with forced heartiness.

He knew only too well what Lora Roberts was like. Fat and lazy, she didn't know when she was well off. Bryn Roberts was a better man than most. A drink or two occasionally, but then, what miner didn't down a few pints on pay night?

She'd always treated young Merrion like a skivvy. Even when she'd been a mere kid Lora had expected her to help with the housework and look after her brothers. That was probably why she was so scrawny, and looked more like ten than sixteen.

'Get along with you!' Dai Williams told her roughly. 'Your mam's the one who needs comforting.' He gave her a push that sent her stumbling on her way.

As the noise of the disturbance faded into the distance, Merrion steeled herself for the ordeal to come. The crying and retribution might last for days, but it was what happened after that ended that she most dreaded. With only the pittance that she and Emlyn earned to live on, how would they manage to pay the rent?

The thought of her dada's body still lying down there in the dark dankness sent a shudder through her. It would be unbearable, knowing that. It would haunt her dreams for evermore, and she'd be listening in case he called out to her. Supposing they were right and there was a pocket of fresh air trapped inside the gallery, then he might linger for days – a week, even. How long could you live without food and water, she wondered.

Old Granfer Thomas from number ten had told her some hair-raising stories about the time when he'd been a soldier and how they'd had to go on advancing long after their rations had been exhausted. And they'd been marching! Mile after mile, they'd travelled, with packs on their backs.

If you were just squatting on your hunkers,

or lying on the ground, you'd probably live twice as long, she reasoned. Unless, of course, you were so badly injured you bled to death. That could take days and days, growing weaker and weaker all the time, until in the end you lost consciousness and became one with the blackness around you.

She began to run, glancing over her shoulder from time to time, fearful in case she saw her father's ghost. Not until she reached her own door did she stop to get her breath back and collect her thoughts.

The rain had stopped and the sky had cleared. The plaintive cry of the new baby cut through the stillness. She heard her mother speaking to Madoc, and her voice sounded so normal that Merrion knew she'd not yet heard what had happened. No one had broken the news to her.

She looked back down the street, putting off the moment when she must go indoors and tell her. One or two shawl-wrapped women stood on their doorsteps watching her, eager for details, but Merrion looked away quickly, not wanting to be drawn into an exchange of words with them. Her mind still seethed with the realisation that she would never see her dada ever again.

As she walked into the house her sense of loss turned to a feeling of desolation as she saw her father's empty chair. The sight of Madoc, standing at the side of her mam, watching in awe as the new baby was being fed, brought a lump to Merrion's throat.

'You've been gone a long time, girl!'

Merrion bit her lip to stop it trembling. With a tremendous effort she forced herself to look at her mother. The expression on her face and the anguished silence said it all. The painful details could come later.

Trembling, Merrion waited for the outburst. She felt she couldn't stand it if her mother shouted, though she feared that the more upset her mam was the louder she would yell.

The tears she'd held in check, even when Pennington had stood up on the cart and read out her father's name, suddenly welled to the surface and erupted.

Lora Roberts freed her nipple from the baby's mouth and laid her youngest back in its cradle, then she held her arms wide open, to offer comfort to her daughter.

'Oh, Mam,' Merrion gulped, staring in disbelief. She couldn't remember the last time her mother had held her close, and here she was holding out her arms like she did to Madoc when he fell over and grazed himself.

With an anguished sob, Merrion sank on to her mother's ample lap, taking refuge in the comfort afforded. They rocked together, tears mingling as Lora Roberts pushed Merrion's damp hair away from her face and kissed her on the brow.

'I'll take care of you, Mam,' Merrion vowed,

33

sitting up and brushing her eyes with the back of her hand. Her gaze lingered on her mother's pale, pudgy face and brown eyes now full of sadness. 'I'll look after you and Madoc, Mam. And the new babba as well. Emlyn will help.'

Resolutely she stood up, squaring her narrow shoulders determinedly. From now on she must be the strong one, the one who did the consoling.

'I know, cariad, I know.'

'We'll manage somehow, Mam. They're bound to let us stay on here in this house for a bit,' she stated confidently, smoothing down her crumpled skirt.

'They might, as long as we can afford to pay the rent. Perhaps if your Uncle Huw stays with us and manages to get some sort of job in the mine, things will work out.'

'When's Dada coming home?' Madoc demanded, tugging at his mother's arm.

'He won't be coming home, cariad. There's been an accident . . .'

His mouth drooped. 'You mean the big 'splosion that broke all our plates?'

'It's all right, Madoc.' Merrion picked him up in her arms as his tears spilled. 'There's nothing to get upset about. I'll take care of you and of our mam and little Dilwyn.'

She would, she vowed. She'd not only give her mam a hand with the cleaning and cooking, but she'd work and scheme to make all their lives better. And one day she'd take

34

all of them away from Back Street and its tragic memories.

At the moment, however, it was only a dream, but it was one she'd make come true. They'd move right away from the grim, shabby, coal-stained miners and the stinking pit. They'd go to live in some place where there were trees and flowers and where the grass was fresh and green; where trees blossomed; where the air was free from sulphurous fumes; and where you could see the stars shining bright every night. There'd be no more explosions to cause misery and death.

Chapter Four

They couldn't mourn, there was no body to bury in its final resting place, no funeral with a horse-drawn cortege and flowers. There was only an empty chair that would bring an ache to her heart whenever she looked at it.

It was as if the mine had simply swallowed up her dad without leaving any trace, like the monsters in her dreams, Merrion thought when she went to the pithead a few days later to ask for any wages due to her dad.

Bevan Davies, the colliery overseer, kept her waiting while he carried on an earnest conversation with Alun Weeks, the gamekeeper from the Pennowen Estates. Neither man expressed any sympathy for her loss, but bombarded her with countless questions before grudgingly handing over the few shillings that were due.

She was still recovering from an angry tirade from her mother because she had brought home such a measly amount when her Uncle Huw came bursting into the house, a look of shock and anxiety on his face.

'Have you seen Alun Weeks? Has he been here?' he asked abruptly.

'He's not been here, but he was in the pit

office when I went to collect the wages due to Dada. He and the colliery overseer asked me all sorts of stupid questions.'

Huw Roberts frowned. 'What do you mean? What were they questioning you about, my lovely?'

Merrion shook her head from side to side in bewilderment. 'I'm a bit confused. Half the time I wasn't sure what they were on about. They even wanted to know what we all had for our supper last night. Alun Weeks kept asking me if I thought that rabbit made a good hot stew.'

Huw stood clenching and unclenching his hands. 'You're sure it was him who was asking about the rabbit stew? What else did he want to know?'

Merrion shook her head. 'I'm not sure. One of them asked me if I knew what a poacher was.'

Huw frowned. 'So what did you say?'

'I said I didn't know what he was on about and he said he was talking about the rabbit!'

Huw passed a hand over his head. 'You mean he implied that the rabbit had been stolen?'

Merrion shrugged. 'He asked if our Emlyn had brought it home or if Roddi Jenkins had given it to me. I told him that you'd given it to us and that it was a present from David Pennowen himself.'

'Dammo di!' Huw Roberts's face contorted with anger. 'What the hell did you say that for?'

'It's what you told us when you brought it

home and I couldn't let them think that Roddi or our Emlyn had pinched it. They'd lose their jobs if anyone thought that they'd done something like that,' she said indignantly.

'They've lost their jobs, all right, as it is. You've put the cat amongst the pigeons this time, my lovely!'

Merrion looked startled. 'I only told the truth!'

'There isn't time to explain,' Huw Roberts said curtly. 'Start packing, girl, all of you. We've got to be out of here before the bailiff arrives to throw you out.'

'I don't understand.' she protested.

'Little Miss Innocence, aren't you, Merri?' Huw sneered. 'Surely you didn't really think that David Pennowen had given me that bloody rabbit?'

'Of course I did, I believed you! Why shouldn't I?' She frowned uneasily. 'If you weren't given it, then how did you get it?'

'I trapped it, of course, my lovely. Every time I go over there for my measly charity handout I always put down a snare somewhere along the track. Sometimes I'm lucky, sometimes not.'

'Oh no!' Merrion's hand covered her mouth in horror. 'That's cruel . . . and it's stealing.'

'Darw, you're as bad as they are! What do you mean, stealing? Filling our bellies, more likely, so what's wrong with that? The rabbits are wild. The Pennowens don't want them. I bet they've never eaten rabbit in their life, so why begrudge us a hot meal?'

'That's true enough,' Merrion admitted, 'but they don't see it like that, now do they?'

'No, and the balloon's gone up this time and no mistake. That Alun Weeks is behind it all, cariad. He's sacked Roddi Jenkins and our Emlyn. Even threatened to have the police on them even though they both said they knew nothing at all about it.'

Merrion gaped. 'Are you saying that Roddi's been sacked? That he's lost his job?'

'Too true he has. The pair of them have been given half an hour to get out.'

'So where are they . . . where is Roddi?'

'By now, with any luck, he's on the train to Cardiff and taken young Emlyn with him. They'll be safe enough there for a few days, and that's all it should take for them to find a boat and get out of the country.'

The colour drained from Merrion's face. 'You mean that they've both left Cwmglo without even saying goodbye to any of us,' she said tearfully.

'It's not their fault, cariad. If they'd hung around long enough to do that then they'd have been arrested and slammed in prison like as not.'

'Mam is upstairs having a rest; she'll be heart-broken when I tell her.'

Huw looked uneasy and avoided her eyes. 'It's not only them who's in trouble,' he said uncomfortably. 'It's our whole family. We ate the bloody thing, didn't we? So that makes us just as guilty in the eyes of the law. Now we've a matter of hours to pack up and leave here . . . the whole lot of us.'

Merrion shook her head in despair. 'Emlyn didn't trap the rabbit and Mam had no idea that it had been stolen. You're the one responsible, Uncle Huw, so how have you managed to get away?'

He ran a hand inside his muffler, easing it away from his neck. 'I know all that, my lovely, but David Pennowen interceded for me, see. He says that I've got to leave Cwmglo, though, the same as the rest of you, mind, even after all I did for him, risking my life to save his.'

Merrion's stared at him bemused, her eyes bright with unshed tears. 'So, what will we do . . . where will we go?'

'Somewhere right away from this damned place, my lovely. So pull yourself together, girl, there's no time to waste.'

'You said that Emlyn and Roddi Jenkins were going to Cardiff to try and get a ship, so where will they end up?'

Huw shrugged. 'Hell, how would I know, cariad! They said they'd take the first boat that would sign them on whether it was bound for China, Australia or America. Neither of them seemed to give a damn where it was going as long as it kept them out of prison. Emlyn says it's the sort of life he wants anyway.'

'Our mam will be distraught when she hears what he's done. It will break her heart. She's had enough turmoil over the last few days as it is.'

'For the moment she'll have too many other things to deal with to let Emlyn's departure worry her too much,' Huw said dismissively. 'You'd better call her, she's got to be out of here right away, the same as the rest of us, and that includes you as well, Merrion, so get a move on.'

'That's impossible, Uncle Huw. Mam's as weak as a kitten and in no fit state to pack up and leave her home. She's barely out of childbed!'

'I know that, my lovely. It's hard on her, but there it is. I tried to plead with them on her behalf, but it was to no avail. They wouldn't listen to a word I said, not even David Pennowen, after all I did for him, risking my life to save his. Come on, let's get started, shall we.'

Merrion hesitated. 'There's only one place we can go and that's Cardiff. Mam'll want to go there and see if she can find Emlyn before he sails for foreign lands.'

Huw shook his head disapprovingly. 'It might be better if you don't tell her what he has in mind. Tell her that he is with Roddi Jenkins so he's not on his own and that Roddi will look after him.'

'No, Uncle Huw, we must go to Cardiff and try and stop him,' Merrion said determinedly.

41

'If we don't, then poor Mam will be worried out of her mind for months, perhaps years.'

Lora Roberts looked dazed when they told her the news. She sat suckling Dilwyn, ignoring the pandemonium all around her as Merrion and Huw began packing up their belongings and making preparations to leave.

Madoc looked bemused, sucking his thumb and clinging on to his uncle's leg until Huw was forced to shout at Lora to keep hold of him so that he could get on or the police would be there before they managed to get away.

'Where will we stay when we get to Cardiff?' Merrion fretted. 'We know no one there. I've never even been there though I think Mam has once, a long time ago. She said it was a terribly bustling sort of place with huge shops and trams clanging up and down the streets one after another. She was frightened out of her wits with all the noise and people.'

'Well, you'll be there shortly, so you can decide for yourself if it is as frightening as your mother said it was.'

'Do you really think it is the best place for us to go?' Merrion persisted worriedly.

Huw shrugged. 'The bigger the place and the more people there are then the more difficult it will be for David Pennowen's minions, or the police, to find us.' He grinned.

'They won't really attempt to find us, will they?' she asked anxiously.

42

'Like as not. The charge of stealing from the Pennowen Estate is a crime they're not likely to overlook.'

Merrion frowned. 'But it's you who's the culprit. You are the one who told lies and let us think that the rabbit had been given to you by David Pennowen. You've broken the trust he placed in you. Has he really been giving you money each week as you claim?'

Huw laughed bitterly. 'Oh yes, he's dibbed up. Hush money because of the things I'd seen go on when I was his batman. He'll be more than pleased to see the back of me and to know that I'm out of his life for good.'

They packed as many of their possessions as they could manage into two battered old suitcases and a large carpetbag and were ready to leave before Lora fully realised what was happening.

'What are you doing? We can't leave here,' she protested, grappling at one of the cases and trying to prise it out of Merrion's hands. 'I've lived here all my life. Born and bred in Cwmglo, grew up here, married here, and all my children have been born here, so why should I move away now?'

'We've been turned out, that's why, Lora,' Huw told her bluntly. 'We have to leave right away. Come on, you carry little Dilwyn and we'll take care of everything else.'

'No!' she shook her head stubbornly. 'It's not

right. I'm not leaving here. Where's our Emlyn? What will he think when he comes home and finds the place empty and us up and gone without a word to him?'

'Emlyn has already gone on ahead,' Huw told her.

Lora looked puzzled. 'Gone ahead? Gone where? What are you talking about? Emlyn's at work up at Pennowen.'

'Not any longer, Lora. We've been telling you about what's happened, but you haven't been listening. He's been sacked and that's why we've got to leave here.'

'We're going to Cardiff, Mam. All of us,' Merrion told her patiently.

'And our Emlyn? Did you mean he's already gone there, Merrion?'

'That's right. He has gone on ahead.' She smiled encouragingly. 'He'll be there by now and he'll be wondering where we are. Come on, let's get a move on or we'll miss the train.'

Lora opened her mouth to speak then closed it again. She looked terribly dazed, and Merrion's heart ached, but she knew there was no time to pander to her mother.

'Look, you take the shopping bag, Mam, and hold Madoc's hand. Uncle Huw will bring the two big cases and I'll carry Dilwyn and the carpetbag with all the baby's bits and pieces in it. Come on, let's move.'

She wound a big Welsh blanket round her own body and then around Dilwyn so that the

44

child was safely cocooned and resting close to her body.

Straggling one behind the other, with Huw leading the way, they headed for the railway station. Huw bought the tickets and they huddled in a silent, nervous bunch until the train arrived.

Madoc was wide-eyed with wonder as it came steaming alongside the platform. The moment they had boarded he curled up against his mam and was asleep almost before they'd pulled out of the station.

'So where are we going to stay when we get to Cardiff, then, Huw?' Lora asked.

'Don't worry, we'll find somewhere, cariad,' he told her confidently. 'Have a bit of a nap, why don't you, while you've got the chance. I'll look after you; it's what Bryn would have expected me to do.'

When she saw her mam's head droop on to her chest and heard her breathing become slow and regular, Merrion looked at her uncle enquiringly. 'Well, what have you in mind? Staying in a top hotel, is it?' she asked sarcastically.

'No, it will have to be a bloody doss house somewhere,' he muttered.

'Where? We don't know anything about Cardiff, so where will we start looking?'

'When we reach there you lot hang on in the station waiting room and I'll scout around and find a bed and breakfast place somewhere for us to stay in,' he told her.

'Can we afford it?'

'For one night. Tomorrow we'll look for a couple of rooms to rent. We'll be OK, cariad,' he told her confidently. 'You and me will have to get work as quickly as we can, mind.'

'What sort of work?'

'Whatever we can manage to find, of course.' He scowled. 'Stop being so sodding difficult, Merri. There's plenty of jobs you can do. There's shops and market stalls, and there's factories. There must be work of some sort you can do, even if it is only skivvying.'

'Well, that's me all fixed up, then,' she retorted, 'so what sort of job are you planning on getting?'

'I've no idea, cariad. I'll find something, though.' He patted her knee. 'It's going to be up to us two, you know, to earn the money. Lora will have her hands full looking after little Dilwyn and young Madoc.'

Chapter Five

It took them almost a week in cheap bed-and-breakfast lodging houses before they found somewhere suitable to live. The two rooms they eventually ended up with were in a rundown terraced house in Sophia Terrace in Tiger Bay.

The living room looked out on to a small backyard that was divided by a high brick wall from the houses that backed on to it, so it was dark and gloomy. The faded striped wallpaper was pock-marked by bugs and the ceiling was so dirty that it looked a dull grey instead of white.

The furniture consisted of oddments, nothing matched. There was a wooden table and three rickety wooden chairs, a lumpy couch and a battered armchair.

The kitchen was at the back of the house and they would have to share this and the pots and pans with three other families who were all crammed into the house. If they didn't want other people making free with their food then they would have to keep that in their living room.

The bedroom was equally squalid. There was only one bed and this almost filled the room and there was hardly space for the cot that was wedged between the bed and the window. A grubby curtain was suspended on a pole across an alcove to serve as a wardrobe and there was a battered chest of drawers for everything else.

As Lora pulled aside the patchwork counterpane to look at the mattress, something small and black scuttled away under the thin fawn blanket.

'Bit of a slummy sort of place, isn't it, Huw?' Lora grumbled. 'I didn't think we'd end up having to live in a place like this.'

'It's the best we can manage for the moment, Lora. As soon as Merrion and me have managed to find decent jobs we'll move again to Grangetown or Canton or somewhere like that.'

'All very well you saying that,' she grumbled, 'I'll be the one who has to make do with this hole. You two will be out all day away from it, you'll only be coming back here to sleep.'

'Damn sight better than where we'll probably end up,' he laughed sourly. 'Some of the factories are not only hot and dirty, but smell to high heavens.'

'We'll move as soon as ever we can, Mam,' Merrion promised. 'At least we've got a roof over our heads and somewhere out of the cold.'

'Nowhere near as cosy as our old place, though, is it, girl?' Lora Roberts sighed. 'It's all right for you, but I've got to make do with someone else's old pots and pans. You'll expect a hot meal ready and waiting when you get in at night the same as though I had a proper kitchen and all my own dishes and things.'

'You'll manage, Mam, I'm sure you will. You know you are a perfect wonder at making-do.'

Lora sniffed. 'I'll have to, I suppose,' she muttered grumpily.

Finding work was difficult. Cardiff was so full of men who'd been discharged from the army and were looking for work that Huw despaired of finding a job. No matter how early he arrived at the docks he found there were long lines of men already there waiting.

To supplement what little food Lora managed to put on the table at home Huw joined the groups at the soup kitchens whenever he could get a place. The watery soup and the hunk of stale bread wasn't a patch on the rabbit cawl Lora had made when they'd lived in Cwmglo, but he ate it nevertheless.

Merrion was more fortunate than Huw. She'd found herself a job although it certainly wasn't the sort of work she wanted to do. Even in her worst dreams she'd never considered cleaning public lavatories, but in the three months they'd been living in Cardiff it was the only employment she'd managed to find.

Each day she lugged her buckets of water from one cubicle to the other, cleaning the lavatories and then scrubbing the tiled walls and paved floors. Her stomach churned at the disgusting state most of them were in, so she filled her mind with the dreams she'd once had for a different life for herself and her family. Had they been mere fantasies, she wondered, or would they come true someday?

As the weather became colder, her hands became rough, reddened and sore. She knew she dare not complain, indeed she should be thankful that she'd been taken on, since it was the only money they had coming in. Huw still hadn't found any employment. She knew he set off each day to look for work and she could see how depressed he was by the situation.

Her mother was no real help. Every night the minute she arrived home her mother started grousing either about the slum they were living in, or about the difficulties of coping on her own with looking after Madoc and Dilwyn. Half the time she hadn't even managed to do any shopping and it was left to Merrion to dash out again to see if there were any corner shops still open and then they had to make do with whatever leftovers were still unsold.

This week, she told herself, when she finished work at midday on Saturday, she'd go home, get cleaned up, and then go to the open market at the Hayes. Someone had told her there were splendid bargains to be found there late in the afternoon. All the perishable stuff that hadn't been sold, and wouldn't keep until the following week, was practically given away.

When she told her mam what she intended to do, Lora was up in arms. 'You're going on a shopping jaunt? What about me? I'm stuck here with a grizzling baby and a whingeing kid. You're out meeting people every day of the week and then the moment you're free you go gadding off into town!'

'Then come with me, Mam. We'll both go! It will give us a chance to see if we can buy any little extras ready for Christmas.'

'How can I do that lumbered with a young baby and a little one you've got to hold by the hand the whole time!'

'Well, we can't leave them here, can we! You take charge of Madoc and I'll carry little Dilwyn. We'll make an outing of it. It'll be something to look forward to, won't it?'

'Yes, I suppose so,' Lora agreed reluctantly.

As soon as Merrion finished work on Saturday they put their plan into action.

'I was hoping that Huw would be here and that he'd agree to keep an eye on Madoc and Dilwyn so that we could go on our own,' Lora grumbled.

'Well, he's not, so we'll have to take them with us. If we don't go now all the best bits will be gone.'

'What happens if there's a crowd and we get separated? I'll be lost if we do. I'm not used to crowds and places like the centre of Cardiff, remember.'

'I'll stick close beside you, so don't worry,' Merrion assured her.

'Well, mind you do,' her mother warned. 'You

take young Dilwyn, then, she's too heavy for me to carry; I still haven't got my strength back.'

'I've already said I would, but mind you keep a tight hold of Madoc's hand, he's not used to busy streets either.'

The Hayes was an eye-opener for them. They'd never seen such crowds or witnessed so much noisy selling. As stallholders shouted about their wares it was as if each one of them was trying to outdo all the others.

At first, Lora and Merrion were so completely overawed by the vast conglomeration of things that were on sale that they couldn't concentrate on what they were looking to buy. They wandered around the crowded stalls, eyeing everything in amazement until Merrion reminded her mother that they were supposed to be buying food, not simply looking at everything.

'Come on, Mam,' she said firmly, 'it's time for us to concentrate on some of the offers there are to be had before they're all snapped up.'

Half an hour later, their bags full of meat and vegetables at knockdown prices, as well as cakes and bread that stallholders knew would be too stale to sell on Monday, they started for home.

Merrion felt exhausted. Although Dilwyn was only a few months old, carrying her as well as the brimming shopping bags was extremely tiring. Lora was trying to drag Madoc away from the stalls which had tempting displays of sweets and chocolate.

'Here.' Merrion held out a halfpenny to him. 'Go and buy yourself a gob-stopper and then we'll be on our way home.'

With a face-splitting grin, Madoc seized the coin and headed for the sweet stall.

'You wait for him, Mam, I'll start walking towards the tram stop and you can catch me up,' Merrion told her. 'It's almost dark, so make sure you have hold of his hand, mind, we don't want to lose him.'

When she reached the edge of the Hayes open market, Merrion paused and looked back to see where her mother and Madoc were. She felt drained, her feet hurt and her head ached. She hoped her mother would hurry up so that they'd be in time to catch the next tram. She was reluctant to go any further because she wasn't sure if her mother knew where the tram stop was.

She longed to get home. The gas lamps had already been lit and a thin drizzle of rain was making everything damp and miserable. She was about to turn and walk back to look for her mother when she heard a terrible scream. It was accompanied by an ear-splitting noise of metal scraping against metal as a tram ground to a jarring halt.

People began rushing towards the spot. There was no sign of her mam and she felt annoyed, wondering if she had stopped to see what was happening.

Worried in case they missed each other she

moved back into the crowd and found herself being swept along towards where the tram had stopped so abruptly.

Suddenly there were policemen moving them all away and the clanging sound of an approaching ambulance.

'A woman and a small boy . . .'

'Caught her foot in the rails, did she?'

'No, it was the kiddie who caught his foot, the woman was trying to free him.'

The snippets of conversation drifted into Merrion's head, but at first they didn't register or make any real sense. Then, when she could see no sign of her mother, fear suddenly gripped her. Elbowing her way forward she strained her neck to try and find out what was happening.

She could see that a woman was lying on the ground and that she was wearing a pair of lace-up boots and a blue serge skirt. It was enough to confirm the fear that was already sending shivers through her.

'Mam . . . no, it can't be you!' she screamed. People turned and stared at her.

'Is it your mam, then?' a woman asked.

'I'm not sure . . .' Merrion said hesitantly.

'There's a young boy as well, brown hair, about four years old . . .'

'Madoc!'

'You know them, then?' the woman persisted.

'I . . . I think it could be my mam and my little brother,' Merrion said agitatedly.

54

'Tell the scuffer, then, cariad,' the woman urged, pushing her forward. 'Here, let this girl through,' she called out officiously to the people in front.

A policeman took her by the arm and pointed to the woman lying on the ground. 'Someone said you knew who she was. Do you?'

Merrion felt numb as she stared down. Now there was no doubt about it. Her mam was lying so still that she was sure she was dead. Even so, she found herself asking for confirmation from the policeman.

'No, no, my lovely, she's only unconscious, see. I'm not sure about the young boyo, though.'

'Poor little Madoc! Where is he?'

He led her to the other side of the tram. Someone had spread a coat over the tiny figure. When the policeman pulled it back, she turned her head away as the tears gushed from her eyes. It was Madoc. He still had a gob-stopper clutched in one hand.

Dazed by grief she let them help her into the ambulance, together with the still forms of her mother and young Madoc. The attendant tried to comfort her, telling her that her mam was going to be all right. There was a lot of blood because she'd gashed her head on the tram-lines. That was why she was unconscious.

She nodded as if she understood what they were telling her, but her mind was a blank. All she could see before her was the sight of Madoc lying there clutching his gob-stopper. She had no idea what had happened. Had he let go of their mam's hand and had she tried to stop him?

If she hadn't given him the halfpenny to buy a sweet, would he still be alive? Would her mam be safe and sound? The questions went round and round in her head as the ambulance drove away, and, after they arrived at the hospital, as she waited in the corridor for them to let her see her mam.

Lora looked almost lifeless as she lay in the hospital bed. Tentatively Merrion touched her gently on the arm. 'Mam . . . Mam, are you all right? Do you know what happened?'

Her mother didn't appear to hear her words. Her breathing was shallow and uneven.

Dilwyn, who up until now had been sleeping, cocooned in the big shawl that held her close to the warmth of Merrion's body, began to cry. A strong, hungry cry, and Merrion realised with a shock that it was well past the baby's feeding time. As she looked down at her mother and wondered what on earth she was going to do, someone touched her on the shoulder.

'You'll have to take that baby outside immediately, before it disturbs the whole ward,' a sister in a starched white cap and apron told her reprovingly.

The sound of Dilwyn's cry seemed to penetrate Lora's subconscience. Her eyes flickered open and she stretched out her arms. 'Give her here to me, cariad, she's hungry.'

56

'Mam!' Joy and wonderment filled Merrion as she heard her mother's voice. Without a moment's hesitation she unwound the enveloping shawl and placed Dilwyn into her mother's arms.

'You mustn't do this,' the sister objected. 'Your mother is desperately ill, there is no way that she has the strength to nurse a baby! Take the child away immediately.'

But, with her ebbing strength, Lora was already clutching Dilwyn to her breast and the child was responding greedily.

'It's like a miracle,' the sister murmured. Then she suddenly became alert as Lora's hold on Dilwyn slackened and the baby rolled from her arms on to the counterpane.

Thrusting the baby into Merrion's arms and pushing her to one side, the sister tried to revive Lora Roberts, but it was too late.

Chapter Six

Merrion was still in a traumatised daze as she left the hospital and made her way back home to their squalid rooms in Sophia Terrace. Dilwyn was once more asleep, but she had no idea how long it would be before she awoke again, and then she would be hungry and demanding to be fed.

Sister Thomas at the hospital had been as helpful as possible. She'd said that there was nothing else that could be done at the moment. 'I'm afraid you will have to come back again tomorrow, though, to make arrangements for the burial of your mother and your little brother,' she told her.

Sister Thomas had also warned her that there would be problems about feeding Dilwyn. She'd sent one of the nurses to fetch a packet of formula from their own stocks and had given her instructions on how to prepare it for the baby.

'She may not be too keen on accepting it at first, but you must be patient and persevere. Eventually she'll be so hungry that she'll feed. There's enough formula here for a couple of days so that will give you time to sort yourself

58

out and buy whatever is necessary. Remember, on no account give her cow's milk, because that will upset her. Cow and Gate will be the best if you can afford it. Do you understand?'

Merrion assured her that she did, but she found it difficult to take it all in. Her mind was clouded by the dreadful situation she was now in. Her mam was dead and so was little Madoc. It had all taken place so quickly, without any warning. She wasn't even sure exactly how it had happened.

Someone in the crowd had said that the woman and boy were crossing the road as they left the Hayes and that the child's foot had become trapped in the tramlines. The tram was on top of them before the woman was able to free his foot, and although she'd tried desperately to pull him clear, the tram had hit both of them.

The child, so they kept telling her, had been killed outright. He wouldn't have known anything because it had all happened so quickly.

Her mother had been knocked unconscious, and although she had been in considerable pain when she came round, at the moment of impact she would have known nothing about it, they assured her.

Huw was almost as shocked as Merrion when she told him all this.

'How on earth could it happen if you were together?' he asked in bewilderment.

Wearily Merrion went over the details again.

Huw ran a hand through his hair. 'I know what you're telling me, my lovely, but I still can't understand it at all. Lora and Madoc! Duw anwyl! It's a double tragedy. What the hell are we going to do about Dilwyn? She can't manage to survive without her mam! She's too little to be weaned, isn't she?'

'Far too young for solid food, but they told me at the hospital what I must do. They gave me a packet of formula to make up for her and advised me what to buy. They even gave me a feeding bottle.'

Huw frowned. 'Are you sure that Dilwyn will thrive on this stuff?'

Merrion shrugged. 'We'll have to wait and see, I suppose. I don't know what else we can do. They told me not to give her cow's milk, leastwise not until she is quite a bit older.'

'So who is going to look after her now, then?' Huw asked worriedly.

Merrion stared at him in bewilderment. 'Well, we'll have to, of course.'

'How can we? You're out at work every day.'

'Then you'll have to do it! You still haven't found yourself a job, have you?'

'Me look after her! I can't be left on my own to look after a baby as young as that, my lovely,' Huw protested.

'There's no one else to do it.'

'No, it's out of the question. Dilwyn is only a few months old, she still needs changing and all that sort of palaver. Now if it had been Madoc . . .' He bit his lip and looked away uneasily as he realised what he'd just said.

'Don't let us talk about it now, my lovely,' he murmured, patting Merrion on the shoulder. 'You've had a hard day. You settle young Dilwyn and I'll get some food ready for us.'

'I couldn't eat anything,' she protested.

'You must,' he said sternly. 'Think of Dilwyn, you have to keep fit and well to take care of her.'

'I can't look after her and go out to work as well. You are going to have to be the one to take care of her,' Merrion repeated stubbornly.

'Put her in her cradle and then we'll talk about it,' he prevaricated.

Although they talked until midnight they resolved nothing. Merrion's head ached and she could hardly keep her eyes open. Almost in a trance she made up a feeding bottle of the formula for Dilwyn in case she wakened, and then she crawled into bed.

She'd expected to fall asleep immediately, but the day's events churned round and round in her mind. She kept seeing Madoc's body, so very small and defenceless, his precious gobstopper clutched in his little hand.

Huw accompanied her to the hospital next day to make the arrangements for the funerals. She left him to sign the various pieces of paper that were put in front of them.

'It'll be a pauper's grave for both of them,

I'm afraid, cariad,' he told her sadly as he laid down the pen.

She stared at him in despair, knowing there was nothing either of them could do about that. As it was, she thought uneasily, they were going to have a hard time.

There was only enough formula to last for one more day and then she would have to buy some more and that would take most of the few shillings that she'd managed to save since she'd been working.

Sister Thomas came and spoke to them before they left the hospital.

'If you have any problems with looking after the baby then come back here and ask for me,' she said.

'Thank you, you've been very kind. I'm not sure I am going to be able to cope . . .'

'Oh come now, you will have your dad to help and advise you. Between the pair of you I'm sure you will be able to manage,' Sister Thomas said briskly.

Merrion shook her head. 'My dad's dead. He died a couple of months back when there was an explosion in the mine where he was working.'

Sister Thomas frowned as she looked from Merrion to Huw. 'You aren't Merrion's and Dilwyn's father, then?'

'No! Indeed I'm not.' Huw laughed awkwardly. 'Lora Roberts was my sister-in-law. After my brother was killed we left Cwmglo where we all lived because of the memories, see. Planning to start afresh in Cardiff, see! Well, that's what we were counting on doing.'

'And now?'

Huw shook his head. 'To be truthful, I don't know. The baby is the problem, see. I don't feel I can look after it, and if Merrion has to do that then she will have to give up her job and she is the only one who has managed to find work.'

'This is very worrying. You do have somewhere to live?'

Huw nodded. 'Two rooms in Sophia Terrace. How long we will manage to stay there, though, I don't know. We'll not be able to pay the rent if Merrion has to give up her job.'

'Then you'll have to find work or else be the one to look after the baby,' Sister Thomas said firmly. 'Otherwise', she added reluctantly, 'the baby will have to go into an orphanage or be put up for adoption.'

'No, we'll not do that. We'll manage somehow,' Merrion told her emphatically. 'Dilwyn is too precious. My mam would be heartbroken if she knew I let her go into one of those places.'

Sister Thomas nodded understandingly. 'I appreciate what you're saying, Merrion. Is she the only family you have left?'

'No, I have an older brother. Emlyn.'

'Ah!' Her face brightened. 'Surely he will be able to help you in some way?'

Huw shook his head. 'Emlyn knows nothing

about what has happened and we have no way of letting him know. He's somewhere at sea. We don't even know which boat he's on.'

The weeks that followed had a nightmare quality for Merrion. As she'd feared, she lost her job. Even though she explained the situation, her boss showed her no compassion.

'You should have thought of letting me know what was going on before you stayed away,' he told her when she arrived at work two days later.

Huw was as upset as she was, but he remained adamant that it was for the best since he wasn't capable of looking after a baby.

'So are you going to get a job so that we can eat and pay for the special food for the baby?' she demanded.

'Dammo di! I'm already doing my damnedest to find work, girl, you know that as well as I do,' he told her angrily.

'Not being very successful, though, are you?' she countered scathingly.

'Stop your bloody nagging. I'll get you some money from somewhere,' he told her bitterly.

Merrion found that Huw had already left the house when she woke up next morning. When he came home around mid-afternoon, without saying a word, he placed a big handful of coins down on the table.

'You found a job and they've given you an advance?'

'No, I got it by begging!' he snapped. 'I promised to find you some money, so there it is.'

Merrion pushed it from her. 'How could you!' she gasped. 'Is that what we're reduced to . . . begging!'

'It's better than stealing and as long as it buys us some food why worry?'

Merrion shuddered. 'I can't touch it!'

'Please yourself.' He scrabbled the money together and put it back in his trouser pocket. 'I don't mind spending it and I don't suppose you'll refuse some fish and chips when I bring some back in half an hour or so.'

As she opened her mouth to speak, Huw held up a hand. 'I'll bring back some Cow and Gate for the baby as well. You don't have to eat the chips if you don't want to do so.'

Merrion spent a sleepless night. She'd not only accepted the feed for Dilwyn, but she'd even given in and eaten some of the fish and chips that Huw brought back because she was so hungry.

She went over and over in her mind what she could do to find some way for them to exist. Their rent was paid until the end of the week, but after that they would be homeless unless a miracle happened.

Worn out, she went back to bed after she'd given Dilwyn her early morning feed. It was almost midday before she wakened. Dilwyn was crying because she was wet and hungry.

She walked into the living room expecting

Huw to be there, but it was deserted. For a moment Merrion thought he must have taken what she'd said to heart and gone looking for work again. Then she saw the note on the table.

She read it over and over again, unable to take in its message:

Merrion, I can't take this sort of life any longer.
Take care of yourself and little Dilwyn.
Goodbye,
Your loving uncle,
Huw Roberts

There was no other explanation and Merrion couldn't believe that he could be so callous as to desert her and Dilwyn when he knew she had no money and that there was no one in Cardiff whom she could turn to for help. What a terrible beginning for 1920!

Her uncle was the cause of all their troubles, she told herself bitterly. His lies and thieving had been the reason why they'd had to leave their home in Cwmglo and come to Cardiff where they knew no one.

If that hadn't happened, then they would still have been living amongst friends. Even though her father had been killed there would always have been someone to give them a hand. Now she was completely on her own and in a few days' time she would be homeless.

Her mam hadn't been happy in her new surroundings. She'd hated the squalid rooms,

66

and all of them, except Uncle Huw, having to sleep in one bed. He'd had to make do with the lumpy bug-ridden couch in the living room, but at least he hadn't had to share it with anyone else.

Her mam had hated the poky, dirty little kitchen which the three other families in the house also used. She had rarely spoken to any of them. Their foreign ways were alien to her. She'd found it hard to accept that their skin was a different colour to hers. She was convinced that if they had a good wash, or a bath, they'd be the same colour as she was.

'Some of them look as though they've been down the pit for a week and not bothered to get scrubbed clean when they've come up,' she had protested.

They had sensed her hostility and ignored her presence both inside the house and in the street. Merrion had tried to speak to some of them, but there hadn't been time to really break down the barriers. One or two had expressed their sympathy after they'd seen the report about the accident in the *South Wales Echo*, but no one had asked her how she was coping.

If they hadn't come to Cardiff, then a tram wouldn't have knocked down her mam and she wouldn't have died, Merrion thought bitterly. Madoc would still be alive, too, and Emlyn mightn't have gone to sea . . . and neither would Roddi.

As she thought of Roddi, a fresh wave of

sadness swept through her and she wondered where he was and if she would ever see him again. They had been close for as long as she could remember. Even at school they'd always confided in each other and shared each other's troubles as well as their secret dreams. If only he was here now she was sure he would be able to find a way out of this terrible dilemma she found herself in. As it was, he didn't know where she was and she had no way of tracing him.

He'd always been clever at sorting out problems. She remembered him telling her how much he hated the idea of working down the mine because of his fear of being trapped underground. He'd done something about it. He'd stood up to his father and boldly defied family tradition. It was something she admired about him so much and she felt it was unforgivable that he had lost his job at Pennowen all because of her uncle's lies.

Next morning, after a sleepless night, her mind was made up. She knew there was only one thing she could do and that was to find out how she could go about getting Dilwyn adopted.

It was the last thing she wanted to happen, but it would be for the best, she kept reminding herself. It felt as though she was betraying her mother's trust in her, but she couldn't let the poor little mite starve to death.

She tried to tell herself that she could always

beg in the streets like Huw had done, but she knew she couldn't bring herself to do that. She had too much pride.

Sister Thomas had told her to come back if she had any problems, so perhaps that was what she should do since this one seemed to be insurmountable.

Brushing away her tears, she dressed Dilwyn and got ready herself. Then, wrapping her little sister in the large carrying blanket, she set out for the hospital.

Chapter Seven

Merrion mulled over the advice Sister Thomas had given her for several days before she plucked up the courage to go along to see the adoption authorities.

Her decision was motivated by the fact that there had been no word from Huw and the landlord was losing patience because she was now almost a week behind with the rent for her rooms.

The other deciding factor was that she had run out of food for Dilwyn. That morning she'd used the last scrapings from the tin of Cow and Gate and it had barely made half a bottle.

She knew it wouldn't satisfy Dilwyn for very long, but she hoped that by the time she was crying again she would be safely handed over to the authorities, who would take care of her, and she would never again go hungry.

She felt nervous about going on a tram on her own after what had happened to her mam and Madoc, so she walked all the way from Sophia Terrace to the City Hall. Her mind was in turmoil as she trudged the full length of Bute Road and then along St Mary Street with all its wonderful shops.

When she reached Cathays Park, the City Hall looked so imposing that she almost turned away. A weak, whimpering cry from Dilwyn reminded her how desperate their situation was. She forced herself to approach the gleaming white granite building, but her voice was shaking with fright as she asked the liveried doorman where she had to go.

When she followed his instructions she found herself in a spartan office in the basement of the building. The walls were a harsh shade of green and there were half a dozen hard wooden chairs arranged around the walls leaving room for a small reception desk at one end. Alongside it was a door leading into another room.

There were two people already waiting: a shabbily dressed middle-aged woman and a younger girl, who had a round, pretty face, shoulder-length fair hair and cornflower-blue eyes. Both of them were heavily pregnant.

The younger one was smartly dressed, her dark red woollen coat had a black fur collar and her matching cloche hat was trimmed with a black fur bobble at one side. Merrion judged that she was only a few years older than she was herself.

The women stared at her without speaking although the younger of the two managed a half-smile, then both of them totally ignored her.

Merrion felt nervous because she didn't know what she was expected to do. She stood

71

leaning against the reception desk wondering if she was supposed to knock on the door or simply sit and wait.

Dilwyn's plaintive cry startled the other two.

'So you've had yours already!' the younger woman exclaimed. 'Come and sit over here so that I can have a peep of her.' She patted the wooden chair next to her.

Merrion loosened the enveloping blanket before she sat down and propped Dilwyn up in her arms.

'Oh, what a little darling! How old is she, then?'

'Three months.'

'What do you call her?'

'Dilwyn.'

'There's fancy! Not really worth giving them a name though, is it? They always change it when you hand them over.'

Merrion suppressed a shiver. Now that she was here and the parting with Dilwyn was so imminent, she felt more wretched than ever.

'So if her name is Dilwyn, then what's yours?' the young woman asked. 'Mine's Rhonda, Rhonda Rees.'

'Merrion Roberts.'

'Is this your first visit, Merrion, or have you come to hand Dilwyn over to them?'

Before Merrion could answer the door near the reception counter opened and a thin stern-faced woman, her brown hair drawn back into a tight bun, came out. There was an uncomfortable silence as she picked up some papers lying on the reception desk and scanned through them, her lips tightly pursed.

'Rhonda Rees?' She lifted her head and stared enquiringly around the room.

Rhonda stood up and walked towards the desk.

'Through here,' the woman ordered coldly, leading the way.

As the door slammed shut behind them Merrion drew in a sharp breath. She knew she was trembling. The thought of parting with Dilwyn was like a knife turning inside her chest. She couldn't do it, yet she knew that for Dilwyn's sake she had to. The turmoil inside her head made her dizzy. If only there was some other way. If only Huw hadn't walked out on them.

Her mother had always said he was feckless, but they'd come to depend on him so much since the tragedy at the pit that never, for one moment, had she thought that he would desert her. Huw Roberts was family, he'd seen them all grow up. He'd been almost as close to them as their own father had been.

Common sense told her that there was no real reason why he should saddle himself with her and Dilwyn. He'd been her father's younger brother so he was still young enough to marry and have a family of his own, though she thought it far more likely that he preferred to be free of any responsibility at all.

73

Huw had never been fond of work, but he had a glib tongue and could charm most people. She had no doubt at all that he would fare far better on his own than he would if he was tied to her and Dilwyn.

If only he had warned her, given her some indication of what he was intending to do, then she could have planned things differently after her mam and little Madoc had died. Quite what she could have done she had no idea, but there certainly hadn't been time to make any arrangements.

She was still mulling over her problems when Rhonda came out of the inner office and the older woman went in.

As Merrion looked up to say goodbye to Rhonda and wish her well she was shocked at the look of anger on the other girl's face.

'Bloody old cow!' she raged. 'Dried up old prune!' She sat down on the edge of the chair next to Merrion and ran a finger gently over Dilwyn's brow and down the side of her tiny face.

'How you can bear to hand this sweet little baby over to that snarling bitch I don't know.'

Instinctively Merrion held Dilwyn closer. 'What do you mean?'

'She spoke to me as if I was daft! Then she gave me a lecture on what a terrible sin I'd committed by flaunting my body and being so weak that I let men take advantage of me. It wasn't like that at all! I was in love with Harvey.

74

I thought he was going to marry me. I had no idea that he already had a wife and three kids.'

'Oh, how terrible!'

'Traveller he was, see. He lived in Newport, but he came to where I was working every few months and when he did we lived it up, if you know what I mean.'

'So how did you find out the truth about him?'

'The minute I told him I was expecting he couldn't leave quick enough.'

'After telling you the truth . . . that he was already married.'

'That's right. Showed me a picture of them all. Lovely family group,' she added bitterly.

Merrion shook her head sadly. 'Don't you want to keep your baby?'

'How can I! My family are very respectable. They turned me out the minute I started to show because they didn't want the neighbours to know how much I'd disgraced them.'

'So how have you managed since then?'

Rhonda smiled. 'I still have my job so I'm able to pay my way. I've pinched and scraped, mind, so that I could save a few pounds to see me through for a few weeks after the baby is born. Then, I thought that with any luck, once I'm free of it, I'll get my job and my life back again.'

'And is that why you are having the baby adopted?'

'Why I *was* having it adopted!' She ran a hand over her mountainous stomach, ending with a tiny affectionate pat. 'I wouldn't hand a dog over to that woman, let alone a defenceless baby. She's cold, vinegary and harsh. You mustn't let her have your little one,' she warned.

'I've really no choice,' Merrion whispered. All her earlier doubts about what she was doing came flooding back. 'How can I work and look after her at the same time?'

'What about her dad, has he ditched you? The bastards are all the same. They want their fun, but they run away from any of the responsibility.'

'It's not like that,' Merrion said quickly. 'Our dad's dead, he was killed a few months ago in a pit explosion.'

Rhonda stared at her wide-eyed. 'You mean she's your sister, not your own kid?'

'That's right. We came to Cardiff intending to make a fresh start, see. My Uncle Huw was looking after us, but . . . but he's walked out on us.'

'So what about your mam?'

Merrion bit her lower lip and the tears rolled down her cheeks. 'She's dead, too. And so is my little brother Madoc. They . . . they were involved in an accident right here in Cardiff, about a week ago at the Hayes.'

'You mean the poor woman who was knocked down by a tram!' Rhonda gasped.

'That's right.'

'Duw anwyl! That's the saddest story I've ever heard.'

76

Before Merrion could answer the door opened and the woman who had been in the waiting room with them came out. Her eyes were red and she was gulping back deep, harrowing sobs.

'She's ready to see you now,' she told Merrion. She looked down at Dilwyn and her ravaged face softened. 'Must you let her have your baby, my lovely?'

As the brisk, official voice called out for the next girl to come in, Merrion and Rhonda exchanged concerned glances.

'Come on.' Rhonda, grabbed hold of Merrion's arm. 'Let's leave. Once we're outside where no one can overhear what we say, we'll discuss what we can do.'

Merrion hesitated for a moment before agreeing. It had taken so much courage to get this far that she wondered if she was being foolish in listening to a complete stranger.

'Let's nip along to Lyon's Corner House and talk about things over a hot drink,' Rhonda suggested once they were out of the building.

Merrion hesitated. 'I'd love to, Rhonda, but I've no money . . .'

'I have! Come on, before we freeze to death. If we ask them nicely they'll give us some sugar water to feed the baby.' She pulled a face. 'I know it's not the right thing to be giving her, but it will keep her quiet while we make some plans.'

Over their hot drink they discussed their plight in greater detail and both of them arrived at the same conclusion. Whatever happened neither of them wanted to hand over their babies for adoption.

'So what can we do?' Merrion sighed dejectedly.

'Well,' Rhonda's bright blue eyes sparkled, 'I've got an idea. Why don't we team up? We're both alone in the world and . . .'

'And have no money and no roof over our heads!' Merrion interrupted bitterly.

'Not quite true. We do have somewhere to live.'

'You might have, but if I don't come up with the rent on my rooms today then me and my few belongings will be out on the street.'

'Right! Now that's the first point. Why don't we move in together?'

Merrion stared at her open-mouthed. 'What good is that going to do?'

'Well, it will save one lot of rent, for a start. It will also mean that when my baby is born then one of us can go out to work and the other can look after both the babbas. What about it?'

Merrion looked taken aback. The reasoning behind the idea was so good that she couldn't fault it, but she was sure there were snags she hadn't thought about. For one thing, they were more or less complete strangers. How would they like living together? They might get on each other's nerves. Even when you were living with your family that could happen, she reminded herself. Yet, for all that, she had to admit that it did seem like a sound idea.

'So where would we live? Your place or mine?'

Rhonda shrugged. 'I've only got one room and since you have two then I suppose it makes sense to go to your place. Where is it?'

Merrion bit her lip. 'Sophia Terrace.'

'Where's that exactly?'

'You go over James Street Bridge heading towards the Pier Head and it's the second road on the right. We've only been there a few months. It's not much of an area but it was all we could find that we could afford.'

Rhonda pulled a face. 'That's Tiger Bay so it's bound to be pretty rough! Still, the room I've got out at Splott isn't up to much, either. At least we'll have each other, so what do you say?'

Chapter Eight

To Merrion's surprise and relief she found living with Rhonda Rees was far easier than she'd dared hope. They were so compatible that it was almost as if they'd known each other all their life.

Their backgrounds were completely different. Rhonda had lived in one of the posh parts of Cardiff near Roath Park. She'd been brought up in a well-furnished detached house with a pretty garden. While she was growing up she'd been pampered, well dressed and even sent to a private school.

'I'm not the academic type, mind,' she laughed. 'Mam and Dad wanted me to become a secretary, so they sent me to Cardiff Technical College to do a shorthand and typing course. I hated it. After three weeks I switched courses. I like doing things with my hands, making things, you know.'

'So what did you decide to do instead, become a plumber?'

'No!' Rhonda laughed. 'I became a milliner. I've quite a flare for it.'

'Really! Do you know, your pretty hat was one of the first things I noticed about you the day we met,' Merrion told her.

Rhonda laughed. 'You should see the collection I have at home. Dozens and dozens of them in all the shapes and colours imaginable. I have a hat to go with every dress and coat, two in some instances. I love making them and I adore wearing them. There're so many different ways you can trim a basic shape.'

'Do you still make them?'

'Of course! It's how I'm earning my living.'

'So you work in a hat shop?'

'Well, not in the shop itself, but in the workrooms behind a shop in St Mary's Street. I'm in the design studio. The shapes are made in a factory and then they are brought to the design studio for trimming. We use ribbons, feathers, fur, or artificial flowers; it all depends on the time of year and the type of hats needed.'

'Is that where you met the man . . . the man who is the father of the baby you're expecting?'

Rhonda nodded. The laughter went from her face. 'Yes, he was a traveller who came into the studio with samples of trimmings once a month.'

She sighed dreamily. 'I really love my job and they've said I can go back after I've had the baby, that's why I was going to get it adopted.'

'Well, you can still go back to work . . .'

'You mean you wouldn't mind being the one who stayed at home and looked after them both?'

'Of course not, it makes sense. You are the one who has a job to go to, I haven't!'

81

'So what sort of work were you doing?'

'Cleaning public lavatories,' Merrion told her. She shuddered. 'It was pretty horrible.'

Rhonda stared at her, open-mouthed. 'Duw anwyl, it must have been awful! Most of them are dirty, smelly places.' She giggled. 'You'll still be doing a dirty, smelly job changing nappies and coping with sick,' she warned.

'It's different, though, when you're doing it for your own, isn't it?' Merrion smiled.

'Only one of them will be yours . . .'

Merrion shrugged. 'It will be like having twins really.'

'Shall we give it a go, then, you staying at home and me going out to work? I'm hanging on by the skin of my teeth at the moment. They don't mind me working because no one who matters can see me. Thank heaven I told them that I would definitely be coming back to work after I'd had the baby.'

'What did you tell them you were going to do with the baby, then?'

'I didn't. I simply said I'd make suitable arrangements.'

The compromise seemed to suit both of them and all they had to do was to wait for Rhonda's baby to be born to test out whether it would work as well as they hoped.

In the meantime, Merrion sorted out the two rooms. They agreed that for the present they'd share the bedroom and replace the double bed with two single ones and use the downstairs one as a living room.

Even so, it was pretty crowded in there with two single beds and two cots. At first they'd intended to have a dividing curtain down the centre of the room, but in the end they decided that would only make the room appear even smaller.

Huw had taken all his belongings with him, but Merrion had the unhappy task of clearing out all her mother's things and the few items that had belonged to Madoc.

She piled them all together and wondered what she ought to do with them. Her mother had been short and fat so Merrion knew that none of the clothes fitted her and there was no point in keeping them. She wondered if she could sell them since she needed every penny that she could get hold of now that she wasn't earning.

Rhonda was paying the rent and handing over money for housekeeping, but Merrion's pride wouldn't allow her to accept anything from Rhonda for her own personal requirements.

'No, there's nothing I want,' she assured Rhonda, 'as long as I can buy Cow and Gate and the things I need for Dilwyn out of the housekeeping money.'

'Of course you can. That's the whole idea of this arrangement now, isn't it? I really do mean it when I say that if there is anything at all that you need for yourself then you must take it out of the housekeeping as well.'

Merrion thanked her, but her self-respect wouldn't let her do that. Instead she debated which way she would get the most money for the things that had belonged to her mam and Madoc.

'Why don't you pawn them and see how much you get for them, then retrieve them and see what the dealers will give you and go for the one who offers the most?' Rhonda advised. 'At least you'll have a bargaining figure when you offer them to the dealers. That's unless you change your mind and decide that you want to keep them.'

'No, there's no point. Anyway, I need to save up for something.'

Rhonda looked at her questioningly.

'We are going to need a pram. Once your baby is born I won't be able to carry two of them around when I go out to the shops.'

'Of course you won't! I'll get one!'

'You can't afford to pay for something like that, we should go halves,' Merrion insisted.

'I can always get a loan from the Provident and then pay it off week by week.'

'No!' Merrion was adamant. 'No loan sharks, please! My mam would turn in her grave if she knew I'd been involved in something like that.'

Rhonda looked miffed, but in the end she agreed with Merrion that they would scout around for a second-hand pram; a big one.

84

Luck was on their side. They managed to hear about a twin pram that was for sale. It seemed huge, and would take up a lot of space, but both of them knew it would be invaluable. Because it was so big they were able to get it at a bargain price and between them they cleaned and polished it and made new bedding and covers for it.

Rhonda refused go into hospital for the birth of her baby. The week before it was due they asked around and found a woman, Phyllis Morgan, living nearby who was prepared to help with the delivery.

The late February evening when Rhonda's contractions started Merrion went to fetch her, but she was told that Phyllis had gone to the pictures. All she could do was to leave a message to let her know what was happening and ask her to come as soon as she got back home.

Although she had only been gone a few minutes, by the time she arrived back Rhonda's contractions were coming so fast that she realised that the birth was imminent.

She tried to keep calm and to assure Rhonda that everything was going to be all right and that she could cope. Inwardly she was shaking with fright. Although she knew what had to be done, being in control with no one else there to help her was very frightening.

While there was still time she fed Dilwyn, hoping that she would go to sleep afterwards since all her attention would have to be on Rhonda until after the baby was born.

The birth seemed to take an exceptionally long time. Rhonda tried stoically to suppress her cries of distress as Merrion talked to her and encouraged her.

Both of them were exhausted by the time Nerys Rees made her entrance into the world some two hours later. Her protesting cry startled them both by its intensity.

Seconds later Phyllis Morgan rapped on the door and was equally surprised to find that it was all over. She examined Rhonda to make sure that everything had been done correctly. Then she helped to clean up the baby and check that she was fit and healthy before handing her back to Rhonda so that she could have her first feed.

'Little Nerys seems to be taking to that all right so you shouldn't have any problems,' she told them as she prepared to leave. 'Even so, don't forget that you can pop along and see me at any time if there is anything you need to know.'

'I'm sure we will be able to manage,' Merrion told her as she handed over the agreed fee.

'No, no, my lovely. I can't take this, you did all the work,' Phyllis told her.

'No, you came as soon as you could and you did help clean little Nerys up!'

'Let's settle on half of it, then, shall we?' Phyllis insisted. 'Now, are you sure there's nothing else I can tell you?'

'Yes, there is something,' Rhonda told her. 'I'm planning to go back to work in a couple of weeks' time. What's the best thing to do about feeding my baby?'

Phyllis frowned. 'Well, breast is best, I always say, but if you're going to be out all day then of course it's going to be difficult.' She shook her head uncertainly. 'You could express some milk and leave it ready for when it is needed, but I don't think you'd be able to do that for very long, not enough to satisfy the little one, that is.'

'Couldn't she be fed on Cow and Gate, the same as Dilwyn is?' Merrion suggested.

'Bit young for that, my lovely.'

'Dilwyn was only a couple of months old when she had to go on the bottle. Her mam died, see, and there was no other way.'

The woman's eyebrows went up. 'So she's not your baby, then!'

'No, she's my sister.'

'There now! Well, she's certainly bonny so she must be thriving on whatever it is you're giving her.'

Rhonda fed Nerys for the first week then gradually they began to introduce bottle feeds during the day. After that, Rhonda breastfed Nerys before she went to work in the morning and again before the baby went to bed at night.

With two young babies to look after, Merrion found her time fully occupied. Some days it seemed that she was continually feeding one baby or the other. As soon as she settled one to sleep the other one was awake and needing attention.

The twin pram was a godsend. With both babies fed she would settle them in it, one at each end, so that she could go out shopping. Usually they slept, lulled by the motion of being pushed down the street.

On her return she would leave them where they were while she scuttled round, cleaning up their two rooms and getting herself a midday snack before they wakened.

Gradually, though, Merrion managed to establish a satisfactory routine, one that included a hot meal for them both when Rhonda returned home in the evening.

It was the highlight of Merrion's day. She told Rhonda all about the progress of Nerys and Dilwyn while in turn Rhonda regaled her with anecdotes about her day at work.

Both of them were so busy in their different ways that Sundays were their only chance to relax. Whenever the weather was fine they made a point of going out for a walk with the babies. Their favourite outing was over James Street Bridge, up Clarence Road and along Corporation Road to the park in Grangetown.

Christmas 1920 was quite a milestone. Dilwyn was fifteen months old and Nerys ten months. Both babies were now beginning to take notice of what was going on around them. They were also becoming much more of a handful for Merrion and Rhonda was beginning to feel that she was missing out on Nerys's development.

'I wish I could be with her more,' she sighed when Monday mornings came round and she had to set off for work. 'By the time I get back home at night she's in bed asleep. I only really see her on Sundays.'

'Perhaps we should try and reorganise our lives,' Merrion suggested. 'I sometimes wish I could get away from them for a while. I'm tied to their routine all day and every day.'

'Well, perhaps we can work out a different way of doing things in the New Year,' Rhonda agreed.

Chapter Nine

There seemed to be no better alternative to their arrangement than that Merrion should care for Dilwyn and Nerys while Rhonda went out to work. They talked about it occasionally, but as Rhonda was quick to point out, she was able to earn a far better wage as a milliner than Merrion would ever be able to do.

'You certainly wouldn't want to go back to cleaning public lavatories, now would you?' Rhonda asked whenever Merrion raised the matter.

Merrion bit down on her lower lip. 'No,' she admitted, 'I most certainly wouldn't want to have to do that.' What she really wanted, she thought longingly, was to be with Roddi, but she was beginning to think that she would never see him again, except in her dreams.

'So what else is there that you can do?'

'Domestic work of some kind, I suppose. Or I could work behind the counter in a shop, perhaps, or as an usherette at one of the cinemas.'

'You'd only be earning a pittance if you did any of those jobs!' Rhonda sighed.

'Perhaps I could do some nursing, then.

Looking after sick people at home, I mean, not in a hospital because I'd need proper training to do that.'

'So what difference would there be in you doing that to looking after Dilwyn and Nerys?' Rhonda frowned. 'You certainly wouldn't be able to earn as much as I'm able to do, so we'd both be worse off.'

More to the point, Merrion thought, you don't want to be the one looking after the children. Much as Rhonda loved Nerys, and claimed that she wanted to spend more time with her, she was not a good mother.

She was prepared to push the pram when they took the children for a walk on a Sunday, but not to help give them their breakfast. She loved dolling Nerys up in pretty dresses, or combing her auburn curls into ringlets, but she hated having to change her nappy.

Merrion could see, without being told, that the thought of having to look after both of the children all the time very much went against the grain. Rhonda became irritated when it came to spooning mashed up food into the child's mouth, or coaxing her to eat when she didn't want to do so. As long as Nerys was smiling or laughing Rhonda was happy to play with her, but she had no patience when it came to rocking her off to sleep when she was teething or mardy for some reason or other.

Nerys sensed this and whenever she was feeling out of sorts it was always Merrion she

91

held out her arms to, never Rhonda. Merrion seemed to be the only one who could calm her down and comfort her when she was in one of her temper tantrums.

Dilwyn was by far the more placid of the two children and much easier to cope with. With her mop of dark hair and huge dark eyes she took after the Roberts' family. She had a sunny nature and never seemed to mind at all when Merrion picked Nerys up and cuddled her because she was crying or unhappy.

Merrion sometimes dreamed of being able to enjoy a life of her own outside their two rooms. The daily routine of constantly washing, feeding and caring for two youngsters and keeping both them and the rooms clean and tidy was so monotonous. Yet, deep in her heart, she had to admit that she would prefer to be the one who was looking after them rather than having to leave Dilwyn in Rhonda's care.

Someday things would come right she told herself. The two little girls were growing up fast so it wouldn't last for ever and, in the mean-time, she must make the best of what she had.

In so many ways she knew she was lucky that Rhonda was not only able to earn quite good money, but also that she was prepared to hand over so much of it. With careful budgeting there was always enough to pay the rent regularly, feed them all, and even to buy clothes for herself and both the little ones.

One day, Rhonda kept on telling her, they

would be able to afford to move out of Sophia Terrace and find somewhere better to live. Exactly when that would be neither of them knew.

Although when she'd first arrived in Tiger Bay Merrion had thought it squalid, she had now grown used to it. Since she had got to know most of the other people living in the house the difficulties of having to share a kitchen had been overcome and occasionally she would join one or other of them for a cup of tea or a chat.

Rhonda had brought so many useful pieces with her from the room she'd had in Splott that now the two rooms in Sophia Terrace, although crowded, had a nice homely feel.

In fact, the only real worry was that Rhonda spent so much of her time working. Often it was nine o'clock, sometimes even ten o'clock, before she arrived home. Frequently she seemed to be too tired, or too keyed up, to eat the hot meal that Merrion had saved for her.

It took quite some time before it dawned on Merrion that these late hours were not because Rhonda was working overtime, as she had thought, but because Rhonda was going out with friends straight after work.

At first she felt resentful, that Rhonda was enjoying herself instead of coming straight home, mainly because Rhonda hadn't told her what was going on. Then common sense prevailed. Why shouldn't Rhonda have some pleasure out of life? She was working hard enough, so why shouldn't she keep a corner of her life private if that was what she wanted to do?

If Roddi turned up out of the blue, Merrion told herself, as she was always dreaming he would do someday, and she had the opportunity to go out with him, she'd jump at the chance. If that happened, then she'd probably not want to talk about it, either.

It was now almost two years since Roddi had gone to sea and it was as if both he and Emlyn had vanished off the face of the earth. She often wondered if they had ever sailed back into Cardiff at all since then. Frequently, when she had the babies in the pram, she walked down to the Pier Head, or along Bute Road, hoping that by chance she might bump into either of them.

It was such a slender chance that she never mentioned it to Rhonda. It was the only way they would ever be reunited, since there was no means of letting either of them know where she was living. She didn't even know the name of the ship they'd sailed on, or where it had been bound. Everything had happened with such nightmare speed that she wasn't even sure if Roddi and Emlyn knew that the entire family had been forced to come to Cardiff. They certainly didn't know about the tragedy that had overtaken them, or that her mother and Madoc were dead and that Uncle Huw had cleared off without a word. She was afraid to write to any of their old friends or neighbours in Cwmglo, even to Ellyn Jones, in case word got back to Alun Weeks or to David Pennowen and they came looking for them.

Merrion dreamed about Roddi most nights. Sometimes they were both back in Cwmglo where they'd spent their childhood. They'd be walking familiar paths hand in hand, stopping to kiss and cuddle in some quiet spot where no one could see them. At other times, she dreamed that they were in some foreign place that she'd imagined from the mental pictures she'd built up from the stories her neighbours or local shop-keepers told her.

Unlike her mother, she had gone out of her way to talk to the other people who lived in the house and shared the kitchen. Most of them had told her about their backgrounds. She in turn had talked about herself and now most of the shopkeepers in and around James Street gave her a friendly welcome and, from time to time, told her things about their own families.

Rhonda laughed at her, ridiculing her enthusiasm whenever Merrion regaled her with stories someone had told her about the exotic countries they came from.

'Half of them were born right here in Cardiff,' she pointed out. 'The stories they're telling you about foreign places are merely hearsay handed down by their own parents.'

'Maybe they are, but they're nonetheless fascinating for that.'

'I know, Merrion. I just thought you ought to realise that they may not always be telling you the truth before you get too involved with any of them.'

'That's not very likely, I only talk to them in the street or in the shops. I don't go visiting them in their homes.'

'No, but you probably think that some of the men are quite attractive when they're chatting you up.' Rhonda smiled knowingly.

Merrion stared at her aghast. 'You think I might take up with one of them . . . as a boyfriend?'

'Well,' Rhonda tipped her head on one side and studied her intently, 'have you taken a good look in a mirror lately? You've improved a great deal since we first met in that awful adoption place. You're still tall and slim but you've matured . . . I'm sure a lot of men would find you quite attractive, you know!'

Merrion's eyebrows shot up. 'You surely don't think I'm likely to find myself a boyfriend when I'm pushing a couple of babies along the street!' she exclaimed in disbelief.

'That might even attract some of the men since it proves that you'd make a very good mother,' Rhonda laughed.

'What a ridiculous suggestion,' Merrion snapped. 'Even if I did find someone, I'd never be free to go out with them.'

'Well, if you did, I'm sure we'd be able to arrange something. We could take it in turns to have a night out ...'

'Oh yes! You mean like you've already started doing,' Merrion said sharply.

Colour flooded Rhonda's face. 'Well, as a matter of fact ...'

'I knew it! All those late nights when you are supposed to be working, doing overtime, you've been spending time with your friends!'

'So what if I have?' Rhonda snapped back. 'Surely I've every right to have friends!'

'Yes, but while I've been stuck here, nursing your daughter when she can't sleep, and making sure there was some hot food waiting for you when you get in, you've been out on the town enjoying yourself.'

'I know, I haven't really played fair,' Rhonda admitted contritely. 'We'll sort things out, you shall have your chance. I promise!'

'You've said all that before,' Merrion told her huffily. 'You're simply talking twaddle to ease your guilty conscience!'

'That's utter nonsense, you'll soon find yourself a boyfriend if you really want one. I'll help you. I'll introduce you to ...'

'I don't need your help or one of your castoff men friends, thank you very much!'

'You already have a boyfriend, haven't you?' Rhonda exclaimed triumphantly. 'You dark horse, Merrion! Come on, tell me all about him.

What is his name? I want to know all the details. Does he live close by? When am I going to meet him?'

Merrion shook her head, wishing she hadn't been stung into making such an admission.

'You're trying to pay me back for holding out on you, aren't you?' Rhonda teased.

'No, of course I'm not!' Merrion ran the back of her hand across her eyes to brush away the sudden tears. 'He was a boy from the village where I lived. We grew up together.'

'Go on, then! Tell me all about him. When did you last see him?'

Merrion shook her head. 'I'd rather not talk about it. Someday we'll be together again and then all my dreams will come true.'

Chapter Ten

Rhonda tried her best to get Merrion to open up and tell her more about her boyfriend, but Merrion was adamant. As far as she was concerned, Roddi meant far too much to her to gossip about him simply to satisfy Rhonda's curiosity.

Rhonda had no such reserves. She was quite prepared to tell Merrion every detail about the man who had fathered Nerys.

'I was young and easily taken in,' she admitted dramatically, 'and he was a rat of the first water, a real Romeo. I wouldn't mind betting he had affairs all over the place. He probably had a girlfriend in every town he visited.'

'Have you ever seen him after he left you?'

Rhonda shook her head. 'He changed his round, as soon as I told him that I was pregnant.'

'You could probably find him again, though, if you wanted to,' Merrion said thoughtfully.

'I don't want to, though, do I?' Rhonda exclaimed bitterly. 'Why on earth should I?'

'Well, he might be prepared to help out with Nerys. After all, he's as responsible for her welfare as you are.'

'Nerys wants for nothing, nor will she ever,' Rhonda said huffily.

'I know that, but it doesn't seem fair, somehow, that you are the one who has to struggle to bring her up and he doesn't help.'

'Not much in life is fair!'

'Nerys might like to be able to see her dad now that she's growing up,' Merrion pointed out.

Rhonda's mouth tightened. 'I told you he was already married . . .'

'And that he already had three children!'

'What?' She looked startled.

'That's what you told me the day we first met,' Merrion reminded her.

Rhonda shrugged. 'Like I said, a real rat. The older they are the worse they are and the faster they run when things go wrong.'

'Well, let's hope that Nerys never asks about him, then, or wants to see him.'

'If she does, then I'll dream up some imaginary dad for her. Someone young and handsome . . . perhaps like your Roddi,' she teased.

In the months that followed, no matter how hard Rhonda tried to persuade her to talk about Roddi, Merrion refused to do so and would immediately switch the conversation to something concerning Nerys and Dilwyn.

Now that both the little girls were walking and talking, Merrion's days were more fully occupied than ever. Throughout the spring and summer of 1924, she spent more and more time taking them out in order to get away from the depressing, claustrophobic atmosphere of being confined indoors.

For all Rhonda's promises that they would move, they were still living in the same two rooms in Sophia Terrace. No matter how hard she tried to keep it clean, Merrion had never been able to get rid of the cockroaches or bed-bugs that infested the entire building. Now that it was summer, there were blue-bottles every-where the moment food was put on the table. In addition, as the girls grew bigger, the two rooms were becoming more and more cramped.

Merrion suspected that the reason they couldn't afford anything better was because Rhonda was spending money that she should be saving on buying new clothes and on going out to enjoy herself.

Merrion liked to keep to a routine and have the girls tucked up in bed before eight o'clock, and three or four nights a week Rhonda didn't get home until long after they were asleep. It annoyed Merrion and so she stopped keeping a meal hot for her.

She'd also stopped commenting about Rhonda being late. On the few occasions when she had done so it had led to a heated argu-ment so there seemed nothing could be gained from making a fuss.

Rhonda's return each evening was no longer one of the highlights of either the children's day, or of Merrion's, because the times were so erratic. When the evenings were warm, knowing that it was unlikely that the two little girls would settle to sleep, Merrion took them out for an hour. Sometimes it was to the Pier Head, to see if there were any new boats in dock, but more often it was to the park.

Dilwyn and Nerys liked nothing better than travelling on the tram from James Street along Corporation Road to Grangetown Park. An hour of chasing each other around on the green grass, or walking along the paths between the well-tended flowerbeds, helped to tire them out.

Several times while she had been sitting on a bench leaving the children free to run around as they chose, Merrion had noticed a middle-aged man watching them intently.

He was neatly dressed in a charcoal-grey suit and a dark trilby hat and he seemed to be there so often that he became part of the background. She assumed he must live close by and she thought he was merely enjoying the enthusiasm with which the two children played.

When, one evening, she saw him rise from the park bench where he was sitting and approach the two little girls, she was immediately alert. When he bent down and spoke to Nerys she felt alarmed. Immediately she called them back to her side and questioned them about what he had said.

'He asked Nerys what her name was,' Dilwyn told her sister.

Although she was concerned, Merrion tried

not to show it. 'Didn't he want to know your name as well?' she asked, smiling.

Dilwyn shook her head. 'He didn't seem to notice me,' she said.

Although Merrion tried to dismiss it as being of no importance she was relieved to find that he wasn't there when they made their next visit to the park.

She didn't mention it to Rhonda, but one hot evening in late July when once again she took the two girls to the park to tire them out before settling them into bed, she felt uneasy at finding him sitting in his usual spot. She became even more alarmed when he walked over to where they were playing and gave Nerys a big shiny ball.

The two little girls were delighted and immediately raced over to show it to Merrion.

When she looked towards the spot where he'd been sitting, she saw that the man had gone.

Merrion was so worried that this time she told Rhonda all about the incident, and about the other times they'd seen him there, as soon as she came home. To her surprise Rhonda didn't seem to be terribly concerned.

'He gives them a ball to play with, so what's so terrible about that?' she laughed. 'He probably found it lying on the grass and thought it belonged to them.'

'I don't think so. It looks far too shiny, I'm sure it is brand new.'

'Then perhaps he did buy it for them. Rather sweet of him really.'

Merrion felt unhappy about the whole incident, but for several days after that the weather was so bad that they were unable to go out at all, so she put it out of her mind.

The following week, however, the episode was brought back to mind when they next visited the park at Grangetown. Once again the man was there and it was quite obvious that he was waiting for them.

As soon as Merrion sat down he came over and spoke to her. As he lifted his trilby, she was surprised to see that he was almost bald and she judged him to be only in his early fifties.

'Two lovely little girls,' he said, smiling. 'Are they both yours?'

When Merrion tensed and didn't answer, he smiled apologetically. 'Forgive me. I have seen you here several times with the children and occasionally there has been another woman with you and I thought I knew her.' He smiled disarmingly. 'I wondered if the little auburn-haired child was hers?'

Trembling and thoroughly frightened, Merrion got up from the park bench and called out to the two children. Taking them by the hand the moment they reached her side she began to walk away as fast as she could.

'I . . . I thought I recognised her, you see,' the man called out, hurrying after them.

Merrion didn't answer, but her heart was thundering as she hurried Dilwyn and Nerys towards the nearest tram stop.

Rhonda was already in when they reached home and was concerned about the agitated state Merrion was in.

'What on earth is wrong, Merrion?' she demanded, picking Nerys up and hugging her.

Merrion placed a finger against her lips and signalled with her eyes that she was not to say anything more in front of the children.

With Rhonda's help she got them ready for bed. The moment the girls had settled down and they had returned to the living room, Rhonda demanded to know what had upset her so much.

She listened to Merrion's account of what had happened without making any comment, then laughed derisively.

'You think I'm making a fuss about nothing don't you?' Merrion said angrily. 'Well, I tell you what, you come with us to the park at the weekend and judge for yourself.'

It was such a lovely sunny morning the following Sunday that Merrion suggested they make some sandwiches and have a picnic in the park.

Dilwyn and Nerys were highly excited by the idea and jabbered away like a pair of magpies as they helped to pack up a basket of food and a bottle of lemonade. They were so eager to be on their way that they could hardly stand still for Merrion to tie back their hair with bows to match the crisp little cotton dresses they were wearing.

To Merrion's relief there was no sign of the stranger. Relaxed, she joined in the games the two girls wanted to play until it was time to eat, and then they found a shady spot in which to sit and have their picnic.

As soon as they'd finished eating the two girls were ready for play again. 'Let's play Hide and Seek. We'll hide and you two must come and look for us,' Dilwyn insisted, grabbing Nerys by the hand and running off laughing.

'All right. But we must clear up all our picnic things first. We won't be long, but it gives you a chance to hide,' Merrion called after them. She began packing the mugs and bottle into the basket and screwing up the paper their sandwiches had been wrapped in.

'Give me the rubbish and I'll take it over to the waste bin,' Rhonda offered.

'I think the girls have gone that way so make sure that you don't discover them before they've had a chance to hide,' Merrion laughed.

'No, I won't do that, I'll look the other way if I see them,' Rhonda promised.

Within seconds, however, she was back, Nerys clutched to her chest and Dilwyn clinging on to her skirt, her little legs pumping up and down like pistons as she tried to keep up with Rhonda's rapid pace.

'What's happened?' Merrion dropped everything on to the grass and rushed to meet them.
Dilwyn flung herself into her arms, sobbing
with fright.

'Let's get out of here,' Rhonda panted. 'I'll
explain everything later,' she called back over
her shoulder as she grabbed the basket and
headed for the road. 'Come on,' she urged.
'We'll catch a tram, the first one that comes
along, it doesn't matter where it's going,' she
said as she led the way towards Corporation
Road.

Immediately the two children started to
protest that they didn't want to go home.

'Perhaps we should get a tram into the city
centre and take them to Cathays Park,' Merrion
suggested.

Even on the tram, Rhonda refused to talk
about what had upset her or why she was so
anxious to get away from Grangetown Park.

Nerys was sitting on her lap with her face
pressed into her mother's shoulder and Merrion
found she had her hands full trying to calm
Dilwyn who was both upset and angry because
their game had been spoiled.

'Never mind, cariad, we're taking you to an
even better park,' Merrion consoled her. 'You'll
love it there, you wait and see.'

Neither of the girls were very impressed by
their new surroundings. Cathays Park was an
oasis of tranquillity, and more suited to grown-
ups than children. There were signs saying they

were not allowed to walk on the grass so they weren't free to run around like they'd been able to do in the park at Grangetown. They openly sulked as they walked along the paths between the neat flowerbeds. Even the fact that there was a brass band playing didn't seem to make it any better.

After half an hour, it became obvious that both girls were fed up and tired. Dilwyn was complaining that her shoes hurt and Nerys kept saying that her legs ached.

When Merrion suggested that since the sun had gone in, and the sky had clouded over, perhaps they should go home, Rhonda agreed with a smile of relief.

'Yes, I think that would be the best thing for all of us. And it's early bed for these two when we get there,' she added for Merrion's ears only.

Chapter Eleven

It was almost eight o' clock before the two girls
were finally tucked up in bed and had settled
down to sleep. Merrion waited patiently to hear
the reason for them rushing away from
Grangetown Park as they'd done.

'Go and put your feet up, Merrion, and I'll
make a pot of tea,' Rhonda offered.

'Great!'

Merrion eased off her shoes and made herself
comfortable. She said nothing until Rhonda had
poured the tea and passed her a cup. 'Well, are
you going to tell me all about it?' she asked
expectantly.

Rhonda frowned. 'About what?'

'The reason why we had to dash out of the
park in such a hurry this afternoon, of course.'

'Oh that.' She shrugged and pulled a face.
'Call it a silly whim, nothing more.'

Merrion sipped her tea and studied Rhonda
thoughtfully. There certainly had been something very wrong, but it was quite clear that
Rhonda wasn't prepared to discuss it so there
seemed to be no point in trying to pursue the
matter.

She tried to control her curiosity as they

drank their tea and talked about nothing in particular.

Rhonda had still not opened up by bedtime. Much as she wanted to have it all out in the open, Merrion didn't question her, although she was quite sure that whatever it was that had upset Rhonda it was something that was still troubling her.

In the days that followed Merrion pushed the matter to the back of her mind because there were so many other things to worry about. Dilwyn had a fall and skinned one of her knees rather badly, and it needed regular bathing and a dressing. Then Nerys had a summer cold that made her hot and feverish and very much out of sorts so that she wanted to be cuddled most of the time.

As soon as they were both recovered, Merrion agreed they could go to their favourite park. The girls were both dancing around excitedly as they reached it. Before letting them run off and play Merrion looked nervously towards the park bench where the man usually sat and she was relieved to see that it was empty. Perhaps Rhonda had been right after all and she'd been making a fuss about nothing, she told herself.

The two girls played happily for almost an hour, then Merrion told them it was time to go home. With one on each side of her, holding her hands, they headed for the tram stop in

Corporation Road. They were halfway along Pentrebane Street when she was conscious that they were being followed.

As she looked back over her shoulder her heart sank when she saw that the man who was usually sitting on the park bench was walking along the road behind them.

She felt frightened. She didn't know whether to try and run or to slow down and let him pass them. If she slowed down then he might think she was waiting for him.

She didn't want to alarm the children so she pretended not to notice, but every few steps she looked back to see if he was gaining on them.

She wondered what she would do when they reached the tram stop if he came and stood by them. Should she ignore him if he spoke to them or talk to him?

Fortunately a tram arrived within seconds of them reaching the stop and they were on it and the conductor had rung the bell before the man was near enough to board it.

The children hadn't noticed. Both of them were tired and hungry and when they alighted from the tram in James Street all they could think about was getting home and having their tea.

Merrion pondered about whether to mention the incident to Rhonda or not. She wondered, if she did, whether it would prompt Rhonda to tell her why they'd left the park in such a rush the previous Sunday.

111

She had thought about it several times since
then and she was sure that it had been because
Rhonda must have come face to face with
the man who had been watching the two girls
and who had given them the ball. The same
man who had been following them today.

Why had Rhonda been so frightened of him,
though, and why had she refused to talk about
it? It had to be someone she knew and was
afraid of meeting again.

The matter became more threatening the
following evening. Rhonda was home early for
once and they were in the middle of their evening
meal when there was a rap on the door.

They looked at each other, startled. They
didn't have visitors very often. If it was
someone living in the house who wanted them
for something then they might have tapped on
the door first, but they would have also called
out to Merrion at the same time. They most
certainly wouldn't have delivered such an
authoritative double rap.

When the knock was repeated Merrion went
to open the door. She drew in her breath sharply
when she saw that it was the man from the
park standing there.

'Who is it?' Hearing her exclamation of
surprise Rhonda came over to the door. Her
immediate reaction was even more dramatic.

Pushing Merrion to one side she tried to slam
the door shut, but the man quickly put his foot
over the sill and spread both his arms wide on

112

either side of the door to prevent her from being able to do so.

'If you don't go away I'll call the police,' Rhonda hissed. 'I want nothing to do with you! Understand?'

'It's not you I want to see,' he told her. 'Are you going to let me come in or . . .'

Before he could finish Merrion had regained her wits. With Rhonda's help she managed to dislodge him and push him back into the passageway.

The noise of their scuffle brought several of the other people living in the house out to see what was going on. Merrion called out to them to help and immediately they came to her assistance.

The stranger was dragged away from their door and pushed out into the street, but not before he'd threatened that he'd be back.

Merrion and Rhonda were both apprehensive about what might happen next. Even the knowledge that he'd not be allowed inside the door again and that they could yell for help if he ever did come back and try to get in, didn't completely reassure them.

Often, during the weekdays, Merrion found herself in the house alone with the two girls. Not only were the men out at work, but so, too, were many of the women who lived there. Even those who didn't work were often out shopping or visting their friends or relations.

In the past she had enjoyed these moments of peace when she was free to use the kitchen without any interruption and the two girls could run up and down the passage and make as much noise as they liked. In the days that followed the man's visit, though, she felt on tenterhooks.

'We ought to move,' she told Rhonda. 'You said we would and yet we've been living here for almost five years.'

'I know, but it's a case of being able to afford something better and still pay our way, isn't it? At the moment you don't go short of anything, now do you?'

Merrion looked uncomfortable. 'Not of food and necessities,' she agreed, 'but have you ever stopped to think what it is like living in this place? I'm here all day, you only see it for a few hours at night.'

Rhonda frowned. 'So what exactly are you saying is wrong with the place then?'

'Oh come off it, Rhonda. You don't really have to ask, do you? Think about the home where you were brought up and then ask yourself if two rooms in a slummy street in Tiger Bay is good enough for your daughter.'

'What she's never had she'll never miss,' Rhonda snapped.

'What about when it's time for her to start school? That's not very far off, you know.'

'Is it Nerys you're worried about or Dilwyn?' Rhonda retorted waspishly, her blue eyes blazing.

'Both of them,' Merrion told her quietly.

Rhonda stared at her angrily for a moment or two then burst out laughing. 'What on earth are we fighting for? We need each other and we should be dealing with this problem jointly not letting it divide us.'

'We can't even start to deal with it if you won't tell me what's going on,' Merrion pointed out coldly.

'I know, I'm sorry. Come on, let's have a cuppa and I'll tell you the whole story.'

Merrion didn't know whether to feel sorry or angry when Rhonda had finished.

'Well, say something,' Rhonda begged. 'Don't look so disapproving.'

'I can't believe what you've told me is the truth! He's bald and middle-aged and he's old enough to be your father, let alone Nerys's!'

'I know. I must have been mad,' Rhonda admitted. 'I was very young, had only just started work, and he was very persuasive and . . . and very generous. He showered me with presents.'

'When we first met you told me that Nerys's father was a traveller?'

'Yes, that part was true. That was how I first met him.'

'So if he's married with a wife and three children then why is he suddenly taking an interest in you again . . . and in Nerys?'

Rhonda looked uncomfortable, 'I don't know. It's what he told me, but I have no idea if it is true or not. I was also telling you the truth when I said that the moment he knew I was pregnant he changed his round and stopped coming to the place where I work.'

'So why is he hanging around now? You're not still seeing him are you?'

'Of course I'm not! When I spotted him in the park it was the first time I'd seen him in years. He must have followed you from the park, or trailed me home from work, or something.'

Merrion shook her head. 'I don't understand what's going on and I don't know whether to believe what you've been telling me or not. You go out at night and I don't know where you go or who you see. You could be meeting him for all I know.'

'I'm not. I promise you! I do have men friends, though. I'm not a one-man girl like you are, Merrion. I don't how you can pin all your hopes and dreams on this Roddi you talk about ever coming back. There's precious little chance of him ever finding you since he has no idea where you are living.'

'That has nothing at all to do with what we are talking about at the moment,' Merrion told her firmly. 'Let's get this problem sorted out, shall we!'

Rhonda shrugged. 'What else can I say? I've put my cards on the table, told you the truth. I should have taken it more seriously when you first mentioned this man because it sounded like Harvey Weldon when you described him.'

116

'So why didn't you say so? It might have saved us a whole lot of trouble if you had spoken up.'

'I thought I was imagining it or reading more into it than I should be doing. It's so long since I saw him, or spoke to him, that I thought I was being fanciful.'

'Well, he seems to be real enough,' Merrion told her grimly. 'What do we do now?'

'There's nothing we can do, except stay away from the park in Grangetown and you make sure you keep the door to our room locked when you and the girls are here on your own. Don't open it to anyone. I have no idea where he lives . . .'

'You told me he came from Newport.'

'Well, that was what he told me, but I can't be certain that he was telling the truth.'

'So, apart from the fact that he's a commercial traveller, and that his name is Harvey Weldon, we don't know him from Adam. We can hardly go along to the police with flimsy information like that. They'd simply laugh at us.'

'Go to the police?' Rhonda bristled. 'No one has mentioned doing that!'

'It makes sense if he's pestering us, especially since there's a small child involved.'

'Oh no! I don't want the police brought into this. Do that and before you know what is happening it will be plastered all over the *South Wales Echo* and then I'll be hiding from my parents as well as from him.'

117

'I thought you said they threw you out?'

Rhonda chewed her bottom lip uneasily. 'Actually, I left home before they could go that far.'

'You mean you ran away. Didn't they come looking for you? They knew where you were working.'

'I told them that I had a new job and that I was going to work in London.'

'And they believed you?'

'No reason why they shouldn't. They were probably glad to see the back of me because I was pretty wild when I first left school.'

'You've not changed very much, have you?' Merrion commented grimly.

'I thought I'd reformed pretty well.' Rhonda grinned. 'I'm holding down a responsible job, I pay my way and . . .'

'You still haven't learned your lesson!'

'What do you mean by that?'

'You're still going out with men at night!'

Rhonda shrugged. 'Like I told you before, I don't believe in dreams like you seem to do. Anyway, I've nothing to dream about.'

'What about what the future holds for you and Nerys?'

'I don't know what is in store for us. At the moment I thought we were pretty settled, or we were until this blew up. That's one of the reasons why I thought it was sensible to go on living here. It's not the best of places, but no one troubles us and you seem pretty settled and content with things the way they are.'

'I've had no alternative but to make the best of things,' Merrion pointed out. 'I don't like having to rely on your earnings, but as I see it we both need each other. Another thing, of course, is that I've grown very fond of Nerys. Dilwyn is so attached to her that they're almost like sisters. I'm quite sure that if they were separated it would upset both of them a great deal.'

Chapter Twelve

Merrion and Rhonda were on tenterhooks for quite a long time after the incident with Harvey Weldon, but gradually life resumed its normal timbre.

The long sunny days were drawing to a close so the two little girls barely noticed that they had stopped going to the park in Grangetown. Instead Merrion took them to the Pier Head, or for walks along the canal bank, so that they could feed the seagulls with scraps of bread.

As autumn approached there was an even greater change about to take place. Although Dilwyn would be five at the beginning of September, Nerys would not reach five until after Christmas. Merrion, however, was anxious that she should be allowed to start school at the same time as Dilwyn.

The head teacher at Bute Street Infants School said it was out of the question. Apart from being too young, she was so tiny that the bigger children might push her over or bully her.

Merrion refused to accept this ruling so she decided to apply to another school, nearby in Hurman Street.

At first she was told much the same thing.

Merrion pleaded with the headmistress, Miss Stevens, explaining how the two little girls had been brought up together right from birth, and emphasised that it would be like separating twins to part them. After some protracted consideration, Miss Stevens eventually gave way.

'Very well,' she conceded. 'Nerys can start school in September, but if I find that it causes any problems then I might deem it necessary for her to be taken out of school until the start of the Easter term,' she told Merrion.

The two girls were very excited about the thought of going to school and looked forward eagerly to their first day. Rhonda had bought them new canvas satchels to take their lunch in each day. She'd also kitted them out with new shoes, skirts and jumpers which they weren't allowed to wear until the day they were to start school.

Several times Merrion walked with them from Sophia Terrace, along James Street, over Clarence Road Bridge and then down Hurman Street to the school gates to work out how long it was going to take them to get there each day.

There were a couple of older children, Pedro and Ella Palerno, living next door to them in Sophia Terrace who also attended Hurman Street School. They were eager to take the two little girls each morning, and bring them home again in the afternoon, but Merrion insisted on walking there with them herself. Dilwyn and

Nerys begged to be allowed to walk to school with the other children, but Rhonda insisted they must let Merrion take them.

'You two always say the same thing when it's something we want to do.' Nerys scowled, her green eyes bright with tears, her mouth screwed up tight and angry.

'That's because we know what is best,' her mother told her sharply.

'Perhaps later on you will be able to walk to school on your own with Pedro and Ella,' Merrion promised, 'but not for the first week or two.'

'Can Pedro and Ella walk along to school with us then?' Dilwyn asked.

'Of course they can if they want to do so.'

On the first day, however, children who were starting school for the first time went in later than the others so there was no problem about Merrion being the one to take them.

When she handed them over to their teacher, Miss Lewis, at the classroom door, Merrion felt herself blinded by tears. It was the first time she had ever been parted from them and as she walked away she felt as if she was deserting them. It had brought back memories of how abandoned she had felt after Roddi and Emlyn had gone out of her life, and the longing to see them again added to her feeling of unhappiness.

The two little girls had no such qualms. Holding hands they advanced confidently into the classroom and joined the little huddle of other five-year-olds who were all waiting to be told what to do next.

Merrion was at the school gates waiting for them when they came out at the end of the afternoon. She had expected them both to be tired out and subdued, but to her immense surprise they were bubbling over with excitement.

After gabbling noisily about what they had been doing they galloped away ahead of her, calling out to Pedro and Ella to wait for them. Merrion left them to walk ahead with the other two children until they reached Clarence Road. Then she called them back and made them hold her hand as they walked over the bridge into James Street.

As she listened to their excited chatter before they went to bed about the wonderful time they'd had, Rhonda, too, was equally relieved that they had settled so well.

'Can we walk to school with our friends Ella and Pedro tomorrow?' they asked eagerly.

'Yes, but not on your own,' Merrion told them.

The same question was repeated every morning for weeks. Then, in November, when it was cold and dark, foggy and wet, they accepted that they needed her to be with them.

When Christmas was over and the evenings slowly began to get lighter they once again began badgering her about being allowed to walk to school on their own with their friends. Merrion agreed that if she accompanied them over the bridge, and as far as the top of Hurman Street, they could run the rest of the way to school with Pedro and Ella.

'It's only a few hundred yards and I stand there until I see them go in the gates. Then I hang around until the bell goes so I know that they have gone inside the school building and that they are quite safe,' she explained to Rhonda.

'I wonder why it is so important to them that they should go on their own?' Rhonda pondered.

'I think it's because very few other parents take their children to school and they don't like feeling that they are different.'

'I still don't like the idea of them going even that short way without you.'

'Neither do I, and I certainly don't intend to let them out of my sight, so don't worry. There's far too much traffic over Clarence Road Bridge for a start.'

It was the week after Easter 1925 and they'd been at school for over six months when tragedy struck. It was a glorious spring day and the two girls were both dressed in pretty blue and yellow cotton frocks, long white socks and shiny black shoes. Dilwyn was wearing a yellow cardigan with hers and Nerys had on a blue one.

Merrion met them out of school and thought

124

how lovely they looked as they skipped along ahead of her holding hands with each other. She was walking with a couple of other mothers and she was completely at ease with the situation. Both the girls knew that when they reached the end of Hurman Street they must wait there for her because she still insisted that they held her hand as they walked over Clarence Road Bridge and into James Street.

As she parted company with the other mothers, who were turning right when they reached Clarence Road, Merrion looked for her own two charges. Dilwyn was tall for her age and was head and shoulders above most of her classmates, so it was usually easy to spot her. Dilwyn's shiny dark head and Nerys's bright auburn hair alongside her stood out from the crowd.

She couldn't see either of them. Then she spotted Dilwyn and a frisson of alarm shivered through her because she was hunched down by a lamp-post sobbing her heart out.

Merrion ran towards her. 'Whatever's the matter?' she asked. She felt apprehensive as she pulled Dilwyn to her feet and hugged her close, wiping away her tears.

'It's Nerys,' Dilwyn sobbed hysterically, snuffling and crying at the same time.

'Nerys? Why, what's she done?'

Dilwyn tried very hard to tell her, but all she could do was choke and stutter.

'So where is Nerys?' Merrion looked round

anxiously for the younger girl, feeling thoroughly unnerved because she couldn't see her anywhere. 'Where is Nerys?' she repeated turning back to Dilwyn.

'Gone!' Dilwyn sobbed. 'She's gone!' Her voice rose in a panicked scream that rasped through Merrion's head.

'What do you mean?' she demanded, her own fear making her voice strident.

Thoroughly frightened she shook Dilwyn. 'Come on, tell me what you mean. Where has Nerys gone?'

'With the man,' Dilwyn choked. 'The man grabbed hold of her and took her.'

Cold fear clutched at Merrion. For a moment she felt paralysed. People bumped into her and traffic moved past her as she stood there, clutching tight hold of Dilwyn, unable to move out of the way. Overcome with dread, her mind was a blank and she was unable to think what to do next.

Instinctively she knew who the man was. It must be Harvey Weldon! There was no one else who could be interested in Nerys or would dream of doing such a thing.

It was one of her worst nightmares coming true. Ever since he had spoken to them in the park she'd felt concerned. After he'd called at their home in Sophia Terrace, and Rhonda had revealed that he was Nerys's father, she'd dreaded that he'd be back again or even that something like this might happen.

Her fears had slowly ebbed in the months since then, but her visions about what could happen had been so vivid that several times she'd been on the point of telling Rhonda about them. She hadn't done so because she'd thought that Rhonda would laugh at her and tell her that she was a scare-monger.

Rhonda rarely saw the dark side to any problem. She would get upset when something didn't work out as she wanted it to do, she'd flare up, but ten minutes later she'd be laughing about whatever it was that was worrying her and the next minute it would be completely forgotten.

Since she'd confessed about Harvey Weldon and admitted that he was Nerys's father, she seemed to have put the whole thing out of her mind. She'd never mentioned the incident about him coming to the house ever again. For a few weeks, she had come home straight from work every night, so perhaps she had felt some anxiety. Then gradually she'd resorted to her previous habit and gone out straight from work two or three nights a week. Merrion accepted the arrangement and neither of them ever discussed it.

Nor did Rhonda refer to Roddi again, she simply accepted that Merrion was a home bird and was content to dream about the past and even about the future, but to do nothing at all about it.

All this flashed through Merrion's mind as

127

she tried desperately to think what to do next. Somehow she had to find Nerys before Rhonda came home from work, but she had no idea how to go about it.

Again she questioned her own daughter about what had happened, but Dilwyn was still too upset to be coherent.

Merrion looked round frantically, wondering where Harvey Weldon might have taken Nerys.

'Why did you let her go with him?' she demanded, turning back to Dilwyn. 'Did you see which way they went?'

'I didn't let her go, he grabbed hold of her and ran off with her,' Dilwyn sobbed.

'So which way did they go?' Merrion repeated impatiently.

'He jumped on a tram with her,' Dilwyn blubbered.

'A tram! Which way was it going?'

'That way!' Dilwyn pointed in the direction of Corporation Road.

Merrion felt panic robbing her of her senses. By now the tram would almost have reached the centre of Cardiff. They could be anywhere. If he got off at the top of Wood Street, by the main railway station, then from there he could travel absolutely anywhere. He could get a train north to Wrexham or Chester, or go to Birmingham or even London. They might never be able to find her again.

As a commercial traveller, Harvey Weldon

probably knew his way around all the main towns in the country.

Merrion took a deep breath, trying to calm down and think clearly. She wiped Dilwyn's tears away and tried to comfort her. Taking her by the hand, Merrion then walked determinedly towards James Street to see if she could find a policeman. She didn't want to have to involve the police, but that seemed to be the only way they would ever manage to find Nerys.

As the constable listened to her story his face became more and more grave. 'You think you knew who the man was,' he probed. 'So why would he want to take this little girl, why not both of them if they were together?'

Reluctantly Merrion admitted that Harvey Weldon was Nerys's father.

'And you are her mother?'

'No!' Merrion shook her head. 'No, I look after her. I share rooms with her mother in Sophia Terrace.'

The officer paused for a moment as he wrote down what she had told him in his notebook. After he had read it back to her he insisted that she accompany him to the police station in Bute Street.

Once there she had to go over all the details again. Dilwyn was questioned. The sergeant interviewing them encouraged the child to give a description of Harvey Weldon. He then asked where they would be able to find Rhonda as they would need to talk to her as well.

Merrion looked at the clock on the wall over his desk and was shocked when she saw how late it was.

'She may be at home by now,' she said hesitantly. 'I can't be sure, because she sometimes goes out with friends straight from work.'

'Right, well one of our constables will walk back to Sophia Terrace with you and if she is there he can ask her some questions.'

Rhonda was already there. She'd been at home for almost half an hour and she was becoming anxious because she knew Merrion was a creature of habit and she couldn't understand why none of them were there. She knew that they always came straight home, and that the girls played together indoors while Merrion prepared their meal, and then it was off to bed because they had to be up early for school the next morning.

Rhonda looked puzzled when she saw the policeman, then when she realised that Nerys wasn't with them the colour drained from her face.

'Has there been some sort of accident?' She looked frantically from one to the other. 'Tell me what's happened. Has Nerys been hurt?'

Merrion and the policeman both tried to answer at once and to try and explain the situation, but Rhonda seemed unable to take it in.

'It's your fault, you knew this could happen,'

she accused Merrion. 'Why didn't you watch over her more carefully. If you hadn't let her run ahead, if you'd been holding her hand . . .' She broke off in floods of tears, pushing Merrion away angrily when she tried to put her arms around her.

Chapter Thirteen

It was shortly before midnight when the police eventually brought Nerys home. The long wait of almost seven hours filled with stress and mental torment had seemed endless for both Merrion and Rhonda.

Nerys was tired and frightened, but otherwise unharmed in any way. She'd been found in Grangetown Park, sitting on a bench with Harvey Weldon, eating fish and chips. Her pretty blue and yellow cotton dress that had looked so crisp and clean when she'd left home that morning was now dirty and crumpled. Her white socks were in wrinkles around her ankles and the toes of her shiny black shoes scuffed.

Merrion's heart thudded as she looked at her, wondering what ordeal she'd encountered in the passing hours to transform her into such a dishevelled state.

Rhonda hugged her, kissed her and cried over her, refusing to let Merrion anywhere near her.

'I think this little one needs a nice warm drink and then to be tucked up in bed where she'll feel safe and sound,' the fatherly policeman advised. 'We'll come back in the morning to talk to her and find out what she can tell us. No more questions tonight, mind,' he went on sternly, looking from Rhonda to Merrion. 'She needs some sleep, understand?'

He waited until they had both nodded in agreement. 'When we come back in the morning we'll also want to talk to both of you as well, of course, and the other little girl. You'll have to keep both of them home from school tomorrow.'

Nerys clung on to her mother while Merrion fussed around making her a drink and trying to coax her to eat a biscuit. Nerys refused to go into her own bed so Rhonda took her in with her, cuddling her close and trying to reassure her that it was all over and that everything was all right now and she was quite safe.

When the police returned the next morning, they needed every detail about the abduction they could extract from all of them. They repeated the same questions over and over, probing deeply to make sure that nothing had been overlooked or forgotten.

Harvey Weldon, they assured them, was in custody, and if found guilty of kidnapping or abducting the child, he would be severely punished. His story, however, did not tally in many ways with Rhonda's.

Rhonda was reluctant to talk to the police and would only give them the barest details. She stuck to the story she'd told Merrion, namely that Harvey Weldon had been a commercial traveller, and that when she'd been very young he'd cajoled her into having an affair with him. Tearfully, she insisted that the moment he'd heard she was pregnant he'd vanished and she'd never heard any more from him. In the last few months, however, he'd tried to get in touch with Nerys.

'According to his version he was forced to move to another area and it was only quite recently that he heard you'd had a baby. When he realised that the child was his he was anxious to find out if you needed any help and also to get to know her. He even goes as far as to say that he wants to marry you and make a home for you both.'

'Stealing her little girl was a funny way to go about it,' Merrion interrupted.

'Foolish, certainly,' the policeman agreed. 'He claims he came here to this house to explain all this to you, Miss Rees, but that you'd have nothing to do with him. In fact, according to his statement, you shut the door in his face.'

'Did he also tell you that he followed me and the girls in the park week after week and even tried to win Nerys over by giving her a ball?' Merrion asked.

To try and bring the matter to a close, Rhonda claimed she didn't want to press charges. 'I simply want him to go away and leave us in peace,' she stated.

'Are you quite sure you don't want to marry Harvey Weldon and give Nerys a proper home?'

134

Merrion asked bluntly once they were on their own.

'Marry him!' Rhonda's pretty face darkened. 'You've seen him! He must be fifty-five if he's a day and he's become paunchy and bald. I wouldn't have him as a husband if he was the last man on earth.'

Merrion could see her point. She'd always held the opinion that Harvey Weldon seemed to be old enough to be Rhonda's father. Furthermore, as far as she could see, there was nothing in the least bit attractive about him.

'What are you going to do if he wants to help support Nerys?' she asked.

'Turn him down flat, of course! If I took a penny piece from him then he'd expect to be allowed to see her and that's the last thing I want to happen. I've managed without any help from him up until now and I'll go on doing so.'

'Are you sure that's wise?' Merrion asked doubtfully. 'What are you going to do when she starts asking why she hasn't got a dad like the other children?'

'Young Dilwyn never seems to ask. What's more, she seems to be doing all right without a dad, doesn't she?'

'Yes, but she has no choice. Sadly, her dad is dead,' Merrion pointed out.

'As far as Nerys is concerned then so is hers,' Rhonda said in a tone that brooked no argument. 'Now, can we forget all about it? That's the end of the matter as far as I am concerned.'

135

It was nowhere near the end of the matter, however. Although the police withdrew charges, and Harvey Weldon was released on the proviso that he never went near Rhonda or Nerys ever again, someone leaked the information to the newspapers.

Neither Merrion nor Rhonda would speak directly to any of the reporters who came to interview them, so numerous different versions of the story appeared in the papers. All of them were garbled accounts and gleaned from information obtained from people living in the same house or from some of their neighbours. As a result it was Merrion's name, not Rhonda's, that appeared as being the mother of the child who'd been abducted.

Rhonda was delighted. 'You don't mind, do you?' she laughed when Merrion appeared to be annoyed about this. 'No one knows you, you've no family in Cardiff, so what does it matter?'

'That's not the point, though, is it?'

Rhonda's boss, Miss Fitch, read the report, however, and she recognised the name Harvey Weldon. She remembered the commercial traveller who had called on them regularly until some five years or so earlier. It didn't take her very long to put two and two together.

She said nothing to Rhonda but went higher. At the end of the week Rhonda was called into the office and told that her services would no longer be needed.

Rhonda couldn't believe what was happening. She knew they were busy because there was suddenly a fashion craze for highly decorated straw hats and she was an expert at producing them.

When she protested and demanded an explanation for her dismissal, the reason she was given by Miss Fitch left her extremely angry.

'This company lost a very useful contact because of you,' Miss Fitch told her. 'Harvey Weldon was exceptionally good at his job and carried an excellent range of products and it was a great loss to us when he stopped calling here.'

'So what has that got to do with me?' Rhonda protested.

'I don't think it is necessary for me to go into the sordid details,' Miss Fitch said stiffly. 'As a result of your wanton behaviour, he obviously had to move to another area.'

'If you were going to sack me, then you should have done so then, not now,' Rhonda railed.

'Yes, we should have done. Had we realised that he was the father of the baby you were expecting we most certainly would have done. As it was we were extremely lenient and kept you on, even taking you back without any questions once your confinement was over.'

'You did that because you knew I was first class at my job and you didn't want to lose me,' Rhonda pointed out indignantly, her face hardening.

'This company is not in the habit of employing married women, or women with young children, as you very well know,' Miss Fitch blustered. 'We made an exception in your case because . . .'

'Because you all knew how experienced I was and how good I was at my job! So what's changed? I've never taken a day off work since Nerys was born . . .'

'Maybe it would have been better if you had, Miss Rees. If you hadn't left your child in some other woman's care, then she might never have been abducted and this sordid affair would never have come to light,' Miss Fitch snapped triumphantly.

'As long as I do my job satisfactorily and I never take any time off, then my private life is none of your affair,' Rhonda persisted.

Miss Fitch looked most disapproving. 'Not as long as it is private, but when one of our employees has an illegitimate baby and then the whole affair is plastered over the news-papers . . .'

'My name is not in the papers, it is only you who believes that it is me.'

'Come, Miss Rees. Let's not bandy words any further. We both know that it is you, even though you gave a false name. The sooner you leave these premises the better it will be.'

Rhonda was determined not to be beaten so

she tried another tack. 'I still have to provide a home and pay someone to care for my daughter while I am working,' she pointed out.

'I'm afraid that is your concern, not ours!' Miss Fitch told her primly. 'Now please leave the building before I call for someone to remove you.'

Merrion was as outraged as Rhonda when she heard the news. 'What will we do now?' she asked. 'We count on your wages, it's the only money we have coming in. Perhaps, after all, you should ask Harvey Weldon for some help,' she added as an afterthought.

'Never! I'll beg in the streets before I take a penny piece from him,' Rhonda snapped.

'Do you think you can find another job or should I try and find work?' Merrion asked.

'Cleaning public lavatories, you mean,' Rhonda sniped. 'That's about all you're trained to do, isn't it?'

'That's hardly fair,' Merrion protested.

'Well, it is your fault that we're in this mess. If you'd taken proper care of Nerys and never let that wretch take her away, none of this would have happened. No one would have known the truth about her or me and I'd still have my well-paid job.'

'There must be other milliners who need your handiwork,' Merrion reasoned. 'What about one of the big Cardiff stores like James Howell's or David Morgan's? You've so much experience . . .'

'And a red-hot scandal attached to my name so that none of them will touch me with a barge pole,' Rhonda snapped bitterly.

'You don't know that,' Merrion told her firmly. 'Remember it was my name, not yours, that appeared in the paper. It was only because your Miss Fitch once knew Harvey Weldon that she managed to put two and two together.'

'Yes.' Rhonda's face brightened. 'You do have a point. It might be worth trying one of the big shops. I'll have to explain why I am leaving my present job, of course,' she said thoughtfully. 'It mightn't be all that easy. It's no good telling them that I simply wanted a change.'

'Let's leave it a day or two, then, and see if we can think up a more plausible story.'

'No, I'll strike now while the iron's hot,' Rhonda insisted. 'If I delay, old Fitch might gossip and spread the word and then I wouldn't stand a chance.'

Rhonda tried all the big stores in Cardiff but without success. They simply weren't interested in taking on any more people in their millinery department. Only once did she even manage to get an interview with one of the heads of department and when she mentioned how much she had been earning in her previous job, they immediately lost interest.

'No matter how proficient you may be, or how much experience you've had, we couldn't possibly pay you the same sort of wage,' she was told frostily.

'Perhaps I could start on less,' Rhonda suggested with a bright smile.

'Thank you for calling, but if that is the sort of money you expect to earn, then I can tell you now you will never get it working for us,' she was told sharply as she was shown the door.

Merrion was even more depressed than Rhonda. She was managing on as little as she possibly could, trying to stretch out the few shillings they still had, but she knew it was hopeless. Because of the publicity even the local shopkeepers, who knew her well, were hesitant to give them credit.

Chapter Fourteen

'I think you are mad not to press charges against Harvey Weldon,' Merrion stated.

'I want to get away from everything to do with him,' Rhonda said sulkily.

'How can you say that after what happened to Nerys?'

'He didn't hurt her.'

'He frightened the life out of the poor little thing; she's scared of her own shadow at the moment,' Merrion pointed out.

'She'll get over it. Now I've lost my job, I'll be able to be with her all the time so that will help.'

'You mean you're not going to look for another job?' Merrion asked anxiously.

'Not for a while,' Rhonda hedged. 'I want to be around for Nerys until she's had time to forget what happened.'

'So what are we all going to live on in the meantime, fresh air?'

'Stop worrying, Merrion. I've got a few bob saved up, enough to keep us going for a few weeks.'

'I suppose it's the money that you were putting aside to help get us out of Sophia Terrace,' Merrion said bitterly.

'Yes, as a matter of fact, it is. Does that spoil all your big dreams for the future?'

Merrion sighed. 'You can laugh at me all you like, Rhonda, but it's trying to be optimistic that keeps me going,' she added with a catch in her voice.

'You mean until lover boy comes sailing into port and sweeps you off to a better life,' Rhonda said disparagingly.

'He will, one day,' Merrion assured her confidently. 'Dreams never fail, they always come true in the end.'

'The bad ones, do you mean? Your dreams about the pit explosion, things like that.'

'Don't mock. I warned you that something was going to happen to the girls.'

'You said an accident! What happened to Nerys could hardly be classed as an accident could it?'

Merrion ran her hands through her straight dark hair, pushing it back from her forehead. 'I'm still haunted by thoughts of Harvey Weldon. There's something I don't understand . . . it's as if I've walked out in the middle of the picture, as if it's still not over yet.'

'Well, don't tell me. I'm depressed enough as it is. I don't want to hear any more of your fanciful stories.'

Merrion sighed and moved across to the other side of the room. She didn't want to quarrel with Rhonda, not when she was still so upset. 'I've made my mind up,' she told her.

143

I'm going to look for work. There must be something I can do.'

'Part-time work where you can start after nine o'clock and finish in time for you to collect the girls from school?'

'If I can. For the moment, though, while you are still not working, you can take the girls to school each day and collect them, can't you?'

Rhonda raised her eyebrows. 'I suppose so.'

'Good! Well, you can make a start today by collecting them this afternoon. I'm going to tidy myself up and go out and have a look around. There must be something I can do . . . apart from cleaning lavatories,' she added with a wry smile.

Merrion had no idea where to start looking. She had no qualifications, no experience except cooking, cleaning and looking after two small girls, so, she mused, what hopes had she of finding anyone willing to employ her?

She wouldn't be able to find a job today, but at least she could enjoy the freedom of an afternoon on her own without the encumbrance of two small girls, and it would be like a holiday.

She caught a tram from the bottom of Bute Street, intending to go straight to the city centre, but she alighted at the Hayes. The noisy, colourful outdoor market was what she needed to clear her head of the grey clouds that whirled inside it, she told herself. From there she'd walk up St Mary Street, and wander through the

144

arcades and the big stores, even though she had no money to spend. There was no law against looking and dreaming. Someday, she vowed, she'd move right away from Tiger Bay, make a decent home for herself and Dilwyn and shop at Howell's and Morgan's and buy whatever she fancied from all the wonderful things they had on display there.

First, she reminded herself, she needed to find a job in order to buy the basic essentials to keep them alive. Food was the priority, that and the rent of their rooms in Sophia Terrace.

The shops were buzzing. Lovely summer clothes, floaty dresses, pretty hats, dainty shoes. She thought how wonderful it would be to have a job where she was selling them, not simply admiring them in the shop windows. She was tempted to go in and ask if they had any vacancies, but knowing that the moment they heard that she had no experience they'd turn her down, she decided not to even think of doing anything like that. Today she was having a holiday, it was to be a day for enjoying her freedom.

It was almost half past four by the time she caught the tram home. There wasn't one going straight to the Pier Head so she took the one that went down Corporation Road and over Clarence Road Bridge. It took a little longer but it would be a pleasant ending to her day.

As they reached Clarence Road there was a hold-up. Traffic had all come to a standstill before the bridge and she could see that there were at least three trams in front of them.

There was a lot of muttering and speculation about the reason for the hold-up, but no one seemed to know exactly what had happened to cause the delay.

'It seems we could be here for quite some time so it might be quicker to walk, that's if the police will let you cross over the bridge,' the conductor announced.

'Why can't you tell us what's happened?' one or two passengers demanded.

'Because I have no idea! There's been an accident or something on the bridge, or so it seems. You can get off if you want to, there will be no extra charge if you do,' he joked.

'And no refund either,' someone retorted.

Merrion decided to walk the rest of the way. She was already much later than she had intended to be and there seemed to be so many children about that she was suddenly anxious in case Rhonda had forgotten to go and collect the girls from school.

When she reached the bridge there was a whole crowd of people clustered there.

'I'm afraid you can't go across, not at the moment,' a policeman told her, barring her way along the pavement.

'Why, what has happened?'

'A man's gone into the Taff,' he said tersely.

'Off the bridge, you mean? How terrible! What happened, was it an accident?'

146

He moved away without answering.

'The fellow jumped in or so it seems,' a woman nearby told Merrion.

'Jumped? How awful! I wonder what on earth made him do a thing like that?'

'It seems the police were chasing him.'

'Oh my goodness! What had he done? Had he stolen something?'

'No, he tried to take away a little girl as she was coming out of school, by all accounts.'

Merrion felt bile rising in her throat, her head swam and she felt herself swaying.

'Here, are you all right, my lovely?' the woman asked anxiously. 'You've gone as white as a sheet. You look as though you'd seen a ghost. It wasn't because of what I said about the man, was it?'

'No, no, I'm all right,' Merrion told her.

'You certainly don't look it! Do you want to lean up against that lamp-post over there for a minute? I'll help you if you like.'

Merrion shook her away. 'I'm quite all right. I felt a bit faint for a moment, that's all.'

'Well, whatever you say . . .'

'So do you know who this little girl was?' Merrion asked her anxiously.

'No, but it seems she was walking along with a bunch of other kids, and he swooped on her, grabbed her by the arm, and tried to drag her off.'

Merrion shivered, her mind filled with thoughts of Harvey Weldon. The words 'with

147

a bunch of other kids' drummed in her head. If it was a child walking home with a group of others, however, it couldn't be Nerys, or Dilwyn, because Rhonda was going to collect them from school. They'd be safely at home by now and probably wondering where on earth she was, she kept telling herself.

She wished she'd caught the other tram, the one that would have taken her down Bute Street. She'd have been home by now. They would all have been sitting down having their meal and she'd be telling them all about her day out.

She tried to think of some way of getting past the police cordon, but Clarence Road Bridge was the only means of crossing the river Taff at that point. The only other way would be to go back into the city and cross over at Wood Street so that she could come down the other side of the Taff. That would take ages. It would be better to stay where she was and wait. The police were bound to let them through soon, she told herself.

She tried not to fret about how late she was going to be and how worried Rhonda would be. There was nothing she could do about it, she told herself. The police were still holding people back and more and more police seemed to be gathering on the bridge.

There was a general sigh of relief when it seemed that at last there was activity going on underneath the bridge. They could see that some of the policemen were now down on the river bank under the bridge and that there was an ambulance waiting there as well.

'They've fished him out . . .'

'He looks dead to me,' the woman who'd spoken to Merrion stated.

'He might only be unconscious . . .'

'No, he's been in the water far too long,' she insisted.

'They're putting him into the ambulance ready to take him away,' another woman observed.

'Taking him to the infirmary, probably . . .'

'We should be able to go soon . . .'

The babble all around her as people voiced their opinions sounded like a chorus in Merrion's ears. It stopped her from thinking the terrible thoughts that filled her mind.

Minutes later the police moved the temporary barriers away and the crowd of people, Merrion amongst them, swept over the bridge, hurrying like the rest of them to make up for lost time.

Merrion was expecting Rhonda to be irate and up in arms because she was so late, but there was no sign of her or the two girls when she reached home.

Rather puzzled, she went next door to ask Ella and Pedro if they knew where Dilwyn and Nerys might be, but there was no sign of them either.

The only answer seemed to be that Rhonda

had taken the girls out somewhere. Remembering the crowds at Clarence Road Bridge Merrion wondered if they had been caught up there. If it had happened as they were coming out of school, then probably the road from Hurman Street might well have been closed off and they would have had to wait the same as she had done. In which case, she told herself, they should be home at any moment.

To stop herself worrying she started to get the meal ready since doubtless they'd all be hungry when they got in.

When, almost an hour later, there was still no sign of them, she began to get very agitated. She knew Rhonda had been annoyed by her insistence that it was time she found some work, but surely she wouldn't respond by taking the girls off somewhere and staying out this late without letting her know. Rhonda knew only too well how nervous she was ever since the incident with Harvey Weldon and Nerys.

Unable to sit still she went back out into the street to see if there was any sign of them, or even of the children next door. It was now well after six o'clock. She wondered if their mother was at home, and she rapped on the door. Mrs Palerno came to the door with both children crowding behind her.

'Terribly upsetting isn't it?' she exclaimed, her face creased with concern, before Merrion could even speak. 'They sent for me at work because my two had to go along to the police station and answer questions about it all.'

'About what?'

'You don't know?' Her dark eyes widened in surprise.

Merrion shook her head. 'No, I've been out all afternoon. Rhonda was collecting our two from school. Only . . . only I'm worried, because they're not back yet.'

'Well, no, they wouldn't be. They're still talking to the police, I expect.' She looked down at her own two children. 'Weren't Dilwyn and Nerys still at the police station when we left?'

'Yes, and so was Nerys's mum,' Ella said quickly. 'They asked them a lot more questions than they did us. Perhaps they think that it was Nerys's fault.'

'What are you talking about, Ella? What might have been Nerys's fault?'

'The man jumping off the bridge,' Pedro piped up, his eyes wide with excitement. 'He was waiting by the school gate and when he took hold of Nerys's hand she started screaming. Her mum hollered out for a policeman and one came round the corner and started chasing the man,' the boy gabbled breathlessly.

'Yes,' Ella chimed in, 'and then the man ran as fast as he could to get away and he climbed up on top of the railings along the side of the bridge in Clarence Road and then all of a sudden he seemed to topple over into the water.'

151

'No one could get across the bridge after that and the children who were on their way home from school had to wait in Hurman Street until they'd fished him out,' Mrs Palerno added.

'Do you know who he was?' Merrion asked shakily.

Solemnly they all looked at each other and then they shook their heads.

'He was a short, fat man,' Pedro said.

'With a dark trilby hat,' Ella added.

'Nerys didn't half scream when he grabbed hold of her arm,' Pedro added.

'Nerys is all right though?' Merrion asked anxiously.

'She was crying a lot,' Ella said, 'but she stopped when we got to the police station because one of the policemen gave her a toffee.'

'They didn't give us one,' Pedro complained.

'Well, you weren't involved, were you,' their mother told them, ruffling Pedro's thick, dark curls.

'We could have been,' Ella stated. 'I was holding Nerys's hand when the man grabbed hold of her.'

'Yes, and you shouldn't have let go of it,' her brother stated accusingly.

'Never mind arguing about it all now,' their mother told them. 'Both of you run along inside, I'll be with you in a moment.'

She waited until they were out of earshot before turning back to Merrion. 'Nerys is all right,' she affirmed, 'and so is your little

Dilwyn. The police probably needed them to tell their story over again after they'd heard what the other children had to say. I expect they'll be home any minute now. By the way,' she asked curiously, 'do you have any idea who the man might be?'

Chapter Fifteen

Merrion found it hard to contend with Rhonda's depression after she learned that Harvey Weldon had died. She realised that it was a terrible tragedy. The fact that Rhonda had witnessed what had happened and, to some extent, had even been involved, was quite dreadful. Even so, since Rhonda claimed she had never cared for Harvey Weldon and wanted nothing at all to do with him, Merrion felt that she should put it all behind her. The publicity had died down very quickly, and most people seemed to have forgotten all about it after a few days. Merrion thought that they should do the same and get on with their lives.

She could understand that Rhonda didn't want to face the outside world for a while. She even accepted the fact that they would have to sacrifice the money they'd saved up towards moving so that they had something to live on.

Merrion also quickly became aware, however, that they couldn't exist day after day, side by side in two small rooms without getting on each other's nerves.

She was used to a well-planned routine. The children were wakened at eight o'clock without fail and both of them were washed, dressed and sitting down to breakfast fifteen minutes later. They left the house promptly at twenty to nine to walk to school. Ella and Pedro were usually waiting outside their own front door. If they weren't, then the girls would knock on their door and shout out their names.

Merrion never waited for them. 'They can run and catch us up, she always said and insisted that Dilwyn and Nerys held her hand and set off with her.

Merrion was proud of the fact that they had never once been late since the day they'd first started school. Now, with Rhonda underfoot in the morning, their routine had to be abandoned. Instead of urging Nerys to hurry up and get dressed Rhonda encouraged her to creep into her bed for a cuddle. As Merrion tried to comb Nerys's hair, Rhonda insisted on giving her another hug and ruffling it so that more often than not Merrion had to comb it all over again.

Although she was at home all day Rhonda made no attempt to help with the cleaning or shopping. Instead she sat drinking cup after cup of tea and leaving a trail of dirty cups everywhere.

As the weeks passed, it worried Merrion that Rhonda seemed to have given up any intention of finding work. They were now down to their last few shillings. The only way she would have

155

enough money to buy food for the weekend, Merrion thought worriedly, would be to take something along to the pawn shop. Or else to try and find a job herself.

The last time she'd mentioned doing so Rhonda had been so scathing about her chances of finding anything that she'd lost what little confidence she had.

Now she wondered if perhaps when she told Rhonda that there was no money at all she'd do something herself about finding work, or at least be a little more tolerant of her idea that she should be the one to try and get a job.

When she mentioned their predicament Rhonda seemed almost uninterested. 'You do whatever you think best,' she said, and shrugged.

'Will you collect the girls from school this afternoon, then?' Merrion asked.

'I suppose I'll have to if you're not here.'

'Well, I can't be in two places at once,' Merrion snapped.

'No one said you could. For heaven's sake go and find yourself a job, if you can. It's what you've wanted to do for a long time now, isn't it?'

'Yes,' Merrion admitted, 'I do sometimes feel fed up with having no outside interest.'

'There was nothing to stop you getting yourself a little job once they started school,' Rhonda pointed out.

'I know, but you said that it wouldn't be easy to find one that fitted in with school hours.'

'Well, now you don't have to worry about that. If you can find any work then you can spend the whole day doing it. The trouble is finding anyone who will employ someone as inexperienced as you are,' she added unpleasantly.

'So what sort of work do you think I should be looking for?' Merrion asked, biting her lip. She was hurt by Rhonda's words but tried to hold her temper in check.

'You mean you really are serious?' Rhonda said in feigned astonishment.

'Very much so.'

Merrion grew more and more disheartened as they wrote down the sort of work that Rhonda thought she was capable of doing, because it seemed there were so very few jobs for which she could apply. None of the ones that they'd listed appealed to her in the slightest.

It wasn't that she objected to manual work, but she had no experience of factory work, so it was unlikely that she would be taken on. When it came to domestic jobs, apart from looking after the children and their home, Merrion's only experience had been cleaning public conveniences and that was something she had no wish to do ever again.

'What would you have done with your life if your dad hadn't been killed in that pit explosion and your mam and little brother hadn't died almost as soon as you came to Cardiff?' Rhonda quizzed.

'I'd probably still be living back in Cwmglo, where I was born and grew up,' Merrion sighed. Her eyes grew dreamy, 'I'd be married by now, I'm sure.'

'To your precious Roddi?'

'Yes, to Roddi! We'd probably have a family of little ones by now,' she said wistfully.

'You still think he'll come back, don't you,' Rhonda murmured in disbelief.

'Of course I do!'

'How can you go on hoping like that when you've never heard a word from him all this time?'

'It's not just hoping,' Merrion said, her colour rising. 'It's my dreams for the future, see. I never stop dreaming about him, and about my brother Emlyn and how wonderful it will all be when they both come back. I can see Roddi as clearly as I'm able to see you,' she added with a deep sigh.

'He's over five years older now, remember,' Rhonda pointed out. 'He's probably grown fat and may even be going bald, just like Harvey Weldon did.'

'No, I shouldn't think so,' Merrion said confidently. 'He wasn't a middle-aged man like that Harvey Weldon, he was young. A big, strong, handsome young man. Going to sea will have kept him fit. He's probably well bronzed by now and even broader than when I last saw him.'

'If you can see him as clearly as all that in your dreams,' Rhonda teased, 'then why can't you see what ship he's on? If you could see the name of it then we could check all the shipping lists and find out when he's likely to be in port.'

'My dreams aren't like that,' Merrion sighed. 'I wish they were. Nevertheless, scoff all you want, but they give me hope that he is still out there somewhere.'

'And that he's still thinking of you? He might have a wife and children by now!'

'No, he'll still be thinking of me and one day he'll return and we'll be married, you'll see.'

'Perhaps you should get a job telling fortunes,' Rhonda said dismissively.

'No, I'm no good at that,' Merrion said sadly. 'If I could see into the future then we'd have been able to avoid all the unhappiness of the past few months wouldn't we? One thing I do know,' she went on, 'is that you'd have had a very different life if you'd never met Harvey Weldon.'

'Perhaps.' Rhonda shrugged.

'Now that it is all over don't you think that perhaps you ought to make contact with your parents and put things right between you? I'm sure if you tried there could be some sort of reconciliation.'

'I don't want to talk about it,' Rhonda snapped.

'Nerys is their grandchild, remember,' Merrion

went on, ignoring Rhonda's frown. 'They are missing out on her growing up.'

'You mean you think that I should go and eat humble pie in the hope they'll give me a handout?'

'No, I didn't mean that at all. I simply thought it might be nice for Nerys to know her grandparents.'

'Well, I don't agree with you, and since she's never met them she's not going to worry about not ever seeing them, is she?'

'It might make you feel better if you saw them again,' Merrion persisted.

'I've made my bed, as my mother would say, so I'll lie on it.'

'I didn't mean that! I only thought that it would be reassuring for all concerned if you made your peace with them.'

'If you think they're going to welcome me back, kill the fatted calf, offer me a home and provide you with one as well then you can forget it,' Rhonda snapped. 'If you're fed up with us living together then clear off. I'll manage on my own, but I'm not so sure you'll be able to survive,' she added vindictively, waving in the air the details of the jobs they'd listed.

Merrion shook her head in bewilderment. Rhonda wasn't simply fed up, she was mutinous. There seemed to be no reasoning with her. Perhaps if they did change roles, even if only for a short time, it would give her a chance to reconsider things.

160

Merrion realised that being dismissed from the job she'd done ever since she'd left school must have come as a terrible shock to Rhonda. It certainly looked very much as if it was going to take her some time to come to terms with the situation.

'Right!' she snatched back the list from Rhonda. 'I'll give these a try then, shall I. We'll reverse roles. You stay home and look after the girls and take them to school and I'll go out to work. Do you think you can cope with that? It means you'll have to do all the cleaning as well as the shopping and cooking.'

'I'll do it with my eyes shut! It will be like a holiday,' Rhonda told her scathingly.

Merrion didn't feel at all confident as she studied the list. She almost decided to close her eyes and stick a pin in and see where it landed.

It was far too serious a matter to do that, she told herself, so she reworked the list into the order of preference according to her capabilities.

Kitchen work, cleaning jobs, skivvying at one of the large houses in Roath or one of the other posh areas, were at the top of the list. Working as a general cleaner or cook at one of the small hotels in Tiger Bay itself, or as a barmaid came next. The others on the list looked less promising because she had no experience of shop work and she didn't like the idea of being a cashier and having the responsibility of handling money in case she made mistakes.

She bought a copy of the *South Wales Echo* and studied the situations vacant column, marking any that might be possible. There was only one and that was for a cleaner at the Seaman's Mission in Bute Road. That wouldn't be much better than cleaning public conveniences, she told herself.

She looked down the columns again and that was when she spotted one for an usherette at the Capitol cinema. She wasn't sure if she could do that, but she liked the sound of it. The Capitol was quite new, it had only been open about three years and it was in the centre of Cardiff. Still, she told herself, she could catch a tram from the Pier Head that would take her all the way there.

She said nothing to Rhonda about where she was going when she left the house. It would be better to see how she got on first before talking about it, she told herself. If they turned her down, she need never mention it at all.

Her heart was thudding as she made her way towards the cinema. Inside it look so new and grand, with its bright lights and plush carpets, that she was sure they wouldn't employ her, especially since she had no experience.

Half an hour later, though, she was outside once more, and she was feeling more excited than she'd ever been in her whole life. She was to start the next day. She had to be there at twelve o'clock midday, and she would finish at ten o'clock at night, except on Saturdays when she wouldn't finish until eleven.

'We open the doors at one o'clock for the afternoon matinee,' the manager told Merrion, so that gives you time to put on your uniform, check that your torch is working properly and find out which aisles you have to look after. There is also general tidying up to be done before you leave at night.'

'What sort of tidying up do you mean?' Merrion questioned suspiciously.

'Simply walking between the rows of seats and picking up any litter, emptying the ashtrays, that sort of thing.'

'Do I have to tidy and clean the toilets?'

He laughed. 'No, of course you don't! We have a proper cleaner to do all that sort of thing. She also scrubs the front steps to the foyer as well as polishes all the brasswork and so on.'

The situation suited Merrion perfectly. The money she would be earning would not be anywhere near as much as Rhonda had earned as a milliner, but at least it would keep a roof over their heads and buy them some food, she reflected jubilantly as she made her way home.

Chapter Sixteen

Merrion felt extremely nervous at the thought of starting work as an usherette at the Capitol cinema. She hadn't worked since Dilwyn had been born and the thought of having to do so now, and mingle with so many new people, scared her.

Rhonda laughed at her fears. 'I don't see what you are so worried about. People are people, whether they're friends, neighbours or work-mates,' she said philosophically.

'It's all right for you to talk like that, you've been used to working and mixing with people. I haven't got your confidence and they're all going to be complete strangers.'

'The people around here were all strangers when you first moved in,' Rhonda reminded her.

'Yes, and most of them still are! I haven't made any real friends at all.'

'You know all the shopkeepers in James Street and quite a few of the neighbours.'

'I'm on speaking terms with the people who live in this house and in the shops we use. I talk to Mrs Palerno and with a couple of the mums I've met at the school gates, but not with anyone else.'

Rhonda looked at her in surprise. 'Why's that, then? I've always thought you must have plenty of friends, and that you visited them or went out with them while I was at work.'

Merrion shook her head. 'Oh no, I've never wanted to do anything like that. I've never made friends very easily. When I was growing up the only one I ever wanted to be with was Roddi.'

'Then it's certainly time you did get out and meet people and this new job will make sure that you do.'

'And what about you?' Merrion said thoughtfully. 'You'll find it very different being stuck here all day on your own.'

'The way I feel at the moment it will suit me fine,' Rhonda told her. 'I've had enough of people to last me a lifetime.'

'Oh, Rhonda! I don't like to hear you talking like that! You're making it sound as though I'm leaving you in the lurch,' Merrion exclaimed contritely.

'Rubbish! You don't have to worry about me,' Rhonda said irritably. 'I'll make friends when I'm good and ready. The girls must have little pals and they will have mums and dads and I'll get to know them while the girls are out playing with their kids.'

'Rhonda, they don't go out to play. I've never let them.'

'You mean they don't have any friends either?'

'They don't need them . . . they have each other.'

'That's not enough, no wonder they seem to be so insular and inseparable. God!' She slapped a hand to her brow. 'Why didn't I know about this? Are you telling me that until they started school they hadn't mixed with other children at all?'

'With us living here in Tiger Bay I didn't dare let them out to play on their own, heaven alone knows who they might have mixed with,' Merrion protested.

'They're mixing with them now that they're going to school,' Rhonda pointed out heatedly.

'Well, there's not much we can do about that, is there? They don't play with them after school though.'

'What about young Ella and Pedro?'

'They walk to school with them, that's all.'

'No wonder those two kids are always so eager to be with Nerys and Dilwyn, they probably think them weird.'

'Rhonda! Whatever are you saying!'

'Well, think about it. You've kept them locked up like pet animals so the local kids are bound to be curious about them. I can't understand how I didn't realise this before.'

'Maybe it's because you've hardly taken any notice of them, except on Sundays when we take them out.'

Rhonda spread her hands in despair. 'Things

are going to change for them from now on,' she vowed.

'I think you should consider the matter carefully before you let them mix with other children, and as for going out to play on their own . . .'

'Merrion, they're nearly seven, old enough to run messages and walk to school on their own. They don't need to be wrapped in cotton wool and protected like you've been doing. Anyway, how do you know that the other children will be a bad influence when you've had nothing to do with them or their families?'

'They're little girls so they need protection,' Merrion defended herself stubbornly. 'If they'd been boys it might have been different, they'd have been able to cope with the rough and tumble of street life.'

The sharp exchange of words with Rhonda made Merrion even more uncertain about going to work at the cinema since it would mean leaving the girls in her care until late at night.

She spent a sleepless night worrying about it and then realised that there was nothing else for it. She had said she was going to find a job and she had done so. She could hardly change her mind. Rhonda had supported them all up until now so it was only fair that she did her bit, she told herself.

The thought of Dilwyn and Nerys being allowed so much freedom worried her, but she tried not to think about it. Rhonda was right, they weren't babies any more, they had to grow up sometime and learn to stand on their own two feet.

Fortunately, since she didn't have to start work until midday, she would be able to take them to school each morning. After that she would be so busy in her own new life that she wouldn't have time to worry about them, she assured herself.

Dilwyn and Nerys sensed that there were a great many changes in the air even though Merrion did her best to hide the friction between herself and Rhonda from them.

There was a lump in her throat on the morning of her first day at work as she accompanied the girls to school and then kissed them both goodbye before walking quickly away.

Visions of what would happen when they came out of school that afternoon filled her mind as she made her way to the centre of Cardiff and by the time she reached Queen Street she was in turmoil. Rhonda had promised faithfully that she would meet them, but supposing she wasn't there on time? Harvey Weldon was gone, but there were so many other hazards.

They knew their own way home, of course, but it was too dangerous for them to walk over Clarence Road Bridge on their own. There was so much traffic. Supposing someone pushed them off the pavement into the roadway! They'd probably be with Ella and Pedro, they'd be excited, running too fast so they might fall over. A hundred possibilities of all the things that could go wrong went round and round in her head making her feel dizzy.

She'd been told to report by ten o'clock as it was her first morning because the manager, Mr Saunders, wanted to go through her duties with her. She was still too early for work, and so she went to a café and ordered a pot of tea to try and calm her nerves before she reached the cinema.

It was no good starting a new job in such a state, she told herself. She would have to take orders and advice from people who were complete strangers to her. She'd be doing work that was so completely different from anything she'd ever done before so she was going to need to have her wits about her.

She had to make a success of it, she reminded herself. Not only her own future and Dilwyn's depended on her doing so, but that of Rhonda and Nerys as well. They were down to their last few shillings and if she failed to hold this job down, and they couldn't pay the rent for their rooms, then all four of them would be out on the street. Determinedly, she drained her cup, paid the bill, and walked briskly in the direction of the Capitol cinema.

When she'd come for her interview she had been impressed by how gleaming and new it had looked from the outside, but too nervous

169

to notice that it was even more opulent inside. Now, as she entered the marble foyer and walked across the soft carpet towards the sweeping wide staircase, she found it quite breathtaking. The lights were all on so she could see the lovely plush red seats as well as the Wurlitzer organ that would rise up from in front of the screen before each performance started and fill the huge building with music.

She listened intently to Mr Saunders's instructions as he showed her around the auditorium and pointed out which aisles she would be responsible for and then explained precisely the way she must show patrons to their seats.

'Remember, there will be no lights on, so because they are in the dark they will be feeling disorientated and nervous and they may stumble if you don't shine your torch in the correct manner and guide them efficiently. Now, if there are people already sitting in the seat that is on the end of the row then there is a correct way to ask them to let the late arrivals pass by them. You'll find some people will simply bend their legs to one side, others will stand up. Make sure the new arrivals can see their way to get past them and reach their seats. Remember to keep your torch trained on the seats until they lower them and settle down. Always keep your torch pointing down as far as possible so that the beam from it doesn't irritate people watching the screen. Ignore any grumbles about the disturbance, they'll forget about it the moment you move away. You should, of course, delay showing new arrivals to their seats if it is a critical moment in the film and if by disturbing other patrons you would be spoiling their enjoyment of what is going on. Is all that clear, Miss Roberts?'

Merrion assured him it was.

'Never forget that when you are wearing your uniform, politeness, courtesy and efficiency are the keynotes of success in this job,' he told her firmly.

'Right! Now, you've seen the auditorium with the lights on I'm going to turn them out and give you a chance to get your bearings in the dark before people start to arrive. I want you to walk up and down the aisles, right to the very front and then right to the back again, until you feel confident that you are going to be able to find your way in the dark.'

Merrion found her first afternoon and evening so strenuous that long before it was time to go home her legs were aching. Even after her twenty-minute break she was still so tired that she wondered if she was going to manage to carry on until ten o'clock.

She felt as if she'd walked miles and what had appeared to be little more than a smooth incline from the front to the back of the auditorium became a hill to climb each time she had to do it.

People's reactions when she had shown them to their seats had astonished her. A few thanked her profusely, others grumbled, some clutched at her or stumbled so that she had to place a steadying hand on their arm.

She also found the action on the screen quite disconcerting. She was so intent on making sure that she showed each person to their seat that she occasionally forgot the warning about making them wait until it was a convenient point in the film before she did so.

When the evening ended Mr Saunders was quick to point all these mistakes out to her and warn her that he expected her to try harder and do better in the future.

Bone weary, she made her way home. Every jolt of the tram made her body ache even more. The stiffness and pain in the calves of her legs, as she walked from the tram stop to Sophia Terrace, brought tears to her eyes.

The rooms were in darkness when she reached home. She'd expected the girls to be in bed, but she was surprised that Rhonda had also gone to bed because she had hoped she'd be waiting to hear all about how she'd got on.

She felt too tired to even make herself a drink. Wearily, she undressed and crawled into bed in the dark. She'd thought she was probably too weary and aching to settle, but the moment her head touched the pillow she was asleep.

She woke next morning feeling refreshed, and was relieved to find that her aches and pains from the night before had all gone. The house was so quiet that it was several minutes before she realised that it was almost half past eight and that Dilwyn and Nerys were not even out of bed. From then on it was a mad scramble to get them up, dressed and ready for school.

They were so disorganised that she had to tell Ella and Pedro to go on ahead otherwise they would be late as well. As it was she'd had to run all the way down Hurman Street with the two girls and only managed to reach the school as the bell rang.

As she walked away, Merrion realised that she'd not had an opportunity to ask either of them how things had gone the previous afternoon.

Perhaps it was as well, Merrion thought, as she made her way back to Sophia Terrace, since it wouldn't do to let Rhonda think that she was checking up on her by asking questions behind her back.

She had plenty of time before she needed to go to work and as she hadn't even had a cup of tea she decided to make some breakfast for herself and Rhonda. It would give them a chance to talk and perhaps Rhonda would tell her how things had gone after school yesterday.

Rhonda's news of the previous day's events stunned Merrion. 'I had a visit yesterday from my family's solicitor,' she told Merrion as they sat down to the tea and toast Merrion had prepared.

'He came to tell me that my mother has died.

He said that she had a heart attack when Miss Fitch called and told them about Harvey Weldon and me. She was rushed into hospital right away. They thought she would get better, but she had a relapse and . . . and . . . she died a couple of days ago.'

'Oh Rhonda, that's terribly sad. If only your father had let you know the moment she went in to hospital.'

Rhonda shook her head. 'The solicitor said she didn't want to see me, that neither of them did. My dad simply thought it was his duty to let me know that I was the cause of her death,' she added bitterly.

'That's was unnecessary and very cruel. Are you going to her funeral?'

'I've not been asked or even told when it is to be.'

'Surely we can find out? If we . . .'

'No! I don't want to go. If my father feels so bitter about me then it is better that I don't go.'

Merrion touched her gently on the arm. 'She mightn't have been bitter, though, only concerned for your welfare.'

'No!' Rhonda pulled her arm away. 'I'm finished with them both!'

'Well, if that's really how you feel then I'll say no more. If you change your mind and decide you want to go then we'll do everything possible to find out when and where the funeral is.'

'Oh that wouldn't be difficult, the solicitor would know,' Rhonda said, 'but if my father doesn't want me there then there is no point in upsetting him any more, now is there? He'd probably have a heart attack and drop down dead at my feet simply to cause me even more grief.'

'Rhonda, don't say things like that!'

'Why not, when it's the truth? You don't know them like I do!'

'Didn't he want to know about his grand-child?'

Rhonda's face hardened and her mouth tightened. 'She was never mentioned. As far as my father and the solicitor are concerned it seems she doesn't exist. It looks like my father feels the same way about me,' she muttered resentfully.

'Then why did he arrange for the solicitor to call and tell you about your mother instead of writing to you?' Merrion asked, perplexed. 'Perhaps it was simply a way of trying to get in touch with you again in the hope that you would let bygones be bygones.'

Chapter Seventeen

Merrion was extremely worried by Rhonda's spells of moodiness and the way she had neglected herself ever since she'd heard about her mother's death. When they'd first met she'd been envious of the way Rhonda always managed to look so attractive. Her fair hair was stylishly cut, her clothes as fashionable as she could possibly make them. She would spend hours transforming one of her frocks with fresh trimmings to make it look like new. She was as clever at doing that as she was in turning a basic felt shape into a modish hat.

Merrion could understand her present feeling of despair, especially since she'd not been informed in time for her to go to the hospital and see her mother before she died. Added to which, not not being invited to attend her mother's funeral, or not feeling that her father wanted her there was an added trauma, even though Rhonda declared that it wasn't.

It wasn't merely grief that seemed to be affecting Rhonda, though. Merrion sensed that there was something else. Whatever it was went deeper and was more complex, and she couldn't work out what it might be.

By the weekend, Merrion had endured Rhonda's moroseness long enough. On Sunday, after they came back from walking the two girls the full length of Bute Road and then back home along the Taff embankment, during which time Rhonda had been both perverse with her and had snapped at the girls for no reason at all, Merrion decided it was time to speak out.

She waited until they'd finished their meal and then packed Dilwyn and Nerys off to bed with some comics to keep them entertained.

As soon as the dishes were washed and put away, Merrion made a pot of tea and took it into the living room where Rhonda was sitting hunched over the fire, staring unseeingly into its glowing depths.

'Come on now,' she said, passing a cup across to Rhonda, 'it's time you told me what's biting you. You've been like a bear with a sore head for the past week so come on, explain what's the matter.'

Rhonda shook her head.

'I insist! It's not fair on the rest of us. If I know what's wrong then perhaps I can help.'

'There's nothing at all you can do,' Rhonda told her flatly.

'Maybe, maybe not, but I'm sure you'll feel better if you unburden yourself.'

Rhonda shrugged. 'I doubt it. Telling you won't make a scrap of difference.'

'Try it and see.'

'Very well!' To Merrion's surprise and relief, Rhonda suddenly capitulated.

'Go on, then, I'm listening.'

Rhonda hesitated and bit her lip and for a moment Merrion thought she was going to back out. Then, in such a low voice that Merrion had to strain her ears to hear what she was saying, Rhonda began to speak almost as if she was talking to herself.

'My mum was only seventeen when I was born. The man she married was thirty-five years older than her.'

'You mean your dad?'

'He's not my dad!' Rhonda said acidly. 'Everyone has always thought that he is, but it was his son who got my mam pregnant. They met at a Christmas Party in 1899. He was a couple of years older than her, good-looking and with a reputation of being a dare-devil. She was crazily in love with him from the moment they first met and they had a whirlwind love affair. Then he went off to the Boer War, became a hero, and was killed before he even knew that she was pregnant with me.'

'Oh Rhonda, how sad.'

'My mum's family were outraged when they found out that she was expecting a baby. Then his dad, who was a widower, stepped in and saved the day by saying that he would marry my mum. He pointed out that this would not only save her from disgrace but would give the child a name.'

Merrion managed to keep silent although she felt appalled by such a state of affairs.

'He was very persuasive,' Rhonda went on. 'He convinced them that it would solve all their problems and that he would take great care of her. He was quite well off, had his own house, and promised that the baby would be well brought up and educated.'

'And they agreed!'

Rhonda smiled grimly. 'You can imagine the sort of discussions that went on. My mum's views weren't taken into account. She was in disgrace and her parents made all the arrangements, anything to save a scandal.'

'Did she like him?'

'My mum didn't even meet him until a few days before they were to be married. It was a very quiet affair, of course. In fact, it was almost secretive. She was seventeen and he was middle-aged, a few years older than her own father, in fact.'

'How dreadful for her! How on earth could they agree to such an arrangement?'

'You've got to remember that my mum was an only child and came from a very devout Catholic family,' Rhonda sighed. 'Her parents were aghast at the thought of the scandal if people knew that their lovely young daughter was having a baby and that she was not married.'

'What about her feelings, though, at being made to marry such an old man?' Merrion persisted.

'He made it clear that it was a wedding of convenience, to save them from embarrassment and to save his son's child from being classed as a bastard.'

Rhonda paused and wiped her eyes. Merrion refilled their cups. 'Go on, tell me the rest,' she encouraged.

'They hoped that once she was married and had moved away to his house that people wouldn't be able to make the connection that her baby was born less than five months after their wedding day.'

'Her husband also went out of his way to make sure that his own friends and neighbours believed that he was the father of the child she was expecting. He didn't want anyone to find out that his son had fathered the child because, in his eyes, that would harm his son's memory.'

'Your poor mam! She must have been heartbroken. Fancy losing the man she loved and then having to make do with his father. It's almost unbelievable that she could bring herself to do that.'

'They were Catholics and she had committed a grievous sin,' Rhonda reminded her. 'Also, she loved her parents and didn't want to bring shame on their heads. Anyway, he promised them all that it would be a marriage in name only. He said she would have her own bedroom, and because he was so much older than her there would be no question of him demanding his full marital rights.'

'And they all believed him?'

'Oh yes, it seems like it. She quickly found out, though, that he'd only said that because her parents had expected it of him. Once they were legally married he expected her to be his wife in every sense of the word. What was more, because of her condition he refused to let her go out or have any visitors. He even barred her parents from seeing her. He said it was on doctor's orders. No one knew if he was telling the truth or not and she had no one to confide in.'

'Surely she could have got in touch with her own mother?'

'She did write to her mother to tell her what was happening and how unhappy she was, but he intercepted her letters and her mother never knew she'd been trying to get in touch until years later. When she didn't get a reply to her letters my mam thought that the silence meant that her own mother condoned what was going on and so she stopped protesting and gave in to his demands.'

'He sounds like a fiend!'

'He was an absolute dictator. She had to do everything he said. She was never allowed to go out on her own, have any friends, or any freedom. He controlled the purse strings all their married life. He was well off and provided her with a good home, but what he didn't supply was love or consideration.'

'Did he ever physically abuse her?'

'No, but he treated her like a prisoner. He broke her spirit in the first few years of their marriage and from then on she was always browbeaten and nervy.'

'Your grandparents did nothing at all to help her?'

'He convinced them that her nervous condition was the result of my birth and asked them not to interfere. I think they were afraid of him. Mum told me years later that he had told her that they didn't want to have anything more to do with her because they were so ashamed of her. After a time she stopped trying to see them because she really did think that they couldn't bring themselves to forgive her for getting pregnant.'

'So what about your own childhood? How did he treat you?'

'He tried to control me the same way as he did my mother. That was one of the reasons why I was sent to a private school, but at least it meant that I was able to escape his authority some of the time. I was never allowed to take any friends home though!' She sighed deeply. 'As I grew older he poisoned my mother's mind against me, and tried to forbid her even talking to me unless he was present.'

'Goodness, he must have been a horrible sort of person.' Merrion shivered.

'He had to have absolute power over people. Before I left Technical College he arranged with an acquaintance of his, who had a millinery business, for me to go there as an apprentice. I wasn't asked if I wanted to do so, I was ordered to start work there.'

'This was where you met Harvey Weldon?'

Rhonda nodded. 'When I got pregnant he saw it as history repeating itself. He said it was positive proof that I had inherited the evil that had been my mother's downfall. He threw me out, told me never to darken their door again.'

'So what happened at the place where you worked when they heard about this?'

Rhonda gave a sharp laugh. 'At first they couldn't believe that he was so heartless. Then, even though the boss was an acquaintance, it was decided that I could stay on at work, as long as I didn't let him know. I think my boss was afraid of what his reaction might be.'

She stopped and covered her face with her hands and her shoulders shook. Then she raised her head, pushed back her hair, and looked Merrion in the face. 'There you are, now you know it all. I've never talked about it before . . . I couldn't! Now do you see why there is nothing you can say or do to change things?'

'I've never heard anything to equal it in all

my life,' Merrion said slowly. 'I'm still trying to work it all out. The man you were brought up to think of as your father was . . . was really your grandfather!'

'Yes, I suppose he was, I've never thought of it like that before.'

'So he's not Nerys's grandfather! In fact, it would seem that he's her great-grandfather!'

Rhonda shrugged. 'I suppose so, but it doesn't matter because she'll never know him. In fact, she'll never meet him.'

'Never?'

'That's right! I mean it, Merrion. I wouldn't want to let her be in the same room as him. He's evil, Merrion, you've no idea what he's like. He has a way of getting inside your head and twisting your mind. He didn't hurt me physically, never slapped me when I did something wrong like other dads did when their kids were naughty; he had more subtle forms of punishment. He made me spend hours on my knees praying for forgiveness. He deprived me of privileges, stopped me from playing with other children. He even took away my most precious toys and possessions because he said I wasn't worthy of them.

'Going to work offered me an escape, but it was shortlived. His dictatorship invaded even there. He checked up on me and, in the early days, Miss Fitch fed him any information he asked for, thinking it was because he was interested in my progress.'

184

'So how was it that he never knew you were going out with Harvey Weldon?'

'I only ever saw Harvey Weldon at work and we always met in secret in some out-of-the-way place. He had the usual glib tongue that's stock-in-trade to commercial travellers. He sweet-talked me into making love and I was so naive that I thought he was a knight in shining armour. When he promised marriage I could see it as a way of escaping from my father's clutches. As you know, he wasn't good-looking, and was quite a lot older than me, but he was my ticket to freedom. Anyway, that's what I told myself. I even imagined that when my dad heard I was pregnant he would want to meet him and even welcome him as my prospective husband.

'As usual I was wrong. He forbade me to bring him home. He was furious at the thought that he would be losing control over me. He obtained a strange pleasure from punishing me for being my mother's daughter and he held her responsible for what had happened. Perhaps if I'd been a boy, a replacement for the son he'd lost, it would have been different. That's something none of us will ever know.'

'This is nothing like what you told me when we first met,' Merrion said in disbelief.

'I know, but I could hardly tell a stranger the whole truth. You wouldn't have believed me if I had done so.'

185

'No, not if you'd said that your father was your grandfather! I don't think anyone, having just met you, would have been able to swallow a story like that.'

'Well, it's not a fanciful tale, it's the absolute truth,' Rhonda snapped.

'I'm sure it is, it's all such a muddle, though, even before you start to hear about the way he treated you when you were growing up.'

'Well, it's all over now. My mum's dead and as far as I'm concerned that's the end of my home life.'

'Perhaps you should go and see him though, Rhonda. It might clear the air. He must be quite an old man now.'

'He's probably in his late seventies.'

'Old and lonely.'

'He has plenty of cronies. Mean-minded old men like himself,' Rhonda said bitterly.

'I'm sure that none of them have a story like his. I've never heard anything like it in my life. I wonder why he took the trouble to contact you after Harvey Weldon died, or even how he connected him to you?'

'Oh, that was Miss Fitch's doing. She was the one who guessed that it was me when she read about Harvey Weldon's suicide in the *South Wales Echo*. I think she was sweet on him herself. Like I said, he had a glib tongue and he always used to flatter her whenever he came into the workroom. He told me it was because she did

186

the buying and that it was his way of securing a good order.'

'So you think Miss Fitch went and told your father about it in order to get even with you,' Merrion murmured. 'It's quite incredible!'

'Well, every word I've told you is the truth. And it was true what I told you about Harvey Weldon, about him clearing off when I told him that I was pregnant. Now I want to forget about it all and put it behind me.'

'Do you think you will ever manage to do that?' Merrion probed.

'Yes! As far as I am concerned, for Nerys's sake, the only family we have is each other. She's growing up as an only child without a father, the same as your Dilwyn is doing, and neither of them are any the worse for that.'

'Dilwyn does have a brother and someday he might come back and she'll meet him,' Merrion reminded her.

'In your dreams, along with that Roddi you go on about. No, I reckon we're both in the same boat. No family, no ties, no one to care whether we live or die.'

'So you won't go and see your father, well, I mean your mother's husband, not even to clear the air?'

'No, never! He's far too cunning. If he found out that I was out of work and needed help he'd let me come back and then before I knew what was happening he'd be imposing his will on me and Nerys. I'd end up being as downtrodden as my mother was and Nerys would be subjected to the same mental torment as I was when I was growing up. We may be living in a slum, we mightn't have two pennies to rub together, but we've got our freedom. You don't realise how important that is until you lose it,' Rhonda said emphatically.

Chapter Eighteen

Merrion found working at the Capitol cinema completely changed her life. In fact, it altered things for all four of them. A new daily pattern gradually evolved, but it took all of them quite a while to adjust to it.

Merrion was affected by the change most of all. She was so used to spending most of the day on her own, doing things to her own routine, and in the way she deemed to be best, that having to take orders from someone else was at first very hard for her to accept. This was especially so when she felt it would be far better if things were done in a different way, but, because she was so new, she dared not say so.

The late-morning start gave her time to make sure that Dilwyn and Nerys ate a good breakfast, were properly dressed, and had their packed lunch in their satchels before she walked them to school.

On her way back she collected any shopping that was required before calling Rhonda, who liked to sleep late now that she didn't have to rush off to work. The two of them would then sit down to a cup of tea and something to eat before Merrion had to leave for the cinema.

Sometimes she even had time to give their two rooms a quick tidy round, or prepare something ready for a hot meal for the girls when they came home from school, before she went off to catch the tram to work.

Exactly what Rhonda did all day she had no idea. She always claimed she'd been busy, but as far as Merrion could see there was very little evidence of it. She was still the one who did all the washing and ironing on a Sunday which meant that apart from collecting the two girls from school each afternoon, giving them a meal and making sure they went to bed on time, Rhonda did very little towards sharing the chores.

She'd certainly become friendly with all their neighbours. Within a few weeks she knew everyone in Sophia Terrace by name as well as most of the people who used the shops in James Street and many of the shopkeepers.

Her training as a milliner didn't remain dormant for very long. In next to no time she was making or decorating hats for many of them for special occasions like weddings or christenings.

In return they brought her small gifts of fruit, cakes, biscuits, a pot of jam, a packet of tea or even a pound of sausages. It added variety to their frugal diet and the children looked forward eagerly to these unexpected treats.

Merrion was very impressed with the lovely hats that Rhonda seemed to be able to produce from just a handful of feathers, fancy buckles or ribbons.

'It's a pity you can't ask them for money instead of gifts,' she laughed wryly as she carefully counted out her week's wages into separate piles for rent, food, repairs, tram fares and other necessities, juggling the meagre amount so as to meet all their needs.

Her pay as an usherette was nowhere near as much as Rhonda had earned when she'd been working and it seemed that there was no prospect at all of it ever being increased.

In spite of that she found her job exciting. The films that were shown not only astounded her, but opened her eyes and her mind to other ways of living. She found the Pathe news reels of tremendous interest and because the same news reel was shown for three consecutive nights she had plenty of time to absorb the contents in between showing people to their seats.

Dilwyn and Nerys loved to hear about what was on, even the news items. When Merrion related the antics of Buster Keaton or Charlie Chaplin they giggled and laughed uproariously. They also listened with considerable interest when she told them about other movies she'd seen.

Every second Saturday afternoon she was allowed to take them along to the matinee. Rhonda came as well and she took the girls home again when the show was over, leaving

Merrion to carry on with her duties at the cinema for the rest of the evening.

Her late finish every night, especially during the dark nights and cold wintry weather, began to take its toll. Late in April 1926, when the worst of the weather was over and she should have been feeling full of energy, she went down with flu.

She was so ill that she was forced to stay home for over two weeks. When she did return it was to learn that the miners' strike, which had been on for a little over a week, had brought chaos in its wake.

Mr Saunders said he was sorry but he couldn't take her back. As a result of the strike, which was rapidly spreading throughout all the other trades, fewer people were visiting the cinema. They were afraid to spend money on such luxuries because of fears that there was going to be widespread unemployment. The unions were supporting the miners and the result was bound to be a general strike which would affect the whole country.

'I'm sorry, Miss Roberts, but you were the last one to join us, and your attendance record lately has been very poor, so I am afraid I have no alternative but to tell you that your services are no longer needed,' Mr Saunders told her.

Merrion stared at him in dismay, unable to believe what was happening. 'I've been ill,' she protested. 'I've had flu! I wouldn't have stayed away if I'd been well enough to come to work because I need the money too badly.'

'I'm sure what you are saying is quite true, Miss Roberts, but because of the strike, I have been instructed by my superiors to cut back on my staff. You are not the only one who will have to go. One of the cleaners has already been sacked and other staff cuts are about to follow.'

Merrion shook her head in astonishment. 'You want me to go right now?'

'I'm afraid so. If you need a reference, then your prospective employers have only to apply in writing and I will see they get one.'

Merrion turned away and stumbled across the foyer and out into Queen Street, She couldn't believe it had happened. How could they be so cruel, so heartless, she railed inwardly.

Having to go back to Sophia Terrace and tell Rhonda that she'd been sacked, and that there would be no money at the end of the week, was a bitter pill. She'd been working for less than six months. Rhonda had been the one working to keep them for the past six years. She felt ashamed at having to admit that as a wage earner she'd been such a failure.

Rhonda was far more understanding than she could have hoped. She insisted that it didn't matter. She decried the manager's action and staunchly proclaimed that it was their loss.

'We don't need their money,' she declared. 'We won't starve, they only paid a measly pittance anyway. You were worth twice as much as what you were earning.'

'That may be true, but we still need money for rent and food,' Merrion pointed out.

'We'll get it, don't worry. We'll do what you suggested last Christmas. I'll make hats for the neighbours and charge them for my work, not simply hand them over in exchange for a bag of biscuits. I've been thinking about it and how you can help me. With the two of us working together we'll make a living!'

It was brave fighting talk, but Merrion was pretty sure in her own mind that they'd never manage to make a go of it.

'I can't even sew very well, Rhonda,' she pointed out, so in what way am I going to be able to help you?'

'We'll find ways to work together. You can take over running things here again. I'm no good at cooking and cleaning, now am I?'

She laughed as Merrion started to defend her prowess. 'Don't make excuses for me. I'm no good at it and I don't like doing it. The girls hate the meals I make for them. They'll jump for joy when you tell them that you'll be doing it in future. They'll also be pleased that you'll be collecting them from school each afternoon instead of me because I'll be too busy making hats.'

'Will you, though?' Merrion frowned worriedly. 'You need money to buy the materials and . . .'

'Ssh! Don't put a dampener on things before we've even got started. I have dreams as well as you.' She smiled. 'Let's think things through first before we turn down the idea because there are so many obstacles in the way.'

Merrion shook her head. 'I hope it does work out, but I think one of us had better find a job of some kind to bring in enough money for the rent and food.'

Rhonda sighed. 'It's going to be touch and go for the first few weeks,' she admitted. 'You are right, of course, I will need money to buy materials to start me off. Perhaps there is something we can sell, or pawn, so as to get things going.'

'I'll look for some sort of work tomorrow,' Merrion promised. 'I feel more confident now that I have been out working so perhaps that will help when I go after my next job.'

'Perhaps we should both look,' Rhonda suggested.

Merrion looked doubtful. 'If you go out to work then you won't have time to make hats, will you?'

'If we both find work, though, it will give me a chance to get some money together to buy the materials I need.'

They talked about it well into the night. Then they compromised and agreed they would both try and find some sort of part-time job and see how things worked out.

'Perhaps it would be better if we didn't let

the girls know anything about this, not until we have solved the problem,' Merrion suggested.

'We'll have to tell them that you aren't working at the cinema any more.'

'Not right away. I take them to school in the morning as it is and . . .'

'They'll soon find out when you don't take them to the Saturday matinee,' Rhonda pointed out.

'Well, that gives us two weeks to solve things. I'll tell them that because I've been at home ill it's not my turn for free passes and by Saturday of next week we should have sorted things out.'

'Yes, with any luck we'll both have good jobs and we won't need free passes because we'll be able to take them anyway and pay for all of us out of our own money,' Rhonda declared.

Once again it was Merrion, not Rhonda, who found work. This time it was in a pub, the Glendower Arms in George Street, which was only a couple of roads away from where they lived.

'I don't think you'd manage to stay there for very long,' the man in the newsagents warned her grimly when he saw her studying the card in his window that had the details of the vacancy on it.

'Oh, why is that?' Merrion asked in surprise.

'I thought men who ran pubs were always happy, jolly types.'

'Twm Rawlands is all right, but his wife's a bit of a tartar.'

'Does she work in the bar, then?'

'She's everywhere you move in the place. He's so bloody easygoing that she's the one who keeps order. They get a lot of seamen in there, see, and sometimes they can be a bit rough, like.'

'So what happens?'

'Brenda Rawlands chucks them out, doesn't she!'

'She's the one who throws them out!'

'That's right. Muscles on her like a navvy, see. Picks them up by the seat of their pants and the collar of their shirt or coat and wham! They're through the door and into the street before they know what's happening.'

'She sounds ferocious!'

'Oh she's that all right. She won't stand any monkey business from the barmaids either. She soon puts a stop to it if the customers try chatting them up. What's more, if she catches the barmaid flirting with them, or playing coy and giving them the eye, then she's out on her neck as well. That's why they're always looking for new staff.'

'Thanks for the warning. It sounds a good job to me,' Merrion told him.

'You mean you're still going to go ahead and try for it?'

197

'I most certainly am. Thank you for putting me wise about the landlady.' She smiled.

'Good luck! Mind you let me know if you get it.'

Merrion went straight to the Glendower Arms. She didn't want to risk someone else spotting the advert and getting there before her. Brenda Rawlands might be formidable yet in some ways Merrion liked the sound of her. At least I'll feel safe from unwanted attentions from any of the customers if she's such a martinet, she told herself.

The pub was still locked when Merrion reached it. Twm Rawlands shouted out for her to come back in a couple of hours, but Merrion stood her ground.

'I've come about the job as barmaid,' she shouted back.

Twm Rawlands didn't answer, but Merrion heard him walking across to the door and then the sound of a bolt being pulled back and a key turning in the lock.

'Come in and lock the door behind you,' Twm Rawlands told her and went back to getting the bar ready for opening time.

'I saw your card in the newsagents,' Merrion told him.

'Have you done bar work before?'

Merrion swung round as the question came from behind her. A tall, buxom woman, her iron-grey hair coiled into a magnificent bun that emphasised her prominent facial features and gimlet-dark eyes, was standing there, looking her up and down speculatively. Twm Rawlands continued with his preparatory work and ignored both of them.

'No,' Merrion admitted. 'I've been working at the Capitol cinema as an usherette.'

'So why are you changing jobs?' Brenda Rawlands asked tersely.

'They're cutting back because of the miners' strike. People can't afford to go to the pictures if they are off work. I was one of the last to be taken on there so I was one of the first to be laid off.'

Brenda Rawlands regarded her in silence for a moment and Merrion felt conscious of her shabby coat.

'So why have you come down to Tiger Bay looking for work?' Brenda Rawlands frowned.

'I live here, in Sophia Terrace.'

Brenda Rawlands's eyes narrowed. 'Are you married and have you got kids?'

'I'm not married, but I have a six-year-old sister, Dilwyn. Both our parents are dead and so I'm bringing her up.'

'So who is going to look after her while you're working? You can't bring her here. This is a pub so kids aren't allowed on the premises.'

'I realise that, but I share rooms with another woman who has a child of the same age so she'll be looking after Dilwyn when I'm at work.'

'When can you start?'

Merrion's eyes widened. 'You mean I've got the job, then?'

'We'll see. I'll give you a chance to prove yourself so come on, get your coat off and buckle in.'

'Very well, but I need to have ten minutes to nip home and let my friend Rhonda know where I am and to make sure she collects the girls from school this afternoon.'

'Ten minutes, then, no longer,' Brenda Rawlands told her grudgingly. 'If you're not back, or someone else comes after the job, then you've lost it,' she added as Merrion went out of the door.

Chapter Nineteen

Merrion's routine barely changed. She still took the girls to school and on her way back along James Street to Sophia Terrace, bought the bread, vegetables, meat or whatever else she knew they needed.

One difference was that Rhonda no longer lay in bed until the breakfast and a pot of tea were ready, but was up and had them waiting for Merrion's return.

Each week, ever since Merrion had started work as a barmaid, they had set aside a few shillings out of her wages to buy materials so that Rhonda could start making hats and, they hoped, sell them to a shop or one of the market stallholders.

She still did the occasional renovation, or even created a new hat for neighbours, but now, even if they supplied the materials, she charged them for her work. Most of them paid up quite happily. Those who were unable to find cash still paid with a gift of some kind, but there were fewer of them doing that when they realised that it was no longer a pastime for Rhonda, but a means of existence.

Merrion found working at the pub even more

tiring than being an usherette at the cinema.
The loud chatter going on all around her, the
swearing, the penetrating smells of alcohol and
the fumes of pipe and cigarette smoke left
her throat dry and sore, and her chest feeling
so tight that by the end of her evening shift
every breath she took was painful.

'Help yourself to a drink,' Twm told her. 'A
mouthful of beer will take away the dryness.'

Merrion shuddered. 'Thank you, but I can't
stand the taste.'

'What about stout or cider, then?'

She smiled and shook her head.

'Here, have a mouthful of this, then,' he said
pouring her out a small glass of port.

Merrion sipped it tentatively. It was sweet and
smooth and comforting, leaving a warm glow.

'Don't let Brenda catch you drinking it, mind,
or she'll blow her top. Expensive, see. It's
considered to be a real ladies' drink, that's why
it suits you. Bit above working in a place like
this, aren't you, girl? I knew it the moment I
opened the door and saw you on the step. I
didn't expect you to last more than a couple of
days.'

'I need the money, I've got my little sister to
look after.'

'What happened to your dad, then?'

'He was a miner and was killed in an explosion about seven years ago.'

'Dammo di! There's sorry I am to hear that.
Come from up the valleys, do you?'

'That's right. A place called Cwmglo.'

'You'd have done better to have stayed there. Hard life here in Cardiff. What about your mam?'

'She died a few months after we moved here. She was knocked down by a tram. We were shopping at the Hayes. My little brother was with us. She was holding his hand and he died instantly.'

'Duw anwyl! What a catalogue of catastrophes! You must be a lot tougher than you look, girl.' Generously he made to refill her glass, but Merrion stopped him.

'It's delicious,' she told him with a smile, 'but a bit pricey for me so I'd best not get to like it too well.'

Twm nodded. 'Sensible you are, too,' he said admiringly. 'You'd better be on your way home. Take care, girl. And mind you're on time in the morning or my wife will have your guts for garters.'

'Her bark is worse than her bite,' Merrion smiled, 'she's been very kind to me ever since I started here.'

'Yes, she likes you well enough, girl. Good to have a steady reliable worker who doesn't make eyes at the customers, see!'

Like all the rest of the pubs in Cardiff, the Glendower Arms didn't open on a Sunday so whenever the weather was good Rhonda and Merrion took the girls out the same as they'd always done. Occasionally they still went to the park at Grangetown, but it had lost its appeal for them ever since the incident with Harvey Weldon.

That summer they sought out new destinations and went to Roath Park and Victoria Park as well as Sophia Gardens and Cathays Park. Sometimes they walked along the banks of the Taff or the Glamorgan Canal.

The girls preferred Victoria Park because they loved watching the antics of Billy the Seal who was such a star attraction there. The minute they neared the lake they ran ahead, crowding in with the mass of other youngsters all clustered by the railings watching the huge creature splashing and twisting. Like all the others they squealed with delight when they saw it almost leaping right out of the water.

All through the summer the miners remained out on strike, but most of the other industries had returned to work. Shipping was back to normal which meant that there was a steady flow of new faces in the Glendower Arms.

Merrion became well known to the regulars. Once they found she didn't rise to their quips and jesting they either left her alone, or treated her with respect. If a stranger tried to become too friendly there was always someone ready to step in and choke him off.

Brenda Rawlands also kept a close eye on what was going on and she approved of the way Merrion conducted herself. She went out of her way to make sure that Merrion was never harassed by anyone.

Her protection, unfortunately, ended when Merrion left the premises. The minute she stepped out into George Street and the pub door shut behind her, then she was on her own.

Most of the men she encountered on her short walk home were customers who had left the pub only minutes before her. Apart from calling out, 'Nos da', 'Goodnight', 'Been a good night', or 'Are you all right walking home on your own?' as she went by, they mostly left her alone.

Steve, a massive surly mannered Swede was the exception. He was huge and brawny, his hair so fair that it was almost white. When he was in the pub his icy-blue eyes followed Merrion's every movement as she served behind the bar or walked round the room collecting up dirty glasses. He never attempted to talk to her and she sometimes wondered if he could speak English. He never even asked directly for a pint, but pushed his glass across the bar counter, pointed to the pumps and grunted and nodded when she selected the right one.

When she found Steve still outside the Glendower Arms as she left one night Merrion thought nothing of it. He had been in the pub all evening drinking pint after pint, speaking to no one. When she saw him leaning against the doorframe she merely thought that he was drunk so she didn't even say goodnight as she walked past him.

She almost jumped out of her skin when he reached out and grabbed her arm.

'You ignore me and I don't like that,' he rasped in a deep guttural tone.

She stopped, shaking with fright and wondering if it was too late to attract Twm's attention. If she hammered on the door, would she be able to make him hear before he went upstairs to the flat he and Brenda had above the bar?

Realising her intention, Steve positioned himself between her and the pub door. He was so massive that she knew it was pointless to try and push past him.

'I'm sorry, Steve,' she said quietly, 'I wasn't ignoring you, but you seemed to be deep in thought so I didn't want to disturb you,' she said placatingly.

His roar of anger startled her. The only thing she could think of doing was making a run for it. As she took to her heels she could hear him lumbering after her, gasping for breath.

Because she had been later than usual leaving, most of the regulars had already made their way home. Whereas on most nights she would pass half a dozen of them along George Street, tonight there was not one of them to be seen.

Her heart was thundering and she had a stitch in her side making it impossible to increase her pace. She was so panic-stricken that she was afraid to ask any of the strangers she ran past to help her in case they were friends of Steve's. Even when one of them called out, 'Are you OK, Missy?' she was too scared to answer.

By the time she reached Sophia Terrace she was breathless and frightened because she knew from the ponderous footsteps behind her that Steve was still following her. When he grabbed hold of her arms and pulled her roughly towards him, Merrion almost blacked out with fright.

Before she could scream or even struggle his huge hands had grabbed her hair, forcing her head back and she felt as if her face was in a vice as his mouth clamped down on hers. She tasted blood as his huge teeth dug into her lower lip as he kissed her savagely over and over again.

Then he began to paw her, his huge hands roaming possessively over her body, and the more she struggled the more aroused he became. Catching hold of the neck of her dress he tore it from her body and began maniacally fondling her breasts.

Revulsion at his touch gave Merrion a burst of ferocious strength. She brought her knee up sharply and jabbed with spread fingers towards his eyes. Her elation when she knew she'd found her targets stunned her almost as much as it hurt him. His bellow of pain and rage as he released her and covered his eyes with his hands gave her the opportunity she needed.

Not waiting to see if he was following her, she sped the rest of the way down Sophia Terrace to their house and burst in through the door, in a state of collapse.

Rhonda, who was making a hot drink ready for when she arrived home, stopped what she was doing and rushed to find out what was wrong. 'My God! what the hell has happened to you?' she gasped as she looked at the dishevelled state Merrion was in. 'It's all right, you're safe, cariad,' she added, holding her close.

She helped her into a chair and listened with mounting anger as Merrion brushed away her tears and, between sobs, told her about Steve the Swede's attack on her.

'You're safe now,' she repeated. 'Have your drink and get off to bed. Have a lie-in tomorrow morning, cariad. I'll take the girls to school.'

Merrion shook her head. 'I'm not letting him get to me,' she declared tremulously.

'Of course not! We'll talk about it in the morning,' Rhonda said firmly.

The next morning Merrion's face was swollen, and her lower lip so cut and bruised that she could barely sip the drink Rhonda brought her in bed. When she examined her body she found that she was a mass of bruises, almost as if she had been in a fight. The moment she tried to get out of bed she found that she ached so much that she was glad to flop back against the pillow.

'Stay where you are, I told you I'd take the girls to school,' Rhonda scolded. 'You don't want them to see you in this state. I'll pick up some bread and milk and whatever else we need on my way back,' she promised.

Merrion felt so utterly weary that she did as Rhonda suggested without argument. She lay drifting in and out of sleep, trying to ignore the pain and the memories of what had happened. Instead she tried to keep her mind on the dreams that sustained her whenever she had problems or felt upset, and the thought that one day she'd once more be reunited with Roddi and then all her troubles would be over.

Rhonda laughed at her for still carrying a torch for a man she hadn't seen for nearly seven years, but the thought of one day being with him again was what kept her going. Now, after being attacked, she needed that dream of someday being with him more than ever.

They'd had such wonderful plans for their future together, but now it all seemed so impossible that she felt a sense of desolation. She wondered if he was still with Emlyn or whether they had also split up and gone their separate ways. Perhaps the time had come for her to give up her dreams, she thought despondently.

She waited until she heard Rhonda return and then she tried once again to get up, wincing as the pain in her arms and chest struck like hot irons.

Rhonda walked into the bedroom in time to witness the look of anguish on her face. 'Right! That's it, you're not putting a foot outside today,' she ordered. 'I'll ask Carol Palerno to collect Dilwyn and Nerys when she goes to meet her two.'

'I must go to work, Rhonda,' Merrion protested. 'We need the money. Anyway, if I don't go in then there's always the chance that I might lose my job altogether.'

Rhonda frowned. 'No you won't,' she argued. 'I'll go and tell them what has happened.'

'They'll be short-handed, so they'll have to get someone else in to do my job,' Merrion fretted.

'They won't need to do that,' Rhonda told her, 'because I'll go and work in your place. It can't be all that difficult to serve pints and clear tables.'

Merrion smiled weakly. 'It's not difficult, but it is tiring. Anyway, I'm not sure that Brenda Rawlands would agree to such an arrangement. Twm wouldn't mind, he's very easygoing, but she is so strict and everything has to be done the way she says, and . . .'

'And she'll be so pleased that someone is there to help out that she'll greet me with open arms,' Rhonda finished with a grin.

Chapter Twenty

Merrion and Rhonda spent such a long time debating and arguing over what was the right sort of dress for Rhonda to wear that she arrived at the Glendower Arms almost ten minutes late.

The door was already wide open and as she went inside she could see that they were extremely busy. Several men were standing at the bar waiting to be served and almost every table in the room was occupied although it was only mid-morning.

Apart from the fact that there were no other women in the place, Rhonda recognised Brenda's formidable figure from Merrion's description of the landlady the minute she stepped inside.

There was a stunned silence as Rhonda entered. Most of the men stopped talking and eyed her up and down appreciatively as she walked up to the bar. There were exclamations of interest and disbelief as she explained to Twm and Brenda Rawlands the reason why Merrion hadn't arrived for work.

'Attacked by Steve the Swede!' Twm shook his head in dismay. 'I can't believe what I'm hearing. He's never given any trouble all the time he's been coming here. I can't believe he would attack anybody. He stands at the bar night after night, drinking pint after pint and I've never heard him say a word to anyone.'

'Maybe not, but I've seen the way he's been watching Merrion,' Brenda Rawlands stated indignantly. 'Mind you, he never once spoke to her as far as I know and I find it hard to believe that he'd go as far as to attack her.'

'Steve had certainly had a skinful by the time he left here last night, mind,' one of the men at the bar commented. 'He was staggering when he went out of the door.'

'He left a long time before Merrion did, though,' one of the men commented.

'So he must have hung around outside waiting for her to finish work,' someone else observed.

'Well, he certainly hurt her pretty badly,' Rhonda told them. 'She's a mass of cuts and bruises and the attack scared her. She was shaking like a leaf.'

'So is Merrion going to do anything about this attack?' Twm asked worriedly.

'Yes, she certainly is! For a start she's going to stay at home for a few days until her bruises have faded.'

'What I meant was is she going to report what happened to the police?'

Rhonda shrugged her shoulders. 'I don't know. She never said she was going to do anything like that.'

'Perhaps it would be better if she didn't,' Twm said thoughtfully. 'You never know, Steve the Swede might turn nasty and try and get even.'

'There wouldn't be much chance of him doing that if they clap him in jail for what he's done,' Rhonda pointed out. 'It's where he ought to be, the callous brute!'

'You never know what mates he's got, though,' Twm warned. 'If he gets put inside, then they might decide to carry out some sort of revenge on his behalf.'

'We don't want the police nosing around here,' Brenda Rawlands said firmly. 'You go back and tell Merrion that he will be banned from the place from now on so she's nothing to worry about because she'll never see him again.'

'Unless he hangs around outside here until she finishes work one evening and then follows her and attacks her again,' Rhonda commented.

Twm and Brenda exchanged uneasy glances.

'No, no, we'll sort that out ourselves,' Twm pronounced. 'We'll get one of our regulars to walk her home when she finishes each evening. That'll solve that problem, she'll have nothing to worry about, tell her.'

'We'll make sure that it is someone we know is thoroughly trustworthy and reliable. It will be someone she knows that she can trust,' Brenda added.

'Yes, you tell Merrion that's what we'll do in

future,' Twm agreed heartily. 'Thank you for taking the time to come and let us know what happened. Tell Merrion to rest up and we hope she'll be back at work as soon as she feels better.'

'I didn't come here only to tell you what happened,' Rhonda smiled, 'I'm going to do her job until she's well enough to come back to work again.'

'You! Work here as a barmaid?' Brenda looked taken aback. 'Well, I don't know about that! Have you any experience of bar work? If not, then I don't see the point of us going to all the trouble of training you when it is only for a couple of days.'

Rhonda shrugged. 'No need to bother with all that silliness,' she said disparagingly. 'Serving pints, wiping the tables down and collecting up the dirty beer glasses doesn't really call for any special training, now does it?'

Twm and Brenda exchanged glances again. He spread his hands wide, and shrugged his shoulders, mutely indicating that the decision was up to Brenda.

'Put like that, I suppose you could fill in for Merrion until she is ready to come back, seeing as it has left us short-handed,' Brenda admitted grudgingly. 'Get your coat off then, girl, and get started. We've wasted enough time gabbing. There's plenty of work to be done, I'm run off my feet as you can see.'

Brenda bustled across the room with a tray

of drinks. When she turned round she gasped in disbelief. 'What on earth do you think you are wearing? You can't work here dressed like that!' she exclaimed, looking in disapproval at Rhonda's short red chenille skirt and matching low-necked beaded jumper top.

'Why not, Ma?' demanded a chorus of voices as they looked Rhonda up and down appreciatively.

They banged their pint pots noisily on the tables in support of the idea and there were a series of low whistles followed by a vociferous outcry of approval throughout the room.

'We don't mind being served by you, my lovely!' one of the men called out.

'Bring a couple pints over here, cariad,' ordered another, 'I'm dying of thirst.'

'Cheers to you, cariad, nice to have you here serving us!' several chorused, raising their glasses in her direction.

'Looks as if you're going to bring a bit of colour into our lives,' another guffawed.

Twm had already drawn some beers and placed them on the bar so, squaring her shoulders to hide her nervousness, Rhonda picked them up and strutted over to the nearest table. She set them down with a flourish and flashed a wide smile at the men sitting there.

'Are you sure you're real, cariad?' a bunch of dockers who'd just come into the pub guffawed, grinning at her as she walked back to the bar. 'Where's our Merrion, then?'

Before Rhonda could answer Brenda Rawlands walked over and pushed her to one side. 'Merrion's not here because the poor dab was attacked last night on her way home!' she told the newcomers.

'Never! Darw! Who'd do a thing like that, then?' several asked in surprise.

'Steve the Swede. Made a right mess of her by all accounts,' Brenda told them.

'Dammo di!'

'Duw anwyl, who'd have thought he'd ever do a thing like that!'

'Bloody brute, he'd better not show his face in here ever again!'

Rhonda was ignored as an outpouring of comments, indicating their disgust and displeasure that anyone should have hurt Merrion, were expressed.

Brenda Rawlands listened to them in poker-faced silence, her hands on her broad hips as she stood waiting for the noise to subside.

As soon as she could make herself heard, she told them, 'From now on, Steve the Swede's barred. The same will apply to any of the rest of you if you dare to lay a finger on our barmaids, this one included,' she warned as she jerked her head in Rhonda's direction.

'Wouldn't dream of touching her,' the men assured Brenda, quaffing their pints as they did so.

'We can enjoy looking, though, can't we, missus?' someone laughed.

216

'Right little fashion plate, this one, by the look of it!' one of the newcomers commented.

'Yes, she's a sight for sore eyes and that's a fact,' several others agreed.

Brenda made a point of repeating her warning to every customer that came into the pub. At the same time they were also informed about what had happened to Merrion after closing time the previous night.

'We'll watch out and see that it never happens again,' the regulars all assured her.

'I'll make sure it doesn't,' Brenda told them. 'From now on our barmaid, whoever she is, will be escorted home when she finishes work at night.'

So many of the customers volunteered their services that Brenda said she'd draw up a roster of the men she felt were suitable.

'One of these chaps will walk home with you when you've finished work here tonight,' she informed Rhonda as she completed the list.

'Oh, I'm sure it's not necessary,' Rhonda laughed. 'I'll be all right.'

'Not in that get-up you've got on, you won't be,' Brenda told her in a disapproving voice. 'You young flappers don't seem to have any idea what you do to men when you dress in such a manner. Skimpy dresses and all that leg showing in those flesh-coloured silk stockings! In your case, half your chest is bare as well,' she added caustically. 'Tomorrow, put on something that covers you up a bit more.

Make it something black, if you can manage it.'

'I'll see what I can do,' Rhonda promised solemnly, trying hard not to laugh.

For all her sharp, critical manner she liked Brenda Rawlands. Merrion had said she had a heart of gold, and that her bark was worse than her bite, and Rhonda could see what she meant. Twm Rawlands was easygoing, and a complete pushover. Without Brenda there to make sure he wasn't put on she was sure that half the time the customers would have probably got away without paying for their drinks.

Rhonda had no idea that there would be so much walking to and fro or that the trays of beer would be so heavy. She was equally surprised that there was so much clearing up to be done. As well as washing and drying an endless stream of glasses, she seemed to be constantly emptying the overflowing ashtrays. In addition, the tables needed wiping down four or five times during the course of the evening.

By the time Twm called last orders, she was utterly exhausted. She wondered how Merrion had coped and certainly how she'd had the energy, at the end of her shift the previous evening, to manage to fight off her attacker.

'Hold on!' Brenda stopped Rhonda as she was about to leave. 'I meant what I said about you not walking home alone.'

'I know you did, but I really will be all right,' Rhonda protested.

Brenda ignored her. 'Sam!' she called out to one of the men who was leaning on the bar talking to Twm. Immediately he turned round and came hurrying over to where they were.

'Ready, are we?'

'I want you to see Rhonda right to her door, mind, and wait until she's safely inside,' Brenda instructed. 'Then come back here and have a nightcap with us. That way I'll know you've done the job properly and not kept her hanging around talking in the cold and dark,' she told him curtly.

'Oh, it wouldn't be standing around talking that we'd be doing, Brenda, now would it?' he said, winking at Rhonda.

'I've picked you to be the one to take her home because I think you can be trusted,' Brenda snapped. 'Now don't let me down.'

'I won't Brenda, you know you can trust me, I was only joking,' he explained.

'Well, after what happened to Merrion last night we can do without those sorts of jokes,' she retorted sharply. 'Now be on your way, and remember what I said about coming back here afterwards so that I can be sure you've done as I asked.'

Chapter Twenty-One

Rhonda worked at the Glendower Arms for the rest of the week. She claimed she could stick it out for as long as Merrion felt under the weather, but she was secretly relieved when Merrion insisted on going back to work the following Monday.

She gave in gracefully, happy not to have to contend with the beery, smoky, atmosphere any longer, but to be able to return to her millinery work. The previous week's experience had been quite an eye-opener. It convinced her that the sooner she was able to drum up enough business making and selling hats so that Merrion no longer had to work in a place like that then the better it would be for all of them.

For a start, the girls would see more of Merrion, who seemed to be able to do a much better job of looking after them than she could. Merrion seemed to have the knack of controlling them without too many arguments. They never seemed to take advantage of her, or played up with her, like they so often did when she was looking after them, Rhonda reflected.

They liked Merrion's cooking better than hers, too. She had to admit she agreed with them about that. Merrion didn't serve things half raw, or overcook them so that there were burnt bits at the bottom of everything, she thought wryly.

She'd miss the company of the men she'd got to know at the Glendower Arms, however. In fact, she was prepared to admit that there were several that she wouldn't mind getting to know a lot better. It was time she had a proper social life of her own, she decided. Nerys was soon to turn seven, and was growing up fast. Rhonda didn't want to end up spending the rest of her life being on her own and lonely.

If Merrion was to be believed then someday that would happen, when this chap Roddi came back and they married. But would that ever happen? Rhonda asked herself. She wasn't convinced that it would. There were times when she wondered if Roddi was simply a figment of Merrion's imagination. Someone from her past whom she'd built into one of the dreams she believed in so strongly.

No, Rhonda decided, working at the pub had been a wake-up call. She had to start rebuilding her life otherwise she'd still be on her own and working to keep a roof over her head when she was fifty.

Even so, for the moment, she had to help to feed and clothe Nerys. and having now had a taste of what being a barmaid involved, she knew she much preferred to follow her own trade of making hats.

She started to make plans in earnest. Real ones, not dreams like Merrion indulged in, but well-thought-out schemes. She'd build up a range of hats, her very best work, which she could sell or use as samples. When she had enough to represent what she could produce then she'd do the rounds of all the milliners and drapers in Cardiff and see if she could get some orders.

It would be hard work. There would be a lot of tramping the streets, and talking to managers and buyers and trying to convince them to order from her samples. But it would be no worse than trudging backwards and forwards with pints of beer and being polite and smiling to half-drunk pub customers, she consoled herself.

Merrion listened to her plans. 'It sounds like a great idea,' she enthused. 'What can I do to help? The sooner you have the samples made up and ready to take out the better.'

'You could help sort out the trimmings ready for each hat. You could also model the hats for me so that I can see how they look when they're being worn.'

'I'll do anything at all to help,' Merrion promised. 'Now the summer is practically over we could spend the whole day on Sunday working on them. That way you could have samples ready in good time for the Christmas trade.'

'What about the girls? They won't be very happy if they have to hang around watching us work instead of being taken out for a walk.'

'They can always go to Sunday School. They're old enough to go on their own, now, so it will be a bit of an adventure for them. The streets are much quieter on a Sunday so they should be all right. It will give them a taste of independence. At eight years old, they shouldn't need us holding their hands all the time.'

The Rawlands had not only banned Steve the Swede, but they had generously paid both of them for the week Merrion had not been well enough to work, so they used the extra money to buy the basic felt shapes and an assortment of other materials to be used for trimming.

'We'd better stick to petersham ribbon, feathers and fur for the trimmings since this is to be a winter collection,' Rhonda decided.

They both worked hard at the project and by the middle of September they had completed thirty very stylish hats. They were piled up everywhere, covered over with spare sheets and pillow cases to protect them from dust. Rhonda was constantly warning the girls not to go near them or touch them.

'Come on, we haven't the space in this place to stockpile any more,' Merrion told her. 'It's time you started trying to sell some of them if we are going to build up a business. With any luck you might even manage to get some repeat orders in the run-up to Christmas.'

'I'll start on Monday,' Rhonda resolved. 'Come rain or shine. Wish me luck.'

'How are you going to carry them?' Merrion queried. 'You don't want them to be crushed when you get to the shops, now do you?'

'They'll stack two or more on top of each other and I can pack about a dozen into my deep suitcase. I don't need to take out very many at a time so that will be perfect. Fortunately, they don't weigh very much, so carrying the suitcase around will be no problem at all.'

'If you sell the whole lot at the first shop you call at then you can always come straight back home and load up with fresh supplies,' Merrion said, grinning.

Merrion could hardly wait to get home on the Monday night so that she could find out how Rhonda had fared on her selling spree. She was in such a hurry that she felt irritated when Brenda stopped her before she could reach the door and insisted she must wait for Evan Bowler to finish his drink so that he could walk her home.

She knew Brenda had her best interests at heart after the horrible incident with Steve the Swede, but she was in a hurry to get home and hear Rhonda's news. However, because the memory of what had happened was still lurking vividly in the back of her mind, she waited patiently until Evan had finished his drink.

Once outside the pub she started walking so fast that he asked her to slow down.

'Oh come on, anyone would think you were

224

an old man from the speed you are walking, yet you can't be much older than me,' she teased, looking up at the tall, broad-shouldered man at her side.

'Indeed, I can walk as fast as the next man if I want to do so, but I don't want to,' he told her.

'Well, I'm surprised you want to dawdle on a wet night like this,' she stated with a suppressed shiver.

'I've been looking forward to walking you home, Merrion, so I want to take my time, otherwise it will all be over much too soon.'

'I'm in a hurry tonight, though!'

'Why is that? Is the boyfriend waiting for you?'

'No, nothing of the sort,' she protested.

'Well, I'm relieved to hear it!'

She turned her head sharply to look at him, slightly unnerved by the tone of his voice.

'I'm very fond of you, you know, Merrion,' he told her seriously. 'Don't worry. I'm not going to pester you in any way. Brenda would kill me if I did. I won't even attempt to hold your hand, but it doesn't mean that I don't want to.'

'I enjoy your company, too, Evan . . . I think of you as a good friend.'

'Does that mean, then, that I have a chance of getting to know you better?' he asked hopefully.

'Oh, Evan, I'm flattered. I do like you, very much indeed,' she said apologetically, 'but—'

'You're already spoken for! Well, whoever he is, he's a lucky man!'

Merrion sighed.

'Have I touched a raw nerve?' Evan asked. 'That sigh seemed to come from the bottom of your heart.'

'It did!'

For some reason she couldn't understand she found herself telling Evan all about Roddi and her dreams for their future together and how she knew that someday he'd find her again.

'You can't live on dreams for the rest of your life, my lovely, no matter how wonderful they may seem to be,' Evan chided when she'd finished.

'It's more than a dream, it's a conviction that we're meant for each other. We'll be together again one of these days, I'm quite sure of it.'

'If he doesn't come back and manage to find you, what then? You could end up alone and lonely all because you've clung on so strongly to your dreams.'

Merrion looked crestfallen. 'Don't say that,' she murmured. 'Dreams do come true, Evan, I'm sure of it. I've had this one for seven years now, ever since the day I left Cwmglo, and came to Cardiff.'

Evan shook his head and gave a low whistle. 'I find such faith is quite frightening!'

'It's what has kept me going through all the bad times. Losing my mam and little Madoc and knowing that I had been left to look after

Dilwyn who was only a few months old came as a terrible blow.'

Evan shook his head sadly. 'That's what I mean, Merrion, you're far too practical a sort of person to build your whole future on a dream,' he pointed out.

'If we haven't got dreams then what have we got?' she defended herself wistfully.

'You could have me, a real, live, flesh-and-blood man,' he said solemnly.

Merrion felt the blood rush to her face. She had no idea what to say to him. She liked him as a friend, but she knew that he could never be anything more than that. Her heart belonged to Roddi and she knew it always would, whether he managed to find her or not.

'Look, I can still be your friend, you know,' Evan said quickly as if sensing her distress. 'There will be no strings attached, cariad, I promise you. You should have someone you can turn to when you need help. In future I'll be the one who walks you home each night.'

'That wouldn't be fair on you when I can offer you nothing in return.'

'It's better than being on a bloody rota and having to let some other fellow do it!' he pointed out.

'Thank you, Evan, that . . . that's very kind of you. I really do appreciate it.'

'Enough to ask me in out of the rain for a cup of coffee now we're on your doorstep?'

Merrion hesitated. She was eager to get in to

227

find out how well Rhonda had done on her tour of the shops with her case of samples. If she took Evan indoors with her then it would spoil everything because they wouldn't be able to talk about it.

'All right, don't try and think up an excuse, I can see you don't want me to come in.'

'No, please, Evan,' she laid a hand on his arm as he turned on his heel ready to walk away. 'I wasn't trying to think up an excuse.'

'Well, you certainly didn't seem to be overjoyed at the prospect of asking me in.'

'I didn't hesitate because I didn't want you to come in. I was thinking that Brenda would be expecting you back and also because I share two rooms with someone else.'

'I know you do. Rhonda Rees told me all about it when she stood in for you last week.'

'She did?' Merrion felt quite taken aback.

'She hasn't said anything that makes you think she might object to me coming in, has she?' he questioned.

'No, of course she hasn't. It's simply that because we only have two rooms it is so crowded that we never invite anyone back,' Merrion said awkwardly.

'I only suggested a cup of coffee, I wasn't planning to stay for good,' Evan protested mildly. 'Anyway, if you feel uncomfortable with the idea, then let's forget about it,' he said as he turned up his coat collar. 'You'd better get indoors yourself before you get soaked,' he added as he lifted his trilby then replaced it, pulling it down firmly over his eyes. 'I'll see you in the pub tomorrow night.'

'No, please, Evan. I didn't mean to sound rude, I was only trying to explain the situation. Come on in. You deserve a hot drink for walking me home in this downpour,' Merrion insisted.

Chapter Twenty-Two

To Merrion's great surprise, Rhonda seemed to be delighted when she walked in accompanied by Evan.

'What's all this?' she teased. 'I thought we had a long-standing rule about bringing fellas home.'

'This isn't a fella, at least not in the way you mean. It's Evan Bowler, one of the regulars from the pub. He was detailed to walk me home and since it's such a terribly wet night I didn't think you would mind if I asked him in for a hot drink.'

'Doesn't he have to report back to Ma Rawlands afterwards, like all the others, to make sure that he hasn't taken advantage of you on the way home?' Rhonda challenged.

Merrion felt the colour rush to her cheeks as she caught the look that passed between Rhonda and Evan when she tried to apologise for Rhonda's outspoken remark.

'Really, Rhonda, that was uncalled for! She didn't really mean anything by it,' she added quickly, smiling at Evan apologetically.

'There's no need for you to try and explain,' Evan laughed. 'Rhonda knows me well enough to know that you are quite safe with me.'

'Oh, no!' Rhonda argued. 'Simply because you wouldn't kiss me when I gave you the chance doesn't mean you feel the same way about Merrion.'

'Exactly what has been going on?' Merrion looked from one to the other of them in surprise.

'You mean he hasn't told you!' Rhonda tossed back her head and smiled at him provocatively. 'Dark horse this one, I can tell you. Probably the only reason he walked you home was so that he could see me. I bet he was the one who suggested you should invite him in for a coffee, not you,' she challenged.

'I think I'd better be off,' Evan said uncomfortably. 'I know when I'm not wanted.'

'Since you're here you may as well have the coffee you were expecting since it's all ready,' Rhonda told him.

'Sit down, Evan, and take no notice of her,' Merrion invited.

'Shall we tell Evan about the millinery venture we are trying to get going?' she said, when Rhonda handed round the cups of coffee. 'I'm sure he'll be as interested as I am to know how you got on today, so come on, tell us all the details. Did you get any orders, or sell any?'

Rhonda pouted and shrugged her shoulders. 'I'll tell you some other time, I'm sure Evan isn't interested. He'd probably sooner talk about boxing.'

'Boxing?' Merrion looked puzzled.

'That's right, hasn't he told you?'

231

'You mean you earn your living by boxing?' Merrion turned to Evan in surprise.

Rhonda's eyebrows lifted. 'I thought he was supposed to be a friend, yet he hasn't told you all about it?' she mocked. 'Surely you must have wondered what he did for a living! You didn't think he was a docker, dressed up in that flash suit, and you knew he didn't go away to sea because he is in the pub every evening.'

'To tell the truth, I've never even thought about it,' Merrion admitted. 'In fact, I've never stopped to think about what any of the customers do for a living.'

'Perhaps you're doing the wrong job, then,' Rhonda told her. 'In my opinion, to be a good barmaid you have to take a genuine interest in the people who come into the pub.'

'Like you did, you mean.' Merrion smiled.

'Well, I might have only been there for one week, but in that short time I seem to have found out more about Evan, and a lot of the others as well, than you've ever done.'

'Yes, and in those six days we probably found out more about you than we have about Merrion in the months she's been working there,' Evan said quietly.

'Well, are you going to satisfy my curiosity and tell me how you got on today?' Merrion pressed in an attempt to end their exchange which seemed to her to becoming embittered for some reason.

232

'Like I said, I'll tell you later,' Rhonda repeated.

'I think that's a signal for me to drink up and leave,' Evan said wryly. 'Thank you for the coffee. I'll see you in the pub tomorrow night, Merrion. If you are still of the same mind about me seeing you home every night, then we'll tell Brenda that she can scrap her rota.'

'So what did Evan Bowler mean by that?' Rhonda asked as the door closed behind him.

'Evan said he will be quite happy to walk me home every night from now on.'

'Every night!'

'Well, as you said, he's always there.'

'I know that, but it doesn't mean he wants to have to walk you home every night.'

Merrion shrugged. 'He volunteered, I didn't ask him.'

'You want to be careful, I wouldn't trust him. He's got something in mind. Once you let down your guard . . .'

'Let down my guard?' Merrion frowned. 'What are you talking about? He's offered to walk me home, not attack me.'

'Have you forgotten about what happened with Steve the Swede already!'

'Of course I haven't, nor has Evan. That's why he has said he'll make sure I get home safely at night.'

'Brenda was the one who said she'd make sure you got back safely,' Rhonda pointed out. 'She'll be hopping mad when she hears what you've done. Anyway, why do you want Evan to be the one who does it every night? Safety in numbers, you know. Unless, of course, you're having a bit of a fling with him.'

Merrion's face flamed with colour. 'Don't talk so ridiculous, Rhonda!'

'It's not ridiculous. He's quite good-looking and he probably earns a good living. He runs the gymnasium at the far end of George Street and he lives there as well.'

'You seem to know an awful lot about Evan Bowler.'

Rhonda shrugged. 'He talked to me a fair bit when I was working at the pub.'

'Then perhaps that's the reason he wants to walk me home each evening, so that he can have a chance to see you!'

Rhonda looked at her with raised eyebrows. 'So you're not keen on him, then?'

'I think of him as a friend and I feel safe with him, but that's all,' Merrion said firmly.

'You mean that even if he wanted to mean more to you than that, you wouldn't be interested because you are still carrying a torch for that Roddi?'

'That's right. I've told you before, there will never be anyone to take Roddi's place,' Merrion said defensively.

Rhonda looked disbelieving. 'You must be mad! He may never come back, you know. He may have settled out in Australia or even in America by now. He could even be married with a wife and three kids.'

234

Merrion shook her head. 'No,' she said confidently. 'He'll come back one day, I know he will.'

'So you are definitely not in the least bit interested in Evan Bowler, then?' Rhonda pressed.

'I've already told you that I'm not. Now, can we stop talking about him? I want to hear how you got on today.'

Rhonda shook her head disparagingly. 'It was a complete waste of time.'

'Why was that? Those hats were absolutely gorgeous!' Merrion said indignantly.

'So a great many people told me.'

'Then how come you didn't sell any of them or at least get some orders?'

'I misjudged the market. The whole thing has been a washout.'

Merrion looked puzzled. 'What on earth are you talking about, what do you mean?'

'All the buyers had bought in their stock for Christmas. They'd placed their orders back in the spring, of course. I should have known that! I was in the business long enough. The fashion trade works at least six months ahead, sometimes longer, and I should have remembered that, now shouldn't I?'

'So we should have been making hats for spring and summer, not winter hats,' Merrion said aghast.

'That's right. Not only all the big departmental stores but even the small shops said the same thing,' Rhonda said dispiritedly.

'They liked them, though?'

'Oh yes, they said come back with them in the spring and if those styles were still in fashion then they'd consider ordering them for next Christmas.'

'Which means, then, that if you offered them some spring and summer styles right now, they'd buy them!'

'They'd probably place an order, but we haven't anything to show them, have we?'

Merrion frowned. 'Can't we alter the trimmings on them? Take off the fur and put on flowers?'

'That's no good. They're all winter-weight and no one wants heavy felt hats in summer. They'll be looking for straw hats in light colours and trimmed with flowers and pretty ribbons to set off their summer dresses, won't they?'

'Then we'll make some straw ones. Surely half a dozen will be enough to start out with. If you take those around and show them as samples, then you'll get some orders for more,' Merrion suggested.

'Great idea, but what are we going to use for money? We've spent every penny we could afford on making up this pile of hats. Until we sell these we won't have the money to make any others.'

'There must be some way out,' Merrion said. 'Perhaps we could borrow enough money to buy the new materials that we need.'

'Oh yes? Who do we know who would lend

us any money? We live in two squalid rooms in Tiger Bay, it's not even a respectable address!'

'There must be some way,' Merrion insisted.

'Perhaps we could ask your very good friend Evan Bowler if he has twenty or thirty pounds that he's willing to lend us,' Rhonda sneered.

'I wouldn't dream of doing that, but he might well know someone who does have the means of doing so.'

Rhonda looked interested. 'What do you mean, exactly? A money lender?'

'Or a bank. He probably has a bank account himself if he runs a gymnasium as you say he does.'

'I doubt it. Everything is probably paid for off the hip in cash so that no one knows how much he earns. Half the boxers he trains are on the dole so they wouldn't want it known what they are doing.'

'You seem to know a great deal about his affairs.'

'We chatted a lot while I was at the pub,' Rhonda reminded her.

'I can believe that.' Merrion smiled. 'Even so, men don't usually give away so much about their private affairs. Mostly they talk about football, the money they've lost on the dogs or horses and what the beer tastes like.'

'To you, perhaps!'

'No, not to me, to each other. They rarely speak to me except to say "hello" or "thanks" when I put their beer down in front of them.'

237

'That's because you're so quiet and tight-lipped. They think you're stand-offish and they're scared of you.'

'Scared of me! You're mixing me up with Brenda Rawlands, aren't you?'

'No, they know where they stand with Brenda because she doesn't pull her punches. You said yourself that her bark is worse than her bite and the men know that. If they stepped over the mark with her she'd either yell at them to behave themselves or cuff them around the ear. If they did it with you then you'd simply freeze up and they don't know how to deal with that sort of reaction.'

'Quite a philosopher since you spent a whole week working there!' Merrion smiled.

'I learned a lot more about most of them in that short time than you've done in all the time you've been there. You never come home with any snippets of gossip about what they've said or what's happened.'

'True,' Merrion admitted. 'Most of the time while I'm there, even when I'm taking orders, I'm thinking about us.'

'Are you? Or are you day-dreaming about when Roddi will be coming home?'

'I'm always dreaming about that,' Merrion admitted. 'No, I meant I spend my time trying to work out how we can get out of these poky rooms and move somewhere better. The girls are growing so fast that we're packed in like sardines. We've got to do something soon.'

'You'd better ask your friend Evan Bowler, then, if he knows anyone who is willing to let us have a sub or if he knows any loan-sharks that he thinks we can trust.'

Chapter Twenty-Three

They were so busy at the Glendower Arms the following night that Merrion had no opportunity to speak to Evan Bowler so she had to wait until they were walking home before she could do so. Nevertheless, the problem nagged at her all evening. The more she thought of asking his advice about borrowing some money the more nervous she became about mentioning it at all. In the end she was even wondering if it would be better not to get him embroiled in their affairs any further. She even regretted telling him at all that she and Rhonda were trying to set up a business venture.

Unlike Rhonda, who would open up to anybody, she liked to keep her private business to herself. Even though she talked to the other people sharing the house, she had never discussed anything more personal than how the children were getting on at school. For one thing, they were so different to her that she felt she had very little in common with them. Generally she talked about the weather, or what she was going to buy for their main meal. They were all so different from the mining families she had grown up with that she found it very difficult to become close friends with them.

Rhonda, on the other hand, spent hours gossiping with them since she'd stopped going out to work. Night after night she related details about the different families. She knew all about their marriage problems, their quarrels with each other and their opinions on practically everything under the sun.

Merrion often wondered how much she had told them about their affairs, not that there was very much she could tell, of course. She doubted that she would explain to complete strangers why, at twenty-seven, she and her daughter had to share two rooms with another woman, who also had a young child. Or tell them that they were both trying desperately to make ends meet.

In their early days it had seemed a challenge, making their money spin out, managing on practically nothing. Lately though, Merrion found that she had grown tired of the constant penny-pinching and longed to splash out on new clothes for herself and Dilwyn. She would have liked to take her little sister on a trip to Barry Island, or to Porthcawl in the summer holidays so that she could paddle in the sea and build sandcastles. Rhonda probably felt the same way about treats for Nerys, she reminded herself, but there was never enough money to spare. In fact, since she'd lost her job at the Capitol cinema the four of them had only managed to afford one outing to the pictures.

They simply had to press on with the idea of building up a millinery business like Rhonda wanted to do, she decided.

Perhaps if she asked Evan in for a coffee, after he'd walked her home later in the evening, she could lead the conversation round to what they were planning to do, she mused. It might be better if Rhonda was the one to ask how they should go about getting a loan because she was far more outspoken.

As luck would have it, Evan himself broached the subject without any prompting. As they sat enjoying a coffee after he had walked Merrion home, he asked Rhonda what sort of progress she was making with selling her hats. Without any hesitation she gave him the entire spiel about how she appeared to have left it too late for buyers to be interested. 'They all said they'd already chosen their Christmas range of hats,' she said despondently.

'You should have known that! They always work months ahead of each season in the rag trade, now don't they?' he reminded her.

For a moment she looked so annoyed by Evan's criticism that Merrion thought she was either going to start a verbal battle with him, or flounce out of the room in a temper. Then she fluttered her eyelashes at him and murmured quite demurely, 'Well, we're not as clever as you men, are we?'

Evan laughed. 'I don't believe that for one moment. Your trouble is that you are much too

242

near to the problem and so you can't see the wood for the trees.'

'That's where you could help,' Rhonda told him, her blue-eyed gaze locking with his dark one.

'Oh really?' He looked quite surprised. 'In what way?'

'Well, we want to prepare in advance for next year which means I should already be making up samples of hats suitable for spring and summer and showing them to any likely customers.'

'So what's stopping you? You're not working, so you should have plenty of time on your hands.'

'Money! We spent every spare penny we had buying the materials to make the collection of winter hats.'

'So you're broke?'

'Absolutely! Can you advise us where we should go for a loan?'

'Borrow money that you won't be able to pay back for at least six months?' he looked dubious. 'It might even be a lot longer than that since many of the big stores keep creditors waiting for months before they settle their bills.'

Rhonda looked taken aback. 'What do you suggest we should do, then?' she pouted.

'Surely the sensible thing to do would be to sell the stock you have and use the money you get for that to buy new materials.'

'I've already told you, I've left it too late to do that,' Rhonda said heatedly.

'No, you haven't.'

'Of course I have. Haven't you been listening to a word I've been saying!'

'I've heard you say that you took them around the big stores and that they didn't give you any orders. In that case, then, you'll have to sell them direct.'

'Persuade the people who live in Tiger Bay to buy posh hats?' she said scornfully. 'Half of them wear turbans or fezes around here and the rest pull a shawl up over their heads when it's cold. I don't think they're likely to buy many, now are they?'

'I wasn't thinking you should hawk your wares around here from door to door,' he told her.

'So what were you thinking, then?' she demanded petulantly. 'I was hoping you would offer some help, not lecture me!'

'I was thinking that you should try the stall-holders at the Hayes market, or even take a stall there and sell them yourself,' he said mildly.

Rhonda's face brightened, and she looked at him with more respect. 'You know, that's not a bad idea!' Then her face clouded. 'I've only got about fifty hats made up, though, and that would hardly justify hiring a stall would it?'

'Possibly not, but I am sure there are stall-holders who would be interested in giving you space, or be willing to sell them on your behalf, if in return you gave them a cut of the profits.'

'Do a deal of that sort with complete strangers? I hardly think so. They'd know I was new to the game and they'd rip me off something rotten.'

'I know several of the stallholders at the Hayes so I could ask around for you,' Evan offered. 'I could even help to work out how much commission you should pay them for handling your hats if you wished.'

Rhonda's eyes narrowed. 'That's very kind of you, but what are you going to get out of it?'

Evan laughed and his eyes went to Merrion who was sitting listening to them, but not saying anything. 'I'll be happy with a cup of coffee each evening when I walk Merrion home.'

Rhonda looked slightly piqued. 'You're wasting your time if you think this is going to impress her enough to take you seriously,' she said tartly. 'Merrion's dream hero is a sailor, one she hasn't seen for seven years, but she firmly believes that he will come back to her one day.'

'I know, she's told me,' he said quietly.

'As long as you know the score.' Rhonda grinned. 'So how much commission do you think I ought to give the stallholder?'

'Probably a lot less than the discount you'd give to the big shops for taking your hats.'

Her eyes widened. 'Really!'

'I'm quite sure.'

'So how do we arrive at the right figure?'

'I can't stop any longer now, but write down what the materials cost you and what you think the hat will sell for and then we'll work it out from that.'

'When?' she asked eagerly.

'Tomorrow night, when I walk Merrion home. You have the details ready and in the meantime I'll make one or two enquiries at the market and find out if anyone is interested.'

Evan was as good as his word. By the end of the following evening he had not only worked out how much commission she would be expected to give on each hat sold, but also provided her with the names of six stallholders who were interested in doing a deal with her.

'Get along there tomorrow and see what you can do,' he told her.

'Which of these names should I try first?' Rhonda asked as she looked down the list he'd handed to her.

'That's up to you. Why don't you take a walk around the market and have a look at the stalls I've listed and then approach the one that you think is most suitable, or whose stall appeals to you the most.'

'So do you think I should stick to dealing with only one trader?'

'That will have to be your decision, Rhonda,' Evan told her.

'I'm asking for your advice,' she pressed.

'Well, I think you should limit the number you have selling your hats, otherwise they might find that they get so few customers that it's not worth the bother of displaying them. You've only got fifty hats at the moment, so why not select two traders, with stands as far apart in the market as possible, and let them have twenty-five each and see how things go?'

'That sounds very sensible,' Merrion agreed, 'but what if one of them says he doesn't want anyone else selling the same sort of hats?'

'You have a point there,' Evan admitted. 'Perhaps you should ask the first trader if he minds if someone else in the market will also be selling them.'

Rhonda looked flustered. 'It all sounded so easy when we started talking about it, but now I'm not so sure.'

'I don't have to be at the pub until eleven o'clock, so why don't we go up to the Hayes first thing tomorrow morning and take a look round?' Merrion suggested. 'You could even introduce yourself to one or two of the traders on Evan's list and find out if they're interested in selling your hats. If they are, then you can go back with the hats in the afternoon.'

'That sounds like a very sensible idea,' Evan agreed as he pushed back his chair and prepared to leave. 'Goodnight and good luck. I shall look forward to hearing how you get on.'

'He'll do anything for you,' Rhonda commented, picking up the list as the door closed behind Evan. 'He must have spent ages working all this out.'

'I don't give him any encouragement,' Merrion assured her.

'No, you make it pretty plain that you're not attracted to him in the slightest. I think you're mad. I'd jump at the chance if he showed any interest in me. Living in a dream world, spending your time thinking about Roddi and expecting him to turn up out of the blue one day is absolutely crazy.'

'It may be for you, but it's what has got me through all our problems down the years.'

'Well, you can go on living in your dream world if you want to, but I'm going to make a life for myself, a proper life. I'm not only going to make a success of making and selling hats, but I'm going to find myself a husband.'

'You've got your priorities wrong, haven't you? Surely moving out of here and finding somewhere better to live should be top of the list.'

'Oh that as well,' Rhonda agreed airily.

'Right, well then, let's get to bed so that we are up bright and early and have time to take a good look at all the stalls at the Hayes before I have to go to work.'

'You probably think that I should have found a proper job before now,' Rhonda sighed.

'No, not at all. Someone has to be around for

the girls when they come home from school and in the holidays.'

'Yes, I suppose that's true!' Rhonda admitted.

'We've both had our fair share of doing that,' Merrion pointed out. 'Now they're getting older, though, things should get easier.'

'Mind, if this comes off, if we can find enough people to buy the hats and I can get more orders for the summer, then you will be able to stop working at the pub and . . .'

'Now who is the one who is building on dreams,' Merrion interrupted teasingly.

'No, I'm simply looking ahead to the future . . . our future.'

'Come on, we'd better get to bed or we won't have a future. We'll both be too tired in the morning to know what we're doing and we're going to need all our wits about us when it comes to dealing with market traders.'

Chapter Twenty-Four

To Merrion's astonishment Rhonda was the first one up the next morning. She even had the tea made and their breakfast ready before Merrion was dressed.

'Aren't you feeling well, Mam?' Nerys asked in surprise.

'None of your cheek, young lady. Come on, get your breakfast, we're in a hurry this morning.'

'Why, where are you going?' Dilwyn asked. 'Why are you wearing your best skirt?'

'Rhonda and I are going out somewhere, that's why we're looking smart,' Merrion told her. 'Now do as you've been asked, eat your breakfast and get yourselves ready for school.'

'Do we have to go to school, can't we come with you, Mam?' Nerys pleaded.

'No, you can't, now stop gabbing and do as you're told,' Rhonda scolded.

'Where are you going?' Dilwyn asked quietly, tugging at Merrion's arm.

'To the Hayes market, cariad. We want to have a good look round there.'

'Why do you want to do that?' Dilwyn asked in a puzzled voice.

250

'Well, it's a secret at the moment, see, so you mustn't breathe a word to Ella or Pedro or anyone else at school, but Rhonda is thinking of selling some of her hats there.'

Both girls looked suitably impressed.

'Are you going to stand behind a stall there all day selling them to people?' Nerys frowned.

'No, not exactly. We're going to ask one of the stallholders to do that for us. That's why you mustn't say anything about it until we've finished making the arrangements.'

'Why does it have to be a secret?' Nerys probed.

'That's enough! Come on now, pack your satchels and put your coats on, and let's get the pair of you off to school,' Rhonda told her impatiently.

The minute the girls were ready, with warm scarves around their necks and woollen mittens to protect their hands against the cold, Merrion and Rhonda put their own coats and hats on.

'You should both have on one of your new hats, Auntie Rhonda,' Dilwyn pointed out.

'No, I want to sell them, not go out in them,' she told her quickly.

'If you and Aunt Merrion were both wearing one of the new hats, though, the people in the market could see them and then they'd want to buy one for themselves,' Nerys said.

Rhonda and Merrion looked at each other.

'They do have a point, don't they! Shall we?' Rhonda questioned.

251

'I suppose they could be right. It's a good way of showing them off.'

Rhonda went into the bedroom and came back with two hats. A blue cloche one, very fancifully decorated with feathers and contrasting ribbon and a green felt hat that was much plainer and trimmed only with a large fur pompom.

'Take your pick,' she invited.

'I'm not sure I can do either of them justice,' Merrion protested as she pulled off her plain brown felt hat and smoothed down her hair.

'Don't talk nonsense, of course you can.'

'You wear the one with the pompom on it,' Dilwyn told Merrion. 'That will suit you because you're tall. The other one with all the feathers will look better on Auntie Rhonda because it's blue, the same colour as her eyes.'

'There you are, the fashion expert has spoken,' Rhonda laughed.

The green hat with its grey fur trim transformed Merrion. It softened the outlines of her thin face and yet gave her a distinctive look.

Dilwyn was right in her selection. The feathery one looked very appealing on Rhonda.

'I feel a bit daft and overdressed, so come on, before I change my mind,' Merrion protested. 'I really ought to have a new coat to do justice to a hat as posh as this one.'

Half an hour later, Merrion and Rhonda were getting off the tram at the corner of Wood Street.

'I feel as nervous as a kid starting school for

the first time,' Rhonda said as they crossed the road to the Hayes.

'Don't say that, I'm shaking in my shoes as well,' Merrion admitted.

'Daft, really, isn't it?'

'We're only going to walk round the market and see what's what. We don't have to persuade any of them to take any stock if we don't feel like it, not this morning.'

'Well, we might as well, if we like the look of any of the stalls Evan has written down on this list,' Rhonda reminded her.

Although it was only a few minutes after nine o'clock, most of the stalls were laid out ready for business and there were quite a few people shopping at the fruit and vegetable stalls where business was brisk.

'There're not many people browsing at the clothes stalls,' Rhonda said disappointedly.

'There will be later on. Most of the people who are shopping now are from small hotels and cafés, or boarding houses, getting their provisions in,' Merrion pointed out. 'They have to come here early because they've got to get back and prepare what they're buying for their lunchtime trade.'

'Yes, I suppose you're right. Perhaps it's a waste of time coming this early.'

'Of course it isn't, cariad,' Merrion chivvied her, 'let's check out the list Evan gave you.'

There were six names on the list. Two of them specialised in a wide range of clothing items and seemed to be very suitable. One of the others seemed to have only children's and baby clothes.

'We may as well cross that one off,' Rhonda stated. 'I don't know what Evan was thinking about, putting it on the list in the first place.'

'Hold on, don't be too quick, think about it first. Who buys clothes for babies and kids? Women of course. If at the same time there's a stylish hat that catches their eye, you never know, they might be tempted and feel they've got to have it. If they've just had a baby they might need cheering up. Or they might buy it as something special to wear at the christening.'

'I suppose you could be right,' Rhonda admitted dubiously.

'Let's try talking to the stallholder and see what the woman says.'

She admired the hats they were wearing and agreed with their theory about mothers who might need cheering up, but she wanted them to give her time to think about it.

'I'll call back again this afternoon, then,' Rhonda told her. 'I'll bring along some more hats for you to see.'

One of the other stallholders on the list turned them down flat. 'I'll stick to what I know I can sell,' she told them. 'I can't afford to clutter up my stall, my lovely. I've got a sick husband to support.'

Rhonda was getting depressed, but her spirits soared when, finally, they went to the last stall on the list. Although it was selling women's clothes that were quite stylish, the stallholder was a man. He was tall, and smartly dressed in a dark grey suit, a grey and white striped shirt and a bright red tie.

'How can I refuse when such a gorgeous lady, wearing such an eye-catching hat, offers me such attractive stock?' he parried, his green eyes challenging as he responded to Rhonda's flirty manner in the same spirit.

Rhonda stared appreciatively at the handsome, dark haired man. 'Haven't you got that the wrong way round?' she teased. Shouldn't it be attractive woman and gorgeous hats?'

'Whatever you say, my lovely. Both are so beautiful that I can't wait to get my hands on them.'

'You don't seem to be the sort of person I'd expect to be selling clothes to women,' she commented flippantly. 'Are you standing in for your wife or your girlfriend?'

'Neither, my lovely! I'm heart whole and fancy free,' he chuckled. 'At least I was until this moment and now I am faced with the dilemma of having to choose between two of the most beautiful ladies I have ever seen.'

Rhonda laughed. 'I bet you say that to all your customers.'

He pretended to look pained. 'If I told you that you are both wearing the most wonderful hats I have ever seen, would you believe that?'

'Depends on whether you'd like to sell them on our behalf.'

'Take the hats from off your heads!' He frowned. 'Ladies, I am utterly lost for words.'

'I bet that doesn't happen very often,' Rhonda laughed. 'Are you Dai Francis, by any chance?'

'Yes, I am. How do you know that? I'm sure we've never met before, I couldn't possibly forget someone like you.'

'Evan Bowler told me to come and see you.'

'He did? The crafty old matchmaker! He knew I'd find you irresistible! His face creased into a beaming smile. Evan's a great buddy of mine. He's always threatening to train me to be a boxer.' He shook his head. 'That's the last thing I ever want to be, though. I hate hurting people.'

'Quite right! I'm glad to hear it.' Rhonda smiled.

'Thank you.' He gave her an exaggerated bow. 'Now, you know all about me, so aren't you going to tell me about yourself and how you come to be wearing such a beautiful hat? Both of you,' he said quickly with a warm smile in Merrion's direction.

'You like them?' Merrion asked, self-consciously putting her hand up to touch hers.

'They're both quite magnificent. You didn't buy hats like those here in this market!'

'No,' Rhonda admitted, 'I made them.'

'You make hats for a living!' His eyes widened in surprise.

'I'm a fully trained milliner,' she assured him,

'and I'm looking for someone to sell the hats that I make. Evan seemed to think you might be interested in doing so.'

'Whew!' He gave a soundless whistle. 'Can I afford them?'

'I'd supply them without charge and I'd pay you a commission when you sell them,' Rhonda said quickly.

'A businesswoman as well as a beautiful one,' he murmured appreciatively.

'Well, are you interested?' Rhonda pressed.

'Very much so! I specialise in fashionable clothes as you can see and what better way to complement them than with the right hat? Have you any more you can let me see?'

'Every hat I make is different in some way, so how many would you like to take?'

'How many do you have to sell?' he parried.

'Fifty!' Merrion said quickly.

'That many!' Again he gave a soundless whistle, fingering his pencil-thin moustache thoughtfully.

Rhonda reached out and slipped her hand into Merrion's and squeezed her fingers so tightly that Merrion winced.

'If that's too many for you then we have someone else in the market who is interested,' Rhonda murmured.

'No, no!' Dai held up a hand as if to stop her from moving. 'If I take them, then I want to be the only trader in this market who will be selling them. Is that understood?'

'A clever businessman who knows a good product when he sees it!' Rhonda smiled. 'So we're agreed you'll take all fifty?'

'Well, we haven't done a deal yet, have we? How much are you charging me for these creations?'

'I told you, I'll fix the selling price and I'll pay you a commission on your sales.'

'You didn't say how much they would be selling for, though, and until I know that I won't know how much I will be making.'

Merrion listened to their semi-serious discussion with growing impatience. She could see that Rhonda was thoroughly enjoying herself, but she was becoming worried about the way the time was flying by. Unless they left now she was going to be late for work and, even though Rhonda's deal seemed to be going very satisfactorily, she certainly didn't want to lose her job. Not yet, at any rate.

Rhonda became aware of her edginess and guessed the reason.

'If you want to go, Merrion, that's fine by me. I'll see you later this evening.'

Merrion looked startled. 'Are you sure?'

'Quite sure. There're still a lot of the finer details to be settled so it may take us a while longer. Isn't that right, Dai?'

'Very true. I like to have things a hundred per cent clear before I make any decisions. I'm sure we can come to a suitable arrangement over delivery and your terms. I don't want to rush things, though, and then to have to go all over it again, or worse still find that it all goes wrong.'

He turned back to Rhonda, 'My assistant will be here in about five minutes. When she arrives then perhaps we could go across to the café and discuss everything in more detail. You are invited of course,' he said quickly, turning back to Merrion.

'I'm afraid I can't spare the time, much as I would like to come along,' she apologised.

'Go on, Merrion. I'll be quite all right,' Rhonda assured her. 'I'll tell you all the details about the deal when you get home tonight.'

Chapter Twenty-Five

Merrion was on tenterhooks for the rest of the day. She hated having to walk away and leave Rhonda to sort out all the details about the hats on her own.

It wasn't that she didn't think Rhonda was capable of completing the transaction, but it was obvious she was quite taken by Dai Francis and she was afraid that might cloud her judgement. Merrion assumed he was quite trustworthy, since Evan Bowler had recommended him, but for her part she thought he was far too good-looking and glib.

She didn't like to mention this fact to Evan when he came into the pub during the evening. She merely said that she'd had to leave them to their negotiating because otherwise she would have been late for work.

'She'll tell us all the details when you walk me home tonight,' she said, smiling.

Rhonda couldn't wait for them to sit down before she started telling them what had happened. She hugged Evan and kissed him on both cheeks as she thanked him for all his help.

'Hey, hey, steady on, my lovely, you haven't

told us the details yet,' he laughed as he freed himself from her embrace.

Merrion went and made a pot of tea for the three of them while Rhonda gave him a blow-by-blow account of the stalls they'd visited and the conversations she'd had with the various stallholders.

'Come on, girl, I'm waiting to hear what Dai Francis had to say. I gather he is going to sell your hats, but did he agree to your terms?' Evan asked as he stirred his tea.

'Your terms, you mean, don't you! You were the one who worked out all the details!' Rhonda reminded him.

'Fair do's. So he accepted them, I take it.'

'He most certainly did, and he has agreed to take all fifty winter hats!'

'All of them!' Merrion looked pleased. 'Have you taken some of them up to him already?'

'He's got the lot! They're already on display. Well, all except one of them, and you were still wearing that one, Merrion.' She laughed.

'How on earth did you manage to get them all to him? You must have been running backwards and forwards all day.'

'Not a bit of it,' Rhonda told her triumphantly. 'Dai has a little van so he came back with me after we'd settled the details and we loaded the whole lot into it. One journey, that's all! And then he took me out to lunch.' She beamed.

Evan and Merrion exchanged amused glances.

'What more can we say, except let's hope he's as quick at selling the hats as he has been in acquiring them,' Evan remarked dryly.

'He's quite confident about that. Three of them had already sold by the time we got back to the stall after lunch.'

'Well, I must say, that's wonderful news!' Merrion smiled in relief.

'That's not all,' Rhonda went on excitedly. 'He wants some more. He's said he's sure he can sell more than fifty winter hats and he's ordered a hundred summer hats even without seeing any samples.'

'You're both rushing things a bit, aren't you?' Merrion frowned.

'Not at all! He knows when he's on to a good thing,' Rhonda said confidently.

'I know that he's an astute businessman,' Evan agreed. 'I thought he would be interested, but I didn't think he'd be this keen.'

'Well he is. What's more, he's offered to arrange for me to buy the materials and trimming that I need at wholesale prices. I'm going along with him next week when he goes to see his suppliers and I'll be able to select whatever I need. It will save me a lot of money and it means we can keep the prices of the finished hats within the range that he knows his customers are willing to pay.'

'You won't be needing any more advice from me, then,' Evan pronounced as he drained his cup and stood up to leave. 'I'm so pleased that it has all turned out so well. Much better than I ever hoped, in fact.'

Long after Evan had left, Rhonda and Merrion sat discussing the new venture. It seemed obvious that Rhonda had agreed with every suggestion that Dai Francis had made and Merrion hoped that she wasn't being too carried away by it all.

Evan seemed to trust the man and to think he was an honest trader, so perhaps she was being too suspicious, Merrion thought after she was in bed that night, but she couldn't help feeling that it all seemed too good to be true.

In the weeks that followed Rhonda had no such qualms. She made plans, drew up lists, worked out new designs, and decided what materials she was going to need for the additional hats that Dai suggested she should make.

'How are you going to pay for all these materials?' Merrion frowned as she studied the lengthy list that Rhonda had compiled. 'This lot is going to cost the earth, you know.'

'That won't be any problem,' Rhonda said airily. 'I told you, Dai said I can get materials from his wholesalers and that they won't need paying until next month. By that time, he says, he will have sold enough hats to cover the costs of my materials and still leave a nice sum over.'

'You are putting all your eggs into one basket, you know,' Merrion warned.

'What do you mean by that?'

'Well, if this arrangement with Dai Francis doesn't work out, if you should start to disagree about anything, or the hats don't sell, then you're in a fine mess.'

'Do you have to be so critical about everything?' Rhonda flared.

'I'm not being critical, cariad. I simply don't want to see you taken in.'

'By Dai Francis!' Rhonda's blue eyes darkened angrily. 'Let me tell you, he's the nicest, most sincere man I've ever met. Even your Evan Bowler says so. He was the one who recommended him, now wasn't he?'

'Yes, I know that. Things are moving so fast, though, that it's making me quite breathless.' Merrion smiled placatingly.

'I don't see that I have anything to lose,' Rhonda argued. 'Dai's taking all the winter hats that I've made and he wants more, which is terrific. I'm getting my materials at cost price and an introduction to the wholesalers, which can't be bad, now can it?'

'What if later he decides he doesn't want to sell hats? It would be such a terrible let down for you.'

'I'm not worried about that. It will have given me the start I need and I can always look for fresh outlets,' Rhonda told her confidently.

Rhonda went ahead with her plans. She accompanied Dai to the wholesalers where she bought so many shapes and such a vast amount of trimming that Merrion wondered where on earth they were going to store it all.

The two of them worked hard at producing the winter hats in the run-up to Christmas. Merrion helped by sorting out the trimmings ready for Rhonda to use each morning before it was time for her to go to the pub. They also worked side by side all day on Sundays when Merrion stuffed the crowns of the finished hats with tissue paper so that they wouldn't get crushed, then packed them into cardboard boxes Dai supplied, ready for him to collect the next day.

Dilwyn and Nerys complained that they were always so busy that they never took them anywhere, and that they never went for walks or to the park on Sunday any more but were packed off to Sunday School instead.

Merrion and Rhonda agreed that they wouldn't trim a single hat all over the Christmas holidays. They also promised that as well as it being the best Christmas they'd ever known they'd also have a special surprise for them both.

When Merrion laughingly told Evan all about this on their walk home one evening, he suggested that they all go to the pantomime that was being staged at the Prince of Wales theatre on Boxing Day.

Merrion thought it was a fabulous idea so he promised to get tickets.

'Since I'm coming with you, this is my treat,'

he told her when she tried to give him the money to buy the tickets. 'It will give me a chance to repay you and Rhonda for all those cups of tea and coffee.'

Rhonda was thrilled by the idea when Merrion told her what they were planning to do.

'Have you ever been to a pantomime?' Merrion asked. 'I haven't. Will it be suitable for Dilwyn and Nerys?'

'Of course it will,' Rhonda assured her. 'Evan wouldn't have suggested it otherwise. It's a sort of play based on one of the well-known fairy tales but with singing and dancing in it. Sometimes there are clowns and acrobats as well. I'm sure the girls will absolutely love it.'

'Right, not a word about it to them, then. We won't tell them until the very last minute.'

'Make sure you warn Evan not to say anything to them!'

'There's really no need to do that, they're always tucked up in bed asleep when he walks me home at night.'

'We've already said we are taking them somewhere special so we'll leave it at that,' Rhonda agreed.

'Do you think we should even have told them that?'

'I think so, because it will stop them feeling so neglected.'

'True, and it will be one way of making sure that they are on their best behaviour from now until Boxing Day.'

266

There were so many exciting things happening for the children in the week leading up to Christmas that Merrion was worried in case the planned outing to the pantomime would come as something of an anticlimax. She hoped not because she knew that tickets for the five of them must have cost Evan quite a lot of money and he was looking forward to them all enjoying the evening.

Thanks to the deal Rhonda had done with Dai Francis they had enough money to enjoy Christmas to the full. They bought new dresses for themselves as well as for the two girls and they also had a splendid Christmas dinner. Both the girls had been delighted by all the celebrations especially when, as if my magic, they'd both found a silver threepenny bit in their helpings of Christmas pudding.

Merrion and Rhonda decided to let the two girls sleep late on Boxing Day morning. There were plenty of leftovers from the previous day so they used them up for their midday meal and had an easy day themselves.

It was a dull grey day when the girls eventually woke up so the four of them agreed to stay indoors. They spent most of the afternoon playing 'Sorry', the new board game that Dai Francis had bought for them.

The girls were surprised when in the early evening they were ordered to go and put on the new dresses they'd been given for Christmas and told that they would be going out.

Immediately they remembered the special surprise they'd been promised and started trying to work out what it could be.

'I thought our new dresses were the big surprise,' Dilwyn said.

'I didn't, I thought it was all the presents in our stocking,' Nerys laughed. 'So what is it then, Mam? Why are we getting dressed up, where are we going?' she demanded.

'Wait and see,' Rhonda told her. 'Put on your new dresses and then come and have your hair brushed. You've got to look very special.'

By the time Evan Bowler arrived they were so excited that they were almost in tears.

'Oh! Are you the special surprise?' Nerys said in a disappointed voice.

'Only one very small part of it!' He smiled. 'Are all of you ready to leave?'

Throughout the tram ride into town they kept up a barrage of questions about where they were going, but neither of them guessed where it would be.

'We can't be going shopping because all the shops are shut and even the market is closed,' Dilwyn pointed out when they got off the tram close to the Hayes.

Holding the two girls by the hand, Evan led the way across to the theatre. The girls stared in awe as they entered the brightly decorated foyer with its fairy lights and artificial snow. It was Rhonda, though, who let out the loudest exclamation of surprise as she saw Dai Francis standing there.

'Fancy seeing you here!' she exclaimed.

'I asked him to join us,' Evan explained. 'You don't mind, do you?'

'The more the merrier,' Rhonda laughed, tucking her hand into Dai's arm.

Inside the theatre they seated the two girls in the centre of the row and Rhonda sat at one end, next to Dai, while Merrion and Evan sat at the other end.

The two girls were entranced by the pantomime which was *Jack and the Beanstalk*. In the interval, Dai and Evan went to procure refreshments for them all. This brought squeals of delight from Dilwyn and Nerys when the two men returned with drinks and chocolates.

When the show ended the girls were so tired that Dai suggested that as his van was parked nearby perhaps he should take them home in it.

'Yes, that sounds like a good idea,' Evan agreed. 'It will be much better than waiting for a tram. Anyway, they'll be so crowded that we mightn't be able to get on one for ages.'

'You'll find it a bit of a squash mind!' Dai warned as he led the way to where it was parked. 'I didn't have time to clear it out so it's half full of stock.'

Rhonda took the passenger seat next to Dai leaving Merrion to climb into the back with the two girls.

'It doesn't look as if there is going to be room for all of us, so I think I'll walk,' Evan stated.

'As you like, boyo. Great night, see you again soon,' Dai told him.

It had been a very enjoyable evening, Merrion reflected as they made their way home. The two girls were starry-eyed with excitement and chattered non-stop about the wonders of what they had seen. Merrion had also enjoyed every minute of it, but she felt rather disappointed that she hadn't been able to thank Evan properly for such a wonderful outing.

Chapter Twenty-Six

Both Merrion and Rhonda greeted the start of 1927 with enthusiasm. Evan had invited them to a party that was being held in his gymnasium in George Street on New Year's Eve and they were looking forward to it.

'Dai has said that he will pick up Rhonda and the two girls in his van at about eight o'clock, so I'll come and collect you when the pub closes,' he told Merrion.

'I'm a bit concerned about Dilwyn and Nerys attending something like this,' Merrion said worriedly. 'They are only seven years old, you know.'

'There will be other kids there, they'll love every minute of it,' he assured her.

'Yes, I suppose you're right,' she agreed dubiously. 'Rhonda has told them about it and they're terribly excited.'

'There you are, then!'

'I'm sure they'll love it,' Merrion agreed, 'but I'm concerned in case it is all rather grown-up for them and it does mean them staying up very late.'

'They'll be bitterly disappointed if you say they can't come!' he laughed. 'And staying up late won't hurt them for one night. You can take them home as soon as they're tired or if you think that it's getting to be too much for them.'

Although they had an extension at the pub so that customers could toast in the new year, Brenda said it was all right for Merrion to go when Evan arrived at half past ten to collect her.

She'd been rushed off her feet all evening, but her tiredness vanished and she felt quite excited as he escorted her the few hundred yards along George Street to the brightly decorated hall of his gymnasium.

Evan had saved her a plate of carefully chosen titbits from the buffet meal they'd had earlier and it gave her a fresh boost of energy. Once she'd eaten and had a glass of wine, Merrion felt more than ready to enjoy the party and take part in all the merriment with the rest of them.

At midnight their glasses were refilled so that they could welcome in 1927 in the traditional way. Evan assured Merrion that the girls were having nothing stronger than sarsaparilla, but he insisted that she should have a glass of the champagne which he'd bought specially for the occasion.

As they all linked hands and sang the old year out and the new one in, Merrion wondered if maybe Rhonda was right and it was time to put her dreams that Roddi would one day return behind her and build a completely new life.

Even so, she was startled and about to protest when on the stroke of midnight Evan took her in his arms and kissed her. Then she realised that everyone was kissing each other. Quickly she told herself that it was nothing more than a seasonal greeting and it would be foolish to make a fuss.

If was the first time Evan had ever kissed her and she felt guilty because she found it so pleasant. Instinctively, she knew that it had been the same for him. He seemed to look at her in a different way and his voice seemed to be warmer, more intimate.

She tried to tell herself that it was the champagne making her imagine it all, but in her heart she knew this wasn't so. Both of them were suddenly very much more aware of each other than they had been before.

It left her strangely disturbed and self-conscious as well as feeling a little bit guilty that she was showing an interest in someone else when her heart belonged to Roddi. Quite soon afterwards she suggested to Rhonda that it was time for the girls to go home, despite their protests that they weren't the least bit tired.

'I'll walk you home,' Evan told her.

'No, really, there's no need for you to do that,' she told him hastily.

'You can't walk home on your own, there will be drunks everywhere,' he told her sharply.

'I'll take them,' Dai volunteered. 'My van's

parked outside. You're going to take Nerys with you as well, Merrion?' he asked pointedly.

'Of course I am,' Merrion said. She frowned. 'What a strange question!'

'I wanted to be sure because Rhonda wants to stay on a bit longer, see,' he explained. 'If you take the two girls home, then I'll bring Rhonda home later on when she's ready to leave.'

Merrion nodded her agreement. Both girls were tired out and struggling to stay awake. She was quite sure that there would be no problems and that Nerys would go to bed without any fuss.

It was a long time before Merrion fell asleep. She lay there listening for Rhonda to come home and trying to analyse her own feelings for Evan. He was very personable: tall, broad, good-looking with thick fair hair and thoughtful grey eyes. She liked him very much and found him to be good company. He'd certainly proved to be a very reliable friend.

She didn't hear Rhonda arrive back. By then she was deep into a dream in which she was back in Cwmglo. She was sitting with Roddi on the low wall by the river, listening to him telling her how much he loved her and making wonderful plans for their future together.

Troubled by her dream, and by her own mixed-up feelings, Merrion resolved to avoid Evan as much as she could in the future.

It was not easy. Evan sensed her coldness and wanted to know if he had done anything to upset her. Despite her protestations that it was only because she was so tired, she knew he didn't believe her.

She struggled to push it all to the back of her mind because she and Rhonda were so busy. They were both working hard at getting the range of spring hats ready and it took all her concentration.

'We are so short of space that there isn't room to breathe,' Rhonda grumbled, as she placed a pile of new hats on top of a cupboard.

'Why don't you ask Dai if he can take the ones we've already finished?' Merrion suggested. 'I'm sure he must have a storeroom somewhere.'

'That's a great idea.' Rhonda beamed. 'First thing tomorrow morning I'll pop up to the Hayes and ask him.'

Merrion was busy serving when Rhonda burst into the Glendower Arms, so excited she could hardly make herself understood.

'Slow down, cariad, I can't make sense of what you are telling me,' Merrion protested.

'Space, and a real place to work,' Rhonda said slowly, emphasising each word.

Merrion shook her head. 'I still don't understand.'

'Remember you were saying that we needed more space and suggested that I should ask Dai if he could help out by taking the hats we had ready?'

'Yes, of course I do. Heavens, we only talked about it last night,' Merrion said as she collected up dirty glasses and stacked them on to a tray.

'Well, when I did he said that he could,' Rhonda enthused.

'That's good. Now we'll have breathing space.'

'That's not all. He said he had space that I could use as a workroom!'

'Really?' Merrion put down the tray of glasses and gave Rhonda her full attention.

'Yes, it's in Loudon Square. It seems he has a house there and he only uses part of it. He's turned the ground floor into a flat and he uses the upper rooms to store stuff in. I think he said that the house is three storeys, but he said I could use the rooms on the second floor. There would be plenty of space to have a workroom as well as a storeroom.

'It sounds marvellous, but how much is he going to charge you for using the place?'

Rhonda looked at her wide-eyed. 'I never thought to ask!' she gulped.

'I'm sure he'll be fair,' Merrion murmured, picking up the tray again and carrying it over to the bar.

'Not a very good businesswoman, am I?' Rhonda said ruefully as she followed her.

'You'd have remembered about it the moment you had time to think it over.'

'No, you're right,' Rhonda said. 'I need to know now so that I can work out whether it's affordable or not.'

'I'm sure it will be. After all, if you have more room you can probably make more hats and if you increase your output then a reasonable rent will be quite manageable.'

'We'll go and look at it tomorrow morning, before you start work, shall we?'

'If that's all right with Dai,' Merrion agreed.

'Oh it will be. He's given me a door key.'

'So you've already agreed to the arrangement.' Merrion frowned.

'Not really . . .' Rhonda murmured hesitantly.

'You mean that Dai's taken it for granted that you'll take the rooms.'

Rhonda shrugged. 'Possibly. I want to see them first, though, make sure they are right for us.'

The rooms were vast. Rhonda walked round and round them in ecstasy.

'We could put both our rooms into one of these and there would still be space to spare,' she exclaimed.

They decided that one room would be big enough for both storeroom and workroom, but Dai wouldn't hear of it.

'He says we can use the entire floor,' Rhonda told Merrion. 'He says it's only going to waste, otherwise. He said he will arrange it so that it is locked off from the rest of the place so that we know all our hats and materials are completely safe.'

'Let's think about it,' Merrion suggested. 'He hasn't said what rent he wants yet, has he?'

'No, but I think he'll play fair.'

'I'm sure he will,' Merrion agreed, 'but as you said yourself we still need to know what it is to be so that we can decide if we can afford it.'

'I suppose you're right,' Rhonda sighed, 'but it would be wonderful to have so much space, though, wouldn't it?'

'If you think the rooms are suitable for your purpose, try working there for a couple of months and then we'll fix the rent,' Dai suggested when Rhonda discussed it with him again.

'I'd love to do that, but I don't think that Merrion will agree to an arrangement like that, see. She likes to have everything cut and dried.'

Dai's green eyes narrowed. 'She's not your boss, cariad!' he laughed.

'No, but we work as a team. Merrion is better at managing money than I am,' Rhonda confessed.

'Use the place for a couple of months and see if you like it here and then we'll talk again,' he insisted. 'No strings. If you decide you don't like the arrangement after all then all you have to do is move out.'

Rhonda laughed nervously. 'That's very kind of you, Dai. It's almost too good to be true.'

'On Sunday I'll help you move your hats and anything else you will need in order to work there,' Dai told her.

Merrion was still dubious about the whole idea, but as with Rhonda the temptation to have more space overcame her scruples.

Dai was as good as his word. He arrived in his van at ten o'clock on Sunday morning and by midday Rhonda was installed in Loudon Square. Her hats were stored in the dozens of boxes that Dai had brought with him. All her materials were neatly stacked in the enormous built-in cupboards and Dai had put up a huge trestle table for her to work on.

'All you need now is a couple of chairs,' he said as he looked round. 'I've got a couple of spare dining chairs. Do you think they'll do?'

'They'll be absolutely perfect.'

Rhonda looked around in delight as Dai went downstairs to fetch them.

'So what happens now?' he questioned as he placed a chair on each side of the table.

'We'll be here as soon as possible after nine o'clock tomorrow morning, immediately after we've walked the girls to school,' Rhonda told him.

'We?'

'Me and Merrion. We work together in the mornings, until it is time for her to go to the pub.'

'After that do you work on your own?' Dai asked.

'Until four o'clock when the girls come out of school.'

'You can bring them back here if you want

to go on working, you know. There're three more rooms on this floor, plenty of space for them to play around.'

'Are you sure?'

'Of course I am,' Dai said enthusiastically. 'Later on, when the weather's a bit warmer, they'll probably prefer to play in the park outside.'

'Well, I don't know about that, we never let them play out.'

'They'll be safe enough.' He took her arm. 'Come over to the window and see for yourself.'

He pulled the curtains wide and pointed to the large green area surrounded by a low stone wall in the centre of the square. 'It's a bit bare at the moment, but that's because it's winter. In a couple of months those trees will be in leaf and the girls will love running around out there. You can keep an eye on them easily enough from the window.'

'It's almost as if he's determined to make us rent the place,' Merrion commented when Rhonda told her what Dai had said. 'I do wish I knew what sort of figure he has in mind for the rent.'

Chapter Twenty-Seven

Merrion and Rhonda both agreed that having more space in which to work was increasing their output. Separating work and home was also making life in Sophia Terrace much easier. Loudon Square was sufficiently far away that when the working day ended there was no going back, so Rhonda spent more time with Dilwyn and Nerys.

The girls still went to Sunday School which gave Rhonda and Merrion a wonderful opportunity to complete outstanding jobs and clear the decks ready for the coming week.

As spring advanced, Dilwyn and Nerys began to spend more and more time in Loudon Square playing outside in the park. They had made quite a few new friends and seemed to be happier than they'd ever been.

Merrion was still worried about whether or not they were going to be able to afford to keep the workrooms. The range of spring hats were selling so well on Dai's stall that she was afraid they wouldn't manage to produce as many as they were doing if they had to move everything back to Sophia Terrace.

Even so, when Dai eventually decided on the

rent she knew that although it was very fair it was rather more than they could afford.

Explaining this to Rhonda was not easy.

'We're doing so well, Merrion, we must be able to afford it,' Rhonda argued. 'Dai says he could sell twice as many hats as he is doing now if we could supply them. I was even hoping that as we have a proper workroom, perhaps you would think about giving up going to work at the pub. If you did that then we could both work full time on the hats.'

'Now who's the one who is doing the dreaming?' Merrion teased.

'These dreams are more likely to come true than yours ever will!' Rhonda retaliated.

'I wish they could, honestly I do, but unless I keep my job I don't think we can manage to pay the rent for Sophia Terrace and for this place as well.'

'That's it! The perfect answer,' Rhonda exclaimed excitedly.

'What is?'

'We give up the rooms in Sophia Terrace and come and live here.'

Merrion looked dubious.

'I mean it,' Rhonda persisted. 'There are three other rooms we're not using as well as the kitchen. It's perfect. There's a good-size room that we can use as a living room and there are two smaller ones for bedrooms. It means far more living space than we have now in Sophia Terrace. We'll have two bedrooms, not all be cramped up in one with a curtain between our beds. The girls can have their own room, or Nerys and I can share and you and Dilwyn share. We can work the details out later. Change around, even, if we decide we haven't made the right choice. The main thing is it would mean only one rent.'

Merrion nodded thoughtfully, then frowned. 'If we decided to live here, though, Dai might want far more rent than he's asking now.'

Rhonda shook her head. 'No, I'm sure he won't. He keeps telling me to use all the space I need. I make use of the kitchen as it is.'

'It's certainly worth thinking about, I suppose,' Merrion admitted.

'There's lino on the floor and curtains at all the windows so we wouldn't have to fork out any money on furnishings.'

'We'd need beds and a table and chairs and a couple of easy chairs . . .'

'If we buy them second-hand from the market it won't cost all that much. Dai is sure to know where we can get some really good bargains.'

'I don't know.' Merrion shook her head. 'As much as I long to get away from Sophia Terrace, moving here would be such a big step . . .'

'Do you have to be such a stick in the mud?' Rhonda pouted. 'It's too good an opportunity to miss.'

'We aren't missing anything,' Merrion defended. 'We don't even know if Dai will agree to us living here. He mightn't mind letting out rooms to be used during the day, but having four of us living permanently in his house is another matter entirely.'

'It won't make any difference to him. His place is on the ground floor and it is completely self-contained and shut off from the rooms we use. I don't see how it can possibly make the slightest difference to him.'

'Even if he agrees to us all living here he is bound to want more money than if he is just letting it out as workrooms,' Merrion reminded her.

'You only surmise that he will ask for more, but you don't know for certain.'

'True, but don't forget he is a businessman.'

'Well, we'll know for certain tomorrow because I'm going to ask him.'

'Shall we leave it for a few days, Rhonda? We ought to make sure there are no other snags that we haven't thought about.'

Rhonda's mind was made up and first thing the next morning she asked Dai if he would mind them moving into Loudon Square and using the spare rooms as a living space.

'I'm surprised it has taken you this long to come round to the idea,' he told her.

She stared at him blankly for a moment before saying very crossly, 'Then why didn't you suggest it?'

Dai shrugged. 'I didn't want to push you into something you might regret. I'm pleased you've made up your mind. Is Merrion happy about it?'

Rhonda hesitated. 'She's wondering how much more the rent will be.'

'I won't be asking you to pay any more,' he told her flatly. 'The rent stays the same whether you use it as a workroom or as somewhere to live as well.'

Rhonda's round face broke into a beaming smile. 'Really! So when can we move in?'

'As soon as you like,' he said casually.

'We've got plenty of bedclothes and pots and pans, but we'll need beds and some furniture. Have you any idea where we should go to buy them second-hand?'

Dai ran a forefinger over his moustache thoughtfully. 'Why don't you take a look in the rooms up over where you're working?' he suggested. 'There's all my mam's household stuff up there. It was her house and after she died I stored everything up there out of the way. When I did the ground floor up for my own use I only wanted the very latest trend, see. You've never seen inside my place, have you?'

Rhonda shook her head. 'You always keep the blinds drawn.' She grinned.

'I don't want to get my new furniture faded by the sun,' he explained quite seriously. 'My mam always used to keep her blinds down, so it comes natural for me to do the same, especially during the day when I'm not there.'

'So you think there may be some bits and pieces stored away up in the attic that we could use?' Rhonda persisted.

'There's plenty of stuff up there, probably everything you'll need. You and Merrion go up and take a look around, then when I get back tonight I'll help you to move down whatever you want to use.'

Rhonda went straight back to Sophia Terrace to tell Merrion the good news and to persuade her to take an hour off work so that she could come with her to Loudon Square and see what was up in the attic rooms.

It was a revelation to both of them. As Dai had said the rooms up there were packed from floor to ceiling with beds, tables and chairs.

'Seeing that he is such a keen businessman, I don't understand why he has stored all this stuff instead of selling it,' Merrion commented.

'Perhaps he's sentimental and doesn't like selling off things his mother treasured.'

'If that was the case then surely he would be using them, not pushing them up here out of sight where they're only gathering dust.'

Rhonda shrugged. 'Does it matter? He said we can make use of whatever we like and that means we won't need to spend our money buying second-hand stuff. I'm sure we can find enough pieces to furnish the rooms downstairs quite comfortably. There're even plenty of beds.'

'It's all old-fashioned, but quite good quality,' Merrion agreed.

'Then let's start selecting the things we want. Dai said he'd come and help bring them down tonight after he finishes on the stall.'

'The big furniture items will be much too heavy for the two of you to lift!'

'The girls can help, they'll have to come with me because you'll be at the pub.'

'I still don't think you'll manage. I'll ask for a couple of hours off this evening and come and give you a hand. If it's too much for us, then perhaps Evan might be willing to come and help.'

'He might if you are the one who asks him.' Rhonda smiled. 'He's still got a soft spot for you even though you don't give him the slightest encouragement.'

'Yes, well, I think that Dai must have a soft spot for you the way he is putting himself out like this,' Merrion told her tartly. 'You are quite sure he isn't going to put the rent up the moment we've given up our rooms in Sophia Terrace and moved in here?'

'Of course he isn't going to do that. Like you said, he's a businessman and he's doing so well out of the hats that perhaps he wants to have us under lock and key.' She grinned. 'Or it may be that he thinks we can supply more hats if we have our home and our workroom all under one roof,' she added more seriously.

Their exploration of the conglomeration of unused furniture in the top rooms had brought back memories to all of them, especially for Dai. For him it was a trip back to the days when the house in Loudon Square had been his family home with his mother in control.

'She was some lady, you know,' he said. 'Feared by many, but with a heart of gold. Mind, she ruled me with a rod of iron. Dad was killed right at the start the war. I was fifteen, and from that moment on she expected me to be the man of the house.'

'So you were the only son?' Rhonda commented.

'I was not only the only son, I was the only child,' Dai affirmed.

'She could be a right tartar, my mam, I can tell you,' he went on. 'She dressed very smartly and held herself very upright, so she always looked very imposing. She was Victorian to her fingertips. She loved lace doilies and anti-macassars, and she had them everywhere.'

'I bet there were lace curtains at every window, and an aspidistra in the best parlour,' Rhonda joked.

'There were, and our home was kept like that till the day she died. I went the other way after that, and had everything as modern as I could find it. You must come and take a look when we've sorted out things here.'

'Are you sure you'll not mind us using her things?' Merrion asked tentatively.

'Of course I am. I should have got rid of all her possessions years ago, but I couldn't bring myself to do so. I couldn't bear the thought of letting everything go to strangers, see. Indeed, I'm more than pleased to think you'll be making use of anything you find suitable.'

Their search was quite productive. They now had beds, a mahogany dining table, and a set of four matching chairs, as well as a couple of armchairs and a matching high-backed couch. They all had intricately carved frames and were upholstered in brown, green and gold plush. They also found a steel fender and a set of fire-irons as well as a plentiful supply of lace curtains and even a beautiful brown chenille tablecloth to use to protect the highly polished mahogany dining table.

'Now all we have to do is try and move this lot downstairs,' Dai said.

'We're here to help so shall we start right away?' Rhonda suggested eagerly.

Dai ran a hand over his chin thoughtfully. 'I think moving this lot is a bit beyond you two, or even the three of us. There're some heavy pieces amongst that old stuff.'

'I agree,' Merrion said. 'It really needs a couple of strong men.'

'Then we'll ask Evan. I'm sure he'll be willing to help. There's no hurry for a day or so, is there? I'll have a word with him and fix it up.'

'You think he'll agree?'

'Yes, of course he will,' Dai said confidently. 'Leave it with me, I'll sort it out. Now, if we've finished up here, how about a cup of tea down in my place and that guided tour I promised you?'

Chapter Twenty-Eight

It took them less than a week to complete their move from Sophia Terrace to Loudon Square. Nerys and Dilwyn were highly excited by their new home. At first they laughed about some of the furniture, but stopped doing so when Merrion reminded them it had once belonged to Mr Francis's mother and he might feel hurt if he heard them.

They had been equally taken aback by the furniture and furnishings in Dai's flat. Even Merrion and Rhonda admitted that they'd never seen anything so modern before except in shop windows.

'Not very cosy, though,' Merrion commented. 'Some of the chairs look like pieces of bent wood and metal glued together. I'm not sure it would be safe to sit down on them. And those wedge-shaped cups, I'm sure they could tip over if you tried to fill them with tea.'

'It's called art deco and I rather like it,' Rhonda mused. 'In fact, I thought that all the chrome and glass was very ritzy,' she added enviously.

Setting out their own part of the house took them some time because they all had different ideas about which rooms should be used for which purpose. There was a lot of arguing when Merrion insisted that she and Dilwyn should share a bedroom and Nerys could be in with Rhonda.

'If we put you two girls in together in the same room then you'll probably stay awake half the night chattering to each other,' she pointed out.

'I wonder if it would be a good time to move them from the school they're attending in Hurman Road to one nearer here?' Rhonda suggested.

Merrion looked uncertain. 'They're happy where they are.'

Rhonda shrugged. 'One school is pretty much the same as another and I was thinking that if they attended St Mary's in Bute Street, then they could walk there on their own. It takes one of us over half an hour to walk them to school every morning and then break off again in the afternoon to go and collect them.'

'Well, we do our shopping in James Street when we take them to school, don't we? And anyway, it wouldn't be good for you to be working all day without a break.'

'Perhaps not, but there are plenty of shops right here in Loudon Square which we could use.'

'I think we've made enough changes for the moment. Let the girls settle into their new home before we uproot them from school, and Pedro and Ella and all the friends they've made there.'

'I was only thinking about the time involved,' Rhonda insisted. 'The more hours we can spend making hats the more money we can earn.'

'We're doing well enough as it is.'

'Yes, but we could be making even more hats and that would mean we'd be earning far more than we're doing at the present. Now that we're living in the same place as our work-room, the girls could take themselves to school if it was nearby, then we'd be able to start work right after breakfast. We could even work through non-stop until tea-time.'

'Yes, and we could end up producing more hats than we can sell.'

'No.' Rhonda shook her head vehemently. 'Dai says he could sell double, or even more, than he does now if he had them. He says I can get all my materials and trimmings from the warehouse he uses.'

'That's more or less what you're doing now, isn't it?'

'Yes, but he also said that if I buy the hat shapes in bulk, I can make terrific savings. If you gave up the pub and we both worked flat out full time, we could build up a really good stock to sell at Christmas.'

'That's a long way off. We have to eat and clothe the girls in the meantime.'

'We should be getting the money for our summer stock any day now. If we plan it carefully, we could live on that for the next three or four months. Then if we get all the material from Dai's wholesaler and don't have to pay until our Christmas stock has sold, it would mean we'd start next year with a really healthy bank balance.'

'And then?'

Rhonda looked smug. 'Well, if we could get a really good sum of money together, I thought . . .' she stopped and looked uneasy and hesitant.

'Go on, I'm listening.'

Rhonda took a deep breath. 'I thought that perhaps we could open our own shop next year.'

Merrion looked stunned. 'What about Dai, what does he think about that?'

Rhonda raised her thin, pencilled brows disparagingly. 'Don't be daft, Merrion! Of course I haven't mentioned anything about it to him.'

'So after all he's done for us you were going to let him down by opening up in opposition.'

'I wasn't planning on having the shop anywhere near the Hayes! And I wasn't thinking of letting him down either,' Rhonda said huffily. 'The hats he sells now, and hopefully will go on selling, will still be our bread and butter until we get properly established . . .'

'And all our outstanding bills to Dai's wholesalers paid off?' Merrion interrupted.

'We'll manage to do that all in good time.'

'What happens if Dai decides to stop you

ordering materials from his suppliers? He's no fool, Rhonda, he will realise that you are ordering at least double what you are using for the hats you are supplying to him.'

'I've already thought about that and I'm one step ahead of both of you,' Rhonda retorted smugly.

'Yes?'

'Yes. When I was talking to Dai about buying in bulk, I persuaded him to open an account with his wholesalers in my own name. What's more, he's guaranteeing the account. He's signed papers to say that if I don't pay my bills by the end of the month, then he will. Clever, eh?'

'Why has he agreed to do that?' Merrion asked in a puzzled voice.

'To make sure I can get all the materials I need whenever necessary without having to bother him to sign order forms each time I go there.'

'So if you don't pay the wholesaler on time, then he has to do so?' Merrion frowned. 'It sounds rather odd to me.'

'Well,' Rhonda shrugged uncertainly, 'he'll pay them, I imagine, and then I suppose he'll stop it out of the money he owes us for hats, now we've changed our previous arrangements. Don't forget he owes us money most of the time, now doesn't he?'

'He's bound to find out that you are stockpiling, though, Rhonda. Especially if you start increasing your orders at the wholesalers and yet you only go on supplying him with the same quantity of hats.'

'I'll be making more for him as well,' she argued.

'How will you manage that? There are only twenty-four hours in the day!'

'Yes, but if you stop working at the pub and you're helping me full time as well, then we can do it, Merrion. Really we can. Think about it. Wouldn't it be wonderful to have our own shop, and be completely independent of everybody? We might even be able to find some premises that have rooms up over them.'

'You mean something like this place only we use the downstairs as selling space?'

'Not here in Tiger Bay, though! I thought perhaps somewhere like Cathays, or Canton, or even out Roath way. It would be lovely for the girls to be living there and now they're growing up we have to think of them.'

'Yes, I know all about that, Rhonda, but it won't be easy and—'

'And your Roddi might come back in the meantime and sweep you off your feet,' Rhonda snapped.

'He'll be back one of these days.'

'Isn't it about time you gave up that stupid dream and faced reality?'

'It's the dream that has kept me going all these years since my mam died, and it's what will keep me going in the future ... until he returns.'

'Oh for goodness' sake, Merrion, be your age. We're both in our twenties now, we've got kids to support. We'll never find anyone wanting to marry us, so it's up to us to make our own future.'

'And we will. We've made the first step and moved from that awful slummy place in Sophia Terrace, but look how long it has taken us to do that.'

'We've done it, though, and we can progress a great deal more if you'll give up your job at the pub and work with me full time helping to make hats,' Rhonda persisted.

'I promise you that I will think about it, but you must give me time to get used to the idea. Moving here has been a big step for all of us.'

'I agree, but now we've started achieving something for ourselves let's, for goodness' sake, push on. Stop now and we'll be in another rut.'

'And if we rush into something before we've considered it carefully, then we may end up pinching and scraping to make ends meet again,' Merrion warned.

'If we do things your way, we'll be stuck here for the next ten years, working flat out to make money for Dai Francis instead of for ourselves.'

'That's not fair, Rhonda. He pays us a reasonable price for the hats and, remember, he has to do all the work of displaying and selling them.'

'Having our hats to display on his stall has made him the talk of the Hayes market. He's got more customers now than he's ever had.'

Merrion refused to rush into making any changes. She was also reluctant to give up her job at the Glendower Arms. She didn't particularly enjoy the work, but she did like the regular wage packet she could count on receiving at the end of each week.

The money from Dai was spasmodic and Merrion was never quite sure how much of it Rhonda was going to have to pay out for materials. The money she earned at the pub was theirs. Over the next few months, she was able to budget and know exactly how much she could afford to spend on food and everything else. Heating the new rooms would become more expensive when the weather turned colder.

She did, however, eventually agree that before the new school year started in September they should do something about the girls changing schools.

'They'll be moving up into new classes anyway, so it seems like a good time to send them to St Mary's,' she agreed when Rhonda brought the matter up again.

'Thank heavens you've seen sense about that at last,' Rhonda muttered. 'Perhaps you'll make your mind up about my other suggestion.'

'I have thought about it every single day as

I walk all the way from here to George Street,'
Merrion admitted.

'You still don't think it is what we should do,
though?'

'I can see the advantages. But I'm scared
because it is such a big undertaking and I'm
worried in case it might mean that we'll fall
out with Dai.'

'Why on earth should we do that?'

'He would be bound to feel annoyed that we
were opening up in opposition to him.'

'Rubbish! He's a businessman. He'd probably admire us for taking the plunge.'

'I'm not so sure that he will. Would you mind
if I talked to Evan about it and found out what
he thinks? After all, he is a friend of Dai's and
it is thanks to him that we ever started selling
hats at the market in the first place.'

'Please yourself, but can we trust Evan not
to mention it to Dai?'

'I'm sure he won't if I ask him not to.'

Evan had mixed feelings about the venture.
He admired Rhonda's spirit, but, like Merrion,
he thought it would be underhand to go behind
Dai's back.

'Why not mention the idea to him. Perhaps
he would come in on the venture with you. He
knows his way around, you know, and he could
be a great help.'

This time it was Rhonda who needed time
to think things over. Unlike Merrion, however,
she didn't take weeks to do so. A few days later

she agreed that she'd mention to Dai what she was proposing to do.

'I shan't press him to come into the new venture with us, though, because I very much want to try and do it alone,' she pointed out.

'If he insists, though, you'll think about letting him do so?'

'I suppose I'll have to. What do you think?'

'Frankly I don't know what to think. I agree with Evan that it's a big undertaking and that Dai knows all the business angles, so at least we would get good advice from him.'

'Yes, I suppose you're right. If we agree that he can come in with us then we won't have to go looking for a place in some other shopping area either. We could have a shop within a stone's throw of the Hayes.'

'Would that be a good idea?'

'I don't see why not. It could be in one of the small side streets behind St Mary Street or Queen Street. We could sell better quality hats there than we do in the market.'

'That might be a good idea. Then Dai could send along any customers who couldn't find what they wanted on his stall.'

'There you are, then. It is a good idea after all,' Rhonda exclaimed triumphantly. 'So can I tell him that you are going to give up your job at the pub and that from now on we'll be working together full time?'

Chapter Twenty-Nine

To Rhonda's surprise and dismay, Dai Francis seemed to be less enthusiastic about her idea of opening a hat shop than she had expected.

'Rushing things a bit aren't you, my lovely?' he commented wryly, fingering his moustache thoughtfully.

'What do you mean?'

'Well, you've only been in business making hats for about a year and here you are already wanting to open a shop. You know nothing at all about selling, now do you, cariad?'

'Well, there's not all that much to it, is there?' she retorted huffily. 'You display the damn things and if a woman sees one she likes, then she tries it on. If it suits her, she buys it, if it doesn't, then she walks away.'

'Exactly. That's precisely what would happen in your shop, I can see that, my lovely,' he smirked. 'The real skill lies in making sure that everyone who comes in buys a hat whether it suits her or not!'

'Do that and she finds out that you've tricked her, then she'll never come back again!'

'If you've convinced her that she looks

wonderful in the hat she's bought, she will come back – again and again,' Dai told her confidently. 'You have to use flattery, see! The great secret is to do it properly and with real sincerity and then the hat's in the bag, girl!'

'If I wanted to I could do all that every bit as well as you do,' Rhonda pouted.

'No, cariad! That's where you are wrong. A man can flatter a woman, but if another woman tries to do so then it makes the customer suspicious and nine times out of ten she will decide not to buy.'

'Rubbish! Women aren't as daft as you seem to think, boyo,' Rhonda flared.

Dai shrugged and gave her a disarming smile. 'I'm basing my advice on over ten years' experience of selling fashion goods to you ladies, my lovely.'

'So does that mean you want no part in our new enterprise?' Rhonda asked huffily.

'*Our* enterprise!' He gave her a hard look. 'You're not going into this on your own, then?'

'No, it will be with Merrion. She's giving up her job at the pub and coming in with me full time.'

'Mmm!' Dai looked thoughtful. 'Where is this shop going to be, then?'

'We haven't decided yet. It won't be near here because I wouldn't want the competition to spoil your sales.'

'So you are planning to go on supplying me with hats the same as always, are you?'

'Of course! You didn't think that I'd cut off your supply, did you?'

He shrugged again. 'How am I to know? You're keeping it all so secret!'

'I intended the shop to be quite separate. In fact, I thought we would find that we were able to complement each other,' she stated.

'Oh?' His eyebrows shot up and he looked puzzled. 'How would we be able to do that, then?'

'The shop could stock a more expensive range, so you could send customers to me when they were looking for something really exclusive. I could send customers to you when they were looking for something a bit cheaper for everyday wear.'

Dai ran a hand over his chin. 'I can see you've got some big ideas, my lovely, but whether they will work or not . . .' He left the sentence unfinished.

'I've told you what I'm planning to do, so you can't say I didn't tell you!' Rhonda pointed out. 'It's your loss entirely if you don't want to join us in our new venture.'

'I never said that I wasn't interested. You're far too impetuous,' he scolded. 'I need time to think it all through, cariad, and to work out which is the best way to proceed.'

'So does that mean that you are considering coming in with us?'

'Of course I am. I never turn down a good business proposition. Give me a couple of days to think over all that is involved.'

Rhonda tried to hide her disappointment that Dai wasn't ready to commit there and then as she'd expected him to do. She was on tenterhooks for the next few days as she waited for him to give her an answer.

Merrion had to take the brunt of her moods. In the end she felt she could stand it no longer. The prickly atmosphere when they were all at home was even upsetting the girls. Without saying anything to Rhonda she went down to Dai's flat and asked him if he'd made up his mind yet.

'If you have, then give Rhonda an answer, because I can't stand the tension any longer,' she told him.

Dai laughed. 'She's headstrong, isn't she! I couldn't let her dash into a new venture like opening a shop until I'd done all the calculations. I had to make quite sure that she wasn't taking on more than she was capable of, now didn't I?'

'So you think the idea of having a shop is quite feasible, do you?'

He shrugged. 'It's bound to be a gamble, but then all business dealings are.'

'With the two of us working together it should be possible.'

'It will be hard work, mind. I understand that you are packing in your job at the pub, so does that mean you will arrange things so that one of you is in the shop all day?'

'Yes, whoever stays home will see to the children.'

'And be prepared to work on making hats at the same time,' he reminded her.

'I'm sure we can manage that, Dai. We're used to working as a team.'

'Well, in that case, if you are both quite sure, I'll ask around to see if there are any shops up for rent. It isn't something that will happen overnight, so you'd better find a way of pacifying Rhonda. She'll have to learn to be patient.'

'I'm sure that once she knows it is going ahead she'll calm down,' Merrion assured him.

'Tell her to come down here tomorrow evening and we'll work out all the financial involvement. There will be a lot of overheads like renting the shop, fitting it out and buying additional materials, all that sort of thing.'

'She intends to buy from the same wholesalers as she does now,' Merrion told him.

'Good, but she'll still need to arrange to have more credit . . .' He stopped and patted Merrion's shoulder. 'Don't worry, it will work out fine. One or two papers to sign and everything will be set up and we can get moving.'

Rhonda was over the moon. 'You'll give your notice in at the pub right away, won't you,' she urged.

'The Rawlands have been good to me, Rhonda, so I'll have to give them time to find a replacement.'

'A week?'

'We'll see. From what Dai says it's going to take much longer than that to set everything up.'

'We need to build up a really good stock though before we open the shop,' Rhonda pointed out.

'Well, you talk to Dai about it tomorrow and work out the details and I'll give you all the support I can.'

'I know I can count on you, we make a great team.' She flung her arms round Merrion and hugged her. 'I'll never forget all you've done for me.'

It took much longer than Rhonda had hoped, but in the end she had to admit that it had been well worth the wait. The shop Dai found was in Morgan's Arcade off St Mary Street. It was a small lock-up, but it was in a prime spot.

'The secret is to have an eye-catching window, something that draws the attention of people as they cut through the arcade,' Dai told her.

Rhonda frowned. 'Does that mean packing the window with as many hats as possible, or limiting it to one or two really modish styles?'

He raised his eyebrows questioningly. 'Well now, let's hear what you think?'

'Both could be good. I think the secret is to alternate. Change the window often, at least three times a week, so that there is always something new to catch people's attention.'

'Yes, I can see you've got the right idea, my lovely,' he told her approvingly. 'As well as varying your display according to the season, you can also have special ones for occasions like St David's Day, as well as at Easter and Christmas. You can use swathes of material in bright colours, fresh flowers, or anything else that takes your fancy, to draw the eye of people passing by. I can't do anything like that on the stall. There it's a matter of pile them high and sell them cheap.'

'I've already got dozens of ideas,' she told him enthusiastically.

'Good!'

'Merrion told me that you'd said something about needing to make new arrangements with the wholesalers.'

'Yes, that's right. I've sorted it all out and here are the forms for you to sign, cariad.'

He took an envelope from the inside breast pocket of his jacket and drew out some papers. 'Sign here and here.' He pointed as he spread them out in front of her.

'Can I use your fountain pen?'

'Of course!'

Rhonda signed her name with a flourish, then handed them back to him, her eyes glowing with the thrill of achievement.

'I hope you've read and understood everything written there,' he laughed as he folded them over and slipped them back inside the envelope.

306

'Not really, but I'm sure you have.'

'Every single word. I'm not a businessman for nothing,' he laughed.

'So how soon can we move into the shop?' she asked excitedly.

'Three weeks' time. Meanwhile, you need to start making those extra hats. I don't want to be the one who has to go short of stock, you know,' he warned.

'You won't,' she promised. 'Merrion has said she will give in her notice at the pub the moment you confirm that we have a shop.'

'Good. She can go ahead and do that now. The sooner the better.'

'The only thing is,' Rhonda said hesitantly, as she chewed on her lower lip, 'we are going to need money to live on until the shop is sorted out, so how soon can you pay us for the summer hats I supplied?'

'Next week, cariad. Will that suit you both?'

Rhonda nodded happily. 'That will be fine. Thank you, Dai . . . for everything.'

'This is such a tremendous adventure that I think we ought to go out on the town tonight and have a little celebration,' he suggested.

Rhonda hesitated. 'It's not easy. Merrion wouldn't want to leave the girls on their own.'

'I really only meant you and me . . . a cele-bration on our own,' he said softly.

'Oh!' Rhonda felt the colour rush to her face. 'I'd like that,' she admitted.

'Right, let's do it, then. We can tell Merrion

that we are going to inspect the shop. She knows I can't get away to do that during the day.'

'It's a bit sneaky, making an excuse like that, isn't it?' she said uneasily.

He shrugged. 'It's up to you. Tell her the whole story if you wish, but she might be hurt because we haven't asked her out as well.' He moved closer and placed his hand gently on Rhonda's shoulder. 'I want to take you out and to get to know you better, cariad,' he said softly. 'At the moment you are merely a business associate, but I'd like us to be something more than that, wouldn't you?'

Chapter Thirty

Merrion felt resigned when she discovered that Rhonda and Dai were now much more than mere business companions. She felt quite hurt, however, that neither of them had mentioned a word about it to her.

She had thought that the upturn in Rhonda's mood was because the decision had been taken to go ahead with the idea of opening a shop in Morgan's Arcade, which was a prime site.

She'd also assumed that Rhonda meeting up each evening with Dai Francis was to do with fitting the shop out. Even when she consistently refused to let her do anything to help, and had laughed when she'd said that it was hardly fair that Rhonda was spending every night working while she stayed at home, Merrion still hadn't realised what was going on between the two of them.

'There's plenty for you to do here and you know how much better you are as a housewife than me,' Rhonda had persisted. 'The girls like it better when you are at home because they know you have more time for them than I do.'

'Nonsense!'

'Oh you do,' Rhonda insisted. 'You listen to

their chatter; I either tell them to shut up or else completely ignore what they are saying.'

'You could be spending the evenings working on designing new hats, though,' Merrion pointed out.

'You are doing something equally important, by baking and washing and ironing our clothes and making life comfortable for all of us.'

'Well, if you change your mind and decide you'd like an evening at home, then you've only to say,' Merrion told her pointedly.

Rhonda shook her head, her eyes sparkling. 'No, I'm enjoying every minute of it.'

'You are certainly in a better mood these days,' Merrion told her dryly.

Things might well have stayed like that if it hadn't been for Dilwyn and Nerys plaguing the life out of Merrion, constantly pleading that they wanted to go and see the new shop.

'It's not ready yet,' Merrion pointed out. Rhonda is working on it, decorating it and so on. She won't want you there under her feet.'

'That's what she told us when we asked her last Saturday if we could visit it.'

'Well, there you are, then.'

'My mam said it was only a very small shop, so she must have finished getting it ready by now. She said it might be opening tomorrow and yet we still haven't been able to go and see it,' Nerys complained.

'Of course you'll be able to go and see it now that it's ready,' Merrion assured her.

'Yes, but when? If it is as small as all that then we'll certainly be in the way when there are customers in there as well,' Dilwyn pointed out.

'Then we'll have to go and see it sometime when it isn't open,' Merrion suggested.

Merrion thought the two girls were happy with her answer, but they went into a little huddle, whispering so that she couldn't hear what they were saying. Then they began pushing each other and giggling.

'Nerys says why can't we go there now, this evening?' Dilwyn asked.

'On a Friday night!'

'Well, we don't have to go to school in the morning so it doesn't matter if we are up late.'

'Please! We have to go to Sunday School on Sunday so we won't be able to go then,' Nerys begged.

The two of them stared up at her so earnestly that Merrion gave in. Everything had happened so fast that she hadn't even had a chance to see it herself.

'All right. As a very special treat. We'll go straight there, have a quick look round, then it's home and to bed and no arguments. Understood?'

The two girls danced around in glee.

'Well go and get your hats and coats on, then,' Merrion told them.

Ten minutes later the three of them were on the tram heading for St Mary Street. As they

entered Morgan's Arcade the girls dashed
ahead, prancing with excitement as they tried
to be the first to see the shop.

'Stop! Come back, you've walked right past
it,' Merrion called out to them.

The girls raced back and then stood by her
side staring in bewilderment at the unlit
window where stands holding six magnificent
hats were displayed.

Merrion tried to handle the situation tactfully
even though it was obvious that the place was
closed and that there was no one inside.

'I think we've left it a bit late,' she murmured.
'It looks as though they've gone home.'

'It doesn't look as if there is anyone in there,'
Dilwyn said as she shaded her eyes with her
hands and peered through the glass door into
the blackness beyond.

'So where is my mam, then?' Nerys asked
tearfully.

'I don't know,' Merrion admitted. 'Perhaps
she has gone for a drink with Dai Francis to
celebrate because the shop is ready at long last.'

'They should have taken us along as well,'
Nerys pouted.

'They probably thought you were tucked up
safe and sound in bed,' Merrion laughed.
'Which is exactly where you should be, so let's
head for home right now,' she added firmly.

Subdued, they caught a tram back home, only
to find the place in darkness.

'It's not fair, though, Merrion,' Dilwyn

protested. 'You've worked hard making hats for the shop, so if they're out celebrating, then they should have asked you to go as well.'

'And who would have been at home to give you two some supper and then tuck you up into bed afterwards if I'd gone out?'

After the two girls were settled for the night, however, Merrion asked herself the same question as Dilwyn had posed. Why hadn't she been invited along to the celebration? After all, the three of them were supposed to be a team.

Merrion didn't wait up. She was in bed and fast asleep long before Rhonda returned home. Rhonda made so much noise coming up the stairs, though, that she disturbed Merrion who woke up with a start, thinking that someone was breaking in.

Rhonda's lipstick and make-up were both smudged and her hair looked mussed up. She was giggly and starry-eyed. 'Now don't you dare start cross-questioning me about where I've been until now,' she stuttered, swaying unsteadily and wagging a finger at Merrion.

'There's no need for me to do anything of the sort. I can guess where you've been and from the state of you I've a pretty good idea about what you've been doing. You are very drunk and the sooner you get to bed and sleep it off, before Nerys sees you looking such a mess, the better.'

'I only went for a little drink with Dai to celebrate the fact that we've finished on the shop.

Everything is ready for us to open at nine o' clock prompt tomorrow morning.'

'Well, that's great news, but are you going to be fit enough to do that?'

'Don't be daft, cariad. I've had a few drinks too many, I'll be right as rain by morning.'

'If you've been drinking since seven o'clock tonight, I think it will take a lot longer than that.'

'What are you talking about? What's seven o'clock got to do with anything?'

'That was what the time was when I brought the girls to the shop this evening.'

Rhonda frowned angrily. 'How dare you check up on me like that.'

'I wasn't doing anything of the sort! Nerys and Dilwyn wanted to see the shop before it opened.'

Rhonda looked confused 'So what did you tell Nerys when I wasn't there?'

'I didn't have to tell her anything. She worked it out for herself that you'd gone for a drink with Dai to celebrate.'

'Clever girl! She was quite right,' Rhonda giggled. 'We certainly did celebrate!'

'So I gather, seeing the state you are in, though I don't know where you found a place that stayed open until three o'clock in the morning,' Merrion commented tartly.

'Is that really the time!' Rhonda giggled again. 'Good job that I only had to come upstairs to get home, or I would have been even later.'

Merrion felt startled as she realised the impli-
cation of what Rhonda was telling her.

'I'm going back to bed, I can hardly keep my
eyes open. Tell me all about it in the morning,'
she said quickly.

Once they knew there was no need to hide the
truth any longer the affair between Rhonda and
Dai flourished apace. The moment the two girls
were in bed at night Rhonda made some excuse
or other to go down to Dai's flat. Usually she
was gone for at least a couple of hours, often a
lot longer.

The change in her manner left no doubt that
she was in love with Dai Francis. Merrion was
pleased for her, but she had doubts about what
effect it might have on their newly established
business.

At the moment things were going swim-
mingly. Rhonda was working at the shop full
time, as they'd agreed she would, and so far
the sales had made it a very worthwhile
venture.

There was a small room at the rear of the
shop that was large enough for Rhonda to use
as a storeroom and workroom. Here she was
able to do the final trimmings and finishing
touches, like adding a fur pompom, diamante
buckle, or a few extra feathers, when she wasn't
serving customers. But the main work involved
in making the hats was still done at the workroom in Loudon Square – mostly by Merrion,

in between running the home and looking after the girls.

At first she missed the daily noise and bustle that she'd become accustomed to at the Glendower Arms. Gradually, however, she adjusted. The only problem was that being on her own so much gave her more time to think about things.

Her dreams of Roddi returning one day were always there. She knew her belief that he would find her again if she waited had come between her and the life she could be having now. Evan had told her several times how much he cared for her, but he had accepted that they could never be more than good friends because her heart already belonged to someone else.

Evan was the only person she knew who didn't think that harbouring such dreams after all this time was futile. He did sometimes say that he wished she would move on and not live in the past, but in the end, he accepted that she was determined to remain steadfast to her dream.

Deep down she suspected that she was being ridiculous. Over eight years had passed now, Roddi was no longer the young boy she had known back in Cwmglo. Nor was she the starry-eyed young innocent who had given him her promises as well as her heart.

Occasionally she envied Rhonda because she had no such commitment and could take advantage of the opportunity to indulge in a loving relationship. She and Dai seemed to be a good match. He was not all that much older than her, he was good-looking, and he was certainly enterprising. Without his help they would never have managed to achieve all that they had done.

A shiver went through her as she remembered the terrible slummy rooms in Sophia Terrace. She'd hated every moment there and looking back she found herself wondering how it was that they'd never moved out long before they did.

Circumstances, of course, she reminded herself. They'd not had the money, so there'd not been the opportunity. The children had been so small that they couldn't be left and they certainly couldn't afford to pay anyone to look after them.

Poor Rhonda, she'd been used to a much better way of life. Falling out with her family after being seduced and left pregnant had left her so completely alone in the world. If eventually she married Dai, it would be a really happy ending for both her and Nerys.

She still wished that Rhonda had told her how things had changed between her and Dai, and not left her to find out by accident. She had thought they were really close friends. In fact, Merrion mused, she would have thought that she would have been the first person Rhonda would have confided in.

Still, she told herself, there was no point in

making an issue of it. It was important that the three of them remained good friends since the success of their new enterprise depended on it.

Chapter Thirty-One

The run up to Christmas was frenetic for all of them. Dilwyn and Nerys were involved in all sorts of school activities which entailed learning lines and needing special costumes.

In the evenings, and at weekends, Rhonda and Merrion were constantly being expected to help them with these. In addition, they were also both working flat out in order to increase the number of hats they produced for the shop as well as for Dai's stall in the market.

Dai played his part by using his van to transport the hats from Loudon Square to the Hayes as soon as they were ready. Often he also collected additional supplies of materials and trimmings from the warehouse whenever Rhonda and Merrion needed them.

From time to time Evan spent an evening, or sometimes a few hours at the weekend, doing what he could to help. Usually he entertained the two girls, leaving Merrion free to concentrate on making the hats.

If the weather was fine he took them to the park. When it was too cold or wet for that he either took them to the pictures or played board games with them at home. Their favourites were Ludo or Snakes and Ladders and there was tremendous rivalry between the three of them.

In return he was invited to join them all for a meal. Dai was always there as well so it resulted in being almost a family atmosphere which the two girls seemed to enjoy.

Whenever they were all together Rhonda and Dai were constantly talking about the plans for their wedding which they hoped would be early in the new year.

Both girls were highly excited at the thought of being bridesmaids. They even decided on the colour and style of dresses they wanted to wear and what sort of flowers they would like to have as posies.

Occasionally, although she never voiced her concern aloud, Merrion wondered what effect it would have on the business and even how it might change things for her and Dilwyn.

She kept telling herself that theoretically, it shouldn't make any difference at all to their working arrangements. They already had their separate parts to play and that would remain exactly the same.

What would have to change would be their living arrangements. Rhonda would obviously move downstairs to Dai's flat, but what about Nerys? She didn't even know if there was a second bedroom down there. If there wasn't, would Nerys have to stay up in their apartment with herself and Dilwyn? Merrion wondered.

She didn't mind, but she wondered how Nerys would feel if she was separated from her mother. Of course, if she did move downstairs, then it would be Dilwyn who would feel lost, for a time at any rate, because they'd been like sisters all their life.

These thoughts floated in and out of Merrion's mind when she was on her own in the workroom. They mingled with her fantasies about Roddi. Even though she had still not heard a word from him, or about him, in her daydreams he returned in time for them to have a double wedding, side by side with Rhonda and Dai.

She would try and snap out of it by telling herself that it was high time she put the past behind her and made the most of what she had. She could start by accepting the hand of friendship Evan had extended.

The trouble was it would be more than mere friendship if he had his way, she thought wryly.

He had certainly been a wonderful friend right from the very first night when he'd walked her home from the Glendower Arms. She liked him a great deal, but that special spark wasn't there and it wouldn't be fair to let him think that it was.

They'd all be together on Christmas Day, though, she was determined about that. Dai and Rhonda would want to spend the day together and since Evan had no family, he was more than welcome to come and join them.

In fact, she decided, she'd insist he joined them.

The girls would enjoy every moment of it. They were as fond of Evan as she was. And, of course, he had been Dai's friend long before he'd introduced Dai to them, so it would be a perfect arrangement.

As she worked she planned out in her mind exactly what they would have to eat and drink. And she worried about how she would find time to do all the necessary baking.

She would try and make sure that the girls were involved. They'd already stirred the Christmas pudding and made a wish. They could also help fill the mince pies when she made them. Then they could help to decorate the room with paper chains and put the baubles on the Christmas tree that Dai had said he would get them from the market.

She mentally listed the presents she would get for them all. And they'd have Christmas crackers. They'd never had them before but she was sure the girls would love them, especially the ones with coloured paper hats in them and funny jokes.

The girls were still young enough to want to hang up their socks. She'd already collected together quite a few little novelties and surprises for that, but they still had to be filled and she couldn't do that until the very last minute.

The sales of their hats went on right up to

Christmas Eve. Although the miners' strike had brought the country to its knees, and countless businesses had closed so that there were hundreds of men out of work, women were still managing to find enough money to buy hats.

'It's one of the cheapest ways of smartening up last year's winter coat and making it look different,' Dai pointed out.

Those customers with well-filled purses usually bought from their shop in the arcade. The profits from these sales were what Rhonda described as being the icing on top of the cake.

Dai's sales, however, were quadruple the number Rhonda managed. Often, they were less than half the price of the ones she sold, so his overall takings were not all that much better than hers. However, it was still far more than any of them had ever dreamed possible when they'd started the venture.

They all kept warning each other that after Christmas there was bound to be a lull. Merrion kept asking Rhonda to let her see the account books because she was anxious to work out exactly what their takings had been, and how much was left after they'd paid off their outstanding debts to their suppliers. She had been trying to keep a rough check and if her figures were anywhere near right, then they'd had a bonanza. Even so, she kept running through her mind exactly how they would need to spend it.

'The girls are growing so fast that they'll both need new clothes for next summer,' she told Rhonda.

'True, and this time there will be no scrimping or cutting corners. We can afford to buy them the best,' Rhonda emphasised.

'And we can let them help by choosing the styles and colours that they like best!'

'We'll buy some new clothes for ourselves as well,' Rhonda insisted. 'As soon as all the spring ranges are in the shops we'll spend a whole day shopping and take our pick.'

'Since we are bound to have done well, what about getting rid of some of the cumbersome old furniture we acquired from Dai and buy something more up-to-date?' Merrion suggested tentatively.

'Art deco, like Dai has in his flat,' Rhonda agreed enthusiastically.

Merrion looked dubious. 'No, I wouldn't go for ultra modern art deco things like Dai has done. It would be nice to have a pair of really comfortable armchairs, though, the sort you sink into, not the stiff upright Victorian ones like we've got now.'

'Well, you can choose whatever style you like.' Rhonda smiled. 'I won't be here for very much longer, now will I?'

'You'll still be a regular visitor,' Merrion smiled back, 'so I'd like to buy something that you find comfortable.'

'Let's get Christmas itself over first,' Rhonda

324

suggested. 'I want it to be the best one ever.'

'It will be, I'm sure about that if nothing else. Having the day off will make it special. I sometimes think I never want to see another hat in my life.'

'We have all worked exceptionally hard these last few weeks,' Rhonda agreed, 'but it has been wonderful that everything has gone so well.'

'Yes, we're certainly on the way up! We're selling all we can make at the market and the demand at the shop is increasing all the time. We can't ask for more, we really can't.'

'Don't say that! Next year trade is going to be even better in some ways,' Rhonda vowed. 'You've not forgotten that Dai and I are getting married.'

'Forget? How can I do that when the two of you talk of nothing else.'

Rhonda's face sobered. 'You don't really mind, do you Merrion?'

'Mind?' She frowned. 'What do you mean? Why should I mind?'

'Well, it means that you will be living on your own and after all you've done for me, I would hate you to feel lonely. Without you . . .' she left the rest unsaid, but they both remembered that terrible day, almost eight years ago, when they had met for the first time at the adoption agency.

'Because you're getting married it needn't affect our friendship in any way,' Merrion pointed out.

325

'It's bound to change things, though. I'll be moving downstairs, for one thing.'

'These days you spend most of your time down there as it is.' Merrion smiled.

'Yes, I suppose I do. Does than mean you are already feeling lonely and neglected?'

'Neglected, with Dilwyn and Nerys pestering the life out of me all the time?'

Rhonda looked guilty. 'Yes, you do take care of them a lot more than I do,' she admitted.

Merrion shrugged. 'I don't really mind, I find them good company.'

'You don't have to be on your own, you know,' Rhonda said tentatively. 'Evan Bowler is madly in love with you, and he'd jump at the chance of moving in with you . . . whether you marry him or not!'

'Rhonda! What are you saying? What sort of proposition is that!'

'You know quite well what I mean. Why don't you forget all about the past, Merrion and take up with Evan. He's good-looking, honest, hard-working, runs a very successful business and, even more to the point, he worships the ground you walk on.'

Christmas Day was everything Merrion had dreamed it would be. The two girls were as excited as three-year-olds with the bits and pieces they'd found in the socks they'd hung on the end of their beds.

They'd helped to lay the table, happily

singing their favourite carols as they did so. Evan arrived in time to lift the roast turkey out of the oven for Merrion. Dai brought two bottles of wine for them to drink with their meal and a bottle of port for them to have afterwards.

The meal was cooked to perfection and as everyone tucked in Merrion felt a glow of pride that all her plans for the day were working out so well.

A peaceful, lazy afternoon followed. They sat around the fire, eating nuts and sampling the huge boxes of chocolates that Evan had given Rhonda and Merrion. Both Dai and Evan had bought new games for the girls and everyone joined in and learned how to play them.

Later Merrion offered to make some turkey sandwiches, but they all groaned that they had already eaten far too much. Even so, they tucked into the mince pies that Merrion and the girls had made followed by slices of the elaborately iced Christmas cake that Evan had brought as part of his contribution to the feast.

The girls were allowed to stay up well past their normal bedtime, but in the end they were so sleepy that they were quite willing to go to bed.

Shortly afterwards, Rhonda and Dai disappeared downstairs. Merrion felt embarrassed that she had been left on her own with Evan and, as if sensing this, he left a few minutes later.

He didn't even give her a farewell kiss, and she had to admit to herself that she felt strangely disappointed as she closed the door behind him.

Chapter Thirty-Two

The weeks of hard work, coupled with the indulgence of too much food and drink on Christmas Day, took its toll. None of them wakened on Boxing Day until mid-morning.

They probably wouldn't have done so even then, but for the fact that when Nerys woke up and discovered that her mother was not there she decided to look for her. She found Merrion and Dilwyn both still in bed asleep, but no sign of her own mother. She woke Merrion to ask where she could be.

Taken by surprise, and still half asleep, Merrion blurted out that Rhonda was probably downstairs in Dai's flat.

Nerys had raced off before she could stop her. The next thing had been the screaming and commotion when she found out the truth about what was going on.

Rhonda and Dai were furious and there was discord in the air for most of the day. There was still a tense atmosphere when it was time for them to leave for the pantomime at the Prince of Wales theatre, but it soon vanished as they remembered how much they'd all enjoyed it the previous year.

The wonderful costumes, the captivating music and the singing and dancing from the chorus held them spellbound. The grown-ups roared at the jokes, but the humour of many of them escaped the two girls although they pretended to understand them. Nevertheless, they loved the show and were completely dazed when they came out into a crisp winter evening.

It was like emerging from wonderland into reality. Even the Christmas lights and shining shop windows couldn't replace the magic they'd just witnessed.

After such a special evening, Merrion felt very unhappy about the discord earlier in the day. To make amends she decided to get started right away on sorting out the accounts. Perhaps if she did that, and showed them what an excellent business partnership they had, then it might help to restore good feelings between them all.

Next day she waited until mid-afternoon to give them time to be up, dressed and have a meal before she went downstairs and knocked on Dai's door.

'Dai, could you let me have the account books and any outstanding invoices you have?' she asked when he answered.

'What on earth do you want those for today?' He frowned.

'I thought I would sort out the accounts so that we can start the new year knowing exactly where we stand financially.'

'We know where we stand. We've had a really bumper season.'

'Yes, I know that, but I thought if we had accurate figures then we could start to make plans for what we want to do in the new year.'

'Plans?' He groaned. 'We'll do the same as we did last year. Make as many hats as we can; cheap ones for the market and posh ones for the shop.'

'Yes, of course! Even so, we do need to know the figures before we start buying any more materials. We don't want to overspend and we need to work out if we are pricing the hats correctly.'

'I don't want to go into all that at the moment, Merrion. I'm having a day off.'

'Yes, Dai, I know that. I'm not asking you to do it. I know you have other things you want to do, but I'm not doing anything. I have time to spare, so I'll do them for you.'

He laughed evasively. 'Afraid I can't help you, Merrion. All the books and invoices are with my bookkeeper, so that he could make sure that all the bills were paid up to the end of the year and he certainly won't be working today.'

'Bookkeeper! I never knew you had any one doing your accounts?'

Dai's eyes narrowed. 'I'm a great one for deputising, Merrion. I find that if you insist on doing everything yourself, you make mistakes, see.'

'You don't do everything yourself,' she pointed out, 'you have an assistant on your stall . . .'

'That's right. But I'm the brains, see. You and Rhonda should know that. I organised things for you, didn't I? I helped make selling your hats a successful venture and helped you open a shop in one of the finest spots in Cardiff. Not something you could have done on your own, now was it?'

'I realise how much you've helped us both,' Merrion told him emphatically. 'Doing the books was my way of trying to repay you for all you've done.'

'Yes, yes.' Dai patted her shoulder. 'It's good of you, Merrion, but you really don't need to worry about them. Take the day off like the rest of us. Put your feet up and take it easy. After all the cooking and organising you did over Christmas you must be feeling dead beat.'

'Well, if you don't have the books or invoices here then there's not a lot I can do about it, I suppose,' Merrion admitted reluctantly.

'Right! I'll get them for you as soon as the holiday ends and then you'll be able to check them over if that's what you want to do.'

'Oh no, if you have a bookkeeper taking care of that side of things, then you probably don't need any help from me,' she pointed out.

'That's true, but you've every right to see them and judge for yourself that everything is going according to plan. It's your business too, after all.'

Merrion smiled and nodded. 'I understand. I wasn't checking up on you, Dai, simply trying to help.'

'Then what about having a drink with me and Rhonda? A toast to our success . . . and to the future.'

Merrion hesitated. 'I'd love to but what about the girls?'

'Leave them where they are. Tell them you are coming downstairs and that they can come down if they want to when they're good and ready. Nerys knows the way,' he added with a wry smile.

Although the friendship between the three of them seemed to be back to normal, Merrion still felt uncomfortable. Why on earth had Dai been so tetchy when she'd first mentioned checking over the accounts? she wondered. She'd only been trying to help.

She thought about it off and on for the rest of the day, unable to understand why he'd been so dismissive. She wished they weren't shut down for the holiday; she'd feel happier if she was busy. The girls were fully occupied with each other and didn't need her. Rhonda was spending all her time with Dai and didn't need her either.

A terrible feeling of loneliness engulfed her. A longing for Roddi swamped her. All her dreams seemed to suddenly build up into an enormous dark cloud that blotted everything else from her mind, and she sat down to have a good cry.

It was now over eight years since he'd gone to sea. Absolutely anything could have happened to him. He may well have been back to Cardiff time and time again. She might even have walked past him in the street and not recognised him.

She dried her eyes and pushed her hair back behind her ears. That was complete rubbish. She'd know him, she'd sense his presence.

There were other things to be considered, of course. Eight years was such a long time that he could be married. He might even have children, she told herself.

She shook her head. She couldn't imagine him marrying anyone else. They'd been so much to each other. From a very tender age they'd known that they were meant for each other. They'd both been sure that nothing would ever come between them. He'd come back one day, she only had to be patient.

She wandered round the workroom which seemed to be more bare than she had ever known it. Almost automatically, she began to tidy it up. The bench she worked on was completely clear and the cupboard where they stored the materials used for creating and trimming their hats was almost empty.

They'd used up practically every scrap of material in the mad rush before Christmas. All that seemed to remain were a few lengths of ribbon, a tray of threads, a selection of needles and pins.

That was good, of course, because the materials needed for their summer stock would be very different. They really should already have them on order, she thought worriedly. Easter was the biggest season of the year. Every woman wanted a posh hat to set off her new spring clothes. And Rhonda was so skilled at designing light, pretty hats, trimmed with flowers.

Once Rhonda had created the style, all she had to do was to repeat the same trimmings on different-coloured straws ready for Dai's stall. The ones for the shop would be trimmed more individually, something Rhonda excelled in doing. No two were ever alike, but all of them were exquisite.

How many new hats they would be able to make for spring depended on how much money was available for materials. This was why she was so anxious to check the books and work out the figures.

She'd had no idea that Dai had an accountant doing their books. Rhonda had never mentioned it and she wondered if she even knew. Common sense told her that she must do so because she'd worked so closely with Dai when they'd been planning the shop, so why had they shut her out?

Not for the first time since Rhonda and Dai

had become close she felt left out of the arrangements. Involuntarily her thoughts turned to Evan and she wondered if she dared to confide in him about all this. Then she remembered that he and Dai were longstanding friends so perhaps it would be better if she didn't, she decided.

Rhonda brushed her concern aside when she mentioned that they ought to have already placed an order with the wholesalers for supplies of straw shells as well as all the trimmings they would be needing.

'Stop going on about it! Dai told you it's a holiday. The warehouse will be closed on New Year's Day. Relax, enjoy yourself, take the girls out, go to the pictures or something, but for heaven's sake stop worrying.'

'I'm not worrying, I'm simply trying to plan ahead,' Merrion responded tetchily.

'Well, don't! A few days off isn't going to make any difference. You know what a terrific team we are. Once we start work again we'll make all the hats we need in good time for Easter. Sales between now and then aren't going to amount to anything worthwhile. As long as we have a few exclusives to sell in the shop we'll be all right. Dai won't need spring stock for his stall until March.'

Merrion tried to put it out of her mind, but it wasn't easy. She would have enjoyed the New Year's Eve celebrations far more if she'd known that they had all the materials they needed to start work on their spring hats the very next day.

In the end, she confided in Evan. He listened to her worries in silence. She was careful not to blame Dai in any way for the fact that she couldn't do as she wanted in order to start planning ahead.

'It's a funny time of the year,' he agreed. 'I never have understood why people need to take a full week off, not in the middle of winter. Given the choice I'd rather work over Christmas and the new year and then have a week off in the summer when its warm and sunny.'

She studied the serious handsome face and noticed the square set of his strong jaw and the integrity in his clear grey eyes and once again felt reassured by his genuine kindness and understanding.

She also knew how Evan felt about her from the look in his steady gaze. The longing in his eyes overwhelmed her. Perhaps Rhonda was right and it was time to put the past behind her and start anew. If only she could forget her dreams about Roddi and settle for what was so readily available.

She looked away quickly, uncomfortable because she couldn't bring herself to respond in the way she knew Evan wanted her to do. She wished she could. She knew it made sense. He not only cared for her, but he was fond of Dilwyn as well. She had only to accept his love and her life would change overnight.

Evan would make such a wonderful, reliable husband. He'd provide them with security and a good home. There would be no more lonely nights and she need never worry about what the future held in store for them ever again.

So why didn't she go along with it? she asked herself. Every fibre of her being said she should, it was only in the deepest recess of her mind, where her dreams were stored, that the image of Roddi rose like a spectre and made it impossible for her to accept that her future was with Evan.

Chapter Thirty-Three

On New Year's Eve, Merrion took the two girls,
who were both wearing the new dresses that
she and Rhonda had bought for them at
Christmas, to the party Evan had arranged
at his gymnasium.

'We came here last year, didn't we?' Dilwyn
asked excitedly.

'Of course we did.' Nerys nodded. 'I can
remember even if you can't. We had new
dresses on then too.'

The evening went well. Music, dancing,
plenty to eat and drink. They were a very
friendly crowd who were all out for a good
time.

Rhonda and Dai had asked Merrion if she
would keep an eye on Nerys since she wanted
to be with Dilwyn.

'We were wondering if you would take her
with you when you go home after the New
Year has been seen in,' Dai remarked.

'I suppose so, as long as she agrees to that,'
Merrion told them.

'Of course she will.'

Remembering how the evening had ended
the previous year, when Evan had taken her in

his arms and kissed her, Merrion was determined to leave before midnight so that it couldn't happen again.

Rhonda raised her eyebrows when she told her that was what she would be doing.

'It's up to you, of course, but I think you're making a mountain out of a molehill.'

'Maybe I am but that's what I've decided,' Merrion said tight-lipped.

'Neither of the girls will be very happy if they miss the midnight celebrations, though, will they? That's what New Year's Eve is all about!'

'I've thought of that. Well, I've thought of what I'm going to tell Dilwyn.'

'I'm listening.'

'That we should go to the Pier Head in time for midnight and listen to all the boats welcoming the new year in.'

'You'll hear them anyway! They make so much racket with their sirens and klaxons that you can hear them from one end of Cardiff to the other!'

'I know, but the girls don't know that and they'll find it exciting, I'm sure.'

'Fair dos, but don't you think that it might be a bit of a rough house down around there at midnight?' Rhonda said rather worriedly.

'I'm sure there will be plenty of police on duty. We won't stay long and then it will be straight home and to bed.'

'Please yourself. I would have thought it

340

would be more fun to stay at Evan's party. Even if he does kiss you the same as he did last year, does it matter? People are all kissing each other, even complete strangers! It's all part of the fun.'

Merrion was determined not to change her mind. 'You might be right, but that's what I'm going to do. If you don't want Nerys coming with us then say so.'

'No, you're in charge, do whatever you want to as long as you look after her for the rest of the night. Don't blame me, though, if she grizzles about standing around in the cold when she could still be enjoying the fun and music.'

Rhonda was wrong. Both girls were really excited at the thought of being at the Pier Head when the clocks chimed midnight and all the ships' hooters and klaxons welcomed in the new year.

For Merrion it was something deeper. It was a way of being reunited with Roddi who might be out there somewhere on the high seas. Perhaps this would be the year when they'd be together again; when the deep love she had for him and that she'd treasured and nurtured for so many long years could blossom at last.

The crowds at the Pier Head were noisy, but overflowing with goodwill. Men, women and children of every nationality mixed shoulder to shoulder. As midnight approached they sang, they cheered, and on the stroke of midnight they wished each other a Happy New Year.

The girls were tired and ready for home when

341

Merrion said it was time to leave. Their steps dragged as they approached Loudon Square. Once indoors they were almost too tired to get undressed. As soon as she had them safely tucked up Merrion made herself a cup of Ovaltine and then followed them to bed.

She fell asleep still thinking of all the good intentions she'd planned for the year ahead and her hopes that their business would become even more successful.

The only way to achieve that was by hard work. The day after New Year's Day, or as soon as things got back to normal, she'd work out what materials they needed. If Rhonda wasn't up to it after all her partying, then she'd go to the warehouse on her own and place the orders. The sooner they started work on their spring range the more they'd produce and the more money they'd make.

Never again, she told herself before she slipped into oblivion, did she ever want to be down to her last penny. She never wanted to have to scrape and pinch to make ends meet. She had to make plans for her own future. Once Rhonda marries Dai then she and Nerys will be taken care of, but I'll still have to go on providing for myself and Dilwyn she reminded herself.

The two girls slept late the next couple of mornings, but the day after New Year's Day, Merrion was eager to get started. Shortly before eleven she went down and tapped on Dai's door.

'You're as bad as Dai,' Rhonda grumbled when she finally answered it. 'He insisted that he had to go and open up his stall.' She yawned. 'It's a good thing he said I needn't open the shop until Saturday. That will be quite soon enough because I feel as if I could sleep for a week,' she muttered, stifling another yawn. 'I've no idea where Dai thinks he is going to get any customers from today, when all the world and his wife will probably still have a hangover after all the partying.'

'That means you have.' Merrion smiled. 'I'll find you a couple of aspirins and once you've had a cup of tea and taken those you'll feel as right as rain in half an hour.'

'It's worth a try, I suppose,' Rhonda agreed with a watery smile as she pushed her hair back out of her eyes.

'It will work wonders! You'll even feel ready to give me a hand to work out what we need from the wholesalers for the new season,' she added.

By the time Rhonda was dressed, Merrion had made a pot of tea and cut some sandwiches for their lunch, Rhonda was feeling much better. Although she still claimed that her head was muzzy she agreed to help Merrion compile a list of what was needed from the warehouse.

'Shall we go and pay them a visit?' Merrion suggested. 'I'd love to see the place.'

'Well, if you like. I've been there with Dai,

343

but there's not much to see. It's a huge big shed like a factory with shelving from floor to roof all filled with bolts of material and hat shapes. All the trimmings are stored in giant bins. It's not anywhere near as glamorous as a shop, or even a market stall, if it comes to that.'

'It would make an outing for the girls. Keep them from driving us mad because they're shut up indoors all day.'

'Yes, all right,' Rhonda sighed. 'A breath of fresh air might help to clear my head, I suppose.'

'You've still got your headache?' Merrion said in surprise.

'It's much better but I could still do with some fresh air to make sure it doesn't come back again.'

The warehouse was in Splott, too far for them to walk. They took a tram from Bute Road for part of the way and then walked the rest.

The warehouse was very much as Rhonda had described it, but to Merrion and the girls, as they walked in through the metal doors, it looked like an Aladdin's cave. They stared in amazement at all the different-coloured stock that was stacked up, shelf upon shelf, right up to the roof.

'Before we can go and select what goods we need we have to pick up an identity tag from the office,' Rhonda told them.

'Hello, Mr Vaughan, have you had a good Christmas?' Rhonda greeted the lantern-jawed middle-aged man who was seated on the tall stool in the small office at the entrance to the warehouse.

He didn't answer her. Instead his thin lips hardened into a tight line as he looked at her. His voice was frosty as he asked, 'Have you come to pay your outstanding bill, Miss Rees?'

Rhonda frowned. 'No, not really. Mr Francis has already dealt with it, hasn't he?'

Mr Vaughan shook his head. 'Indeed he has not! He assured us that you would be paying all the invoices since they are in your name. I'm afraid the amount outstanding has to be met before you can have any more goods from us.'

'I've come all this way to place a substantial order,' Rhonda blustered.

He shook his head. 'No more credit, not until the overdue bills are paid, Miss Rees.'

'I haven't received any invoices. As I told you, Mr Francis said he would be taking care of them.'

Again Mr Vaughan shook his head. He pulled a stack of invoices from a pigeon-hole above his desk and thrust them at her. 'The total is four hundred and thirty-three pounds, four shillings and four pence, three farthings,' he pronounced.

'How much!'

Mr Vaughan tore a sheet off the pad in front of him and wrote it down, then turned it round so that she could read it.

345

The colour drained from Rhonda's face. For a moment Merrion thought she was going to faint, so she stepped in quickly and held out her hand for the invoices. 'I'm Miss Rees's business partner. May we take those away with us so that we can check them over?' she asked.

Mr Vaughan held on to the invoices, looking at them both in a doubtful manner.

Rhonda leaned forward and snatched the invoices from his hand, her eyes wide with shock and disbelief as she riffled through them.

'These go back months!' she gasped. 'What's more, they're for things Mr Francis ordered for his stall so they are nothing to do with me and should have been sent to him!' she declared angrily. 'They ought to have his name on them and have been sent to *him*. Do you understand?'

'He said you were the one who would settle them,' Mr Vaughan said firmly.

'Absolute rubbish!'

'Then you'd better take the matter up with him,' Mr Vaughan muttered.

'We'll show these invoices to him, don't you worry,' Rhonda assured him.

'Come on!' she grabbed Merrion by the arm and turned to leave.

'Let me remind you that every one of those invoices is overdue,' Mr Vaughan pronounced. 'Unless they're settled in full within the next seven days, we will be handing them over to a debt collector.'

'What does that mean?' Merrion asked.

346

'It means that since they are all in Miss Rees's name the next step will be the bailiffs calling on you. If you can't pay then they'll take your possessions. Understand?'

Stunned, they walked away from the warehouse in complete silence. Even the girls realised that it was no time for chatter. Holding each other's hands they followed closely behind Rhonda and Merrion.

They caught a tram and not a word was spoken until they reached the centre of Cardiff.

'We'll go to the market and see what Dai has to say about all this,' Rhonda said, waving the bunch of invoices she was still clutching in her hand.

'Wouldn't it be better to wait until he comes home tonight?' Merrion said quietly.

'No it wouldn't! By then I mightn't be in such a flaming temper. The way I feel at the moment I could make mincemeat of him.'

'Perhaps it might be better to approach him quietly and ask what has happened,' Merrion suggested. 'There's obviously some sort of mistake.'

Rhonda was not to be dissuaded. 'We'll see!' she muttered ominously.

She was in such a tearing rage that she practically ignored the chorus of greetings from the other stallholders. When they reached Dai's stall they stopped abruptly.

'Where is he, where's Dai?' She stared at the empty stall in disbelief.

347

Those on nearby stalls either shrugged or looked the other way.

'Has Dai been here at all today?' Rhonda asked the man at the next stall.

He shook his head. 'Not seen sight nor sound of him, my lovely. He must have decided to stay off for another day. Perhaps he's ill.'

Rhonda didn't answer. Grabbing Nerys by the hand she hurried away leaving Merrion and Dilwyn to follow, or not, as they chose.

'Where are you going Rhonda?' Merrion called, hurrying to catch her up as she walked past the tram stop and headed for St Mary Street.

'To my shop, of course.'

As they reached the shop, Merrion subconsciously noted that it was the only one in the arcade with its blinds down.

Rhonda fumbled in her handbag for the key. Her hand was shaking so much that she found it impossible to fit it in the lock, so Merrion took the key from her.

She too had difficulty in getting it into the keyhole. 'Is this the right key?' she asked, frowning.

'Of course it is, it's the only one I have except for the key to the door in Loudon Square.'

Merrion looked at the key in her hand. 'Well it certainly isn't that one,' she agreed. 'I'll have another go. Is there a knack about the way you put it in the lock?'

Rhonda snatched it from her hand and tried

again herself. 'No,' she snapped. 'There's no knack . . . I think the lock has been changed!'

She shaded her eyes and peered into the interior, then gasped.

'Duw Anwyl! Everything has gone, the place is empty. There are no hats, no furniture, no mirrors, nothing.'

They stared at each other in horror. Merrion took her arm.

'Let's go home,' she said. 'There's absolutely nothing we can do here.

'What on earth is going on?' Merrion questioned as she sat down next to Rhonda on the tram.

'I don't know, I can't understand it,' Rhonda said miserably. 'Dai said he was going to open up his stall as usual; but he said there weren't likely to be many people out shopping, so he didn't think it was worth my while opening the shop.'

'The first thing we'd better do when we get home is sort out these invoices,' Merrion advised.

'What's the point? We haven't got the money to pay them. Over four hundred pounds! We've never had that much money in our lives.'

The girls sensed that there was something seriously wrong and after Merrion had made them a hot drink and given them a mince pie each, they went off to play on their own.

Rhonda drained her cup and stood up. 'I'm

349

going downstairs to see if Dai is back home yet and to see what he has to say about all this.'

'Hadn't we better check over these invoices first?' Merrion suggested.

Rhonda shook her head.

Minutes later she was back, her expression livid.

'Wasn't he there?' Merrion asked.

'He's not there and neither are any of his belongings. Clothes, furniture – in fact, every trace of him – have all gone.'

Merrion looked stunned. 'What does it all mean?'

Rhonda shook her head, too choked to answer.

'I've been looking through these invoices,' Merrion said awkwardly. 'There's something strange. Half the things listed are nothing to do with the sort of stuff he would order for his stall, even.'

'What do you mean?'

Merrion shook her head. 'I don't understand it. A lot of the items are general goods ...'

'The rotter! You know what he's been doing? He's been ordering stuff for other people and then charging it up to our account.'

Merrion frowned. 'I thought the arrangement was that you charged stuff to his account and then he billed us. Isn't that what was in all those papers you signed when you opened the shop in Morgan's Arcade?'

Rhonda flushed uncomfortably. 'I think so,

but I didn't read them properly! Dai said he'd done so and that they were all in order. I trusted him, Merrion.'

'Of course you did, I understand that, but it's obvious he has tricked you. It's a huge sum outstanding, so what are we going to do now?'

Chapter Thirty-Four

Merrion and Rhonda spent the whole of the next day trying to work out what steps they should take next. They knew they could never find the money to pay the enormous bill they were faced with, especially when their business no longer existed.

'I think we'd better ask Evan what he knows about Dai's movements and if he has any idea what he's playing at,' Merrion suggested after the girls had gone to bed.

'Yes, but that means letting Evan know what a couple of silly fools we've been to let ourselves be taken in like this,' Rhonda said dubiously. 'Do we want to do that?'

'He was the one who introduced us to Dai, so I think he should be told,' Merrion insisted stubbornly.

'Fair dos! Tell him if you want to, I couldn't care less,' Rhonda said resignedly.

'I think it is for the best, Rhonda,' Merrion insisted. 'He'll possibly know what we ought to do.'

'I'll nip down to the Glendower Arms, then, and leave a message with Brenda that we want a word with him.'

352

'Yes, it might be best if we ask him to come and see us here,' Merrion agreed. 'We don't want everyone to know what has happened and if we talk about it in the pub, then someone is sure to overhear what we're saying.'

Evan was as shocked as they were. 'I really don't understand the situation, I can't make head or tale of it,' he said as he went through the pile of invoices they showed him.

'No, well, neither can we,' Rhonda sighed. 'He's left us completely in the lurch with no stock, no premises and an enormous bill for things we've never bought. There's so much money owing that we couldn't pay it if we lived to be a hundred.'

'Mr Vaughan at the warehouse said that if we haven't paid it in seven days' time, then they'd send the bailiffs in to take our possessions,' Merrion pointed out.

'We can't let that happen, our home is all we've got left,' Rhonda said shakily.

'They can only take our furniture, they can't turn us out of our home, can they, Evan?' Merrion asked dubiously.

'Dammo di!' Evan clapped his hand to his forehead. 'I'd forgotten that this property belongs to Dai Francis!'

Rhonda frowned. 'I don't understand. Dai can't take this away as well, can he?'

Evan looked perplexed. He ran a hand through his thick fair hair. 'I don't really know

353

about that. You did say that he's cleared all his own stuff out, didn't you?'

'Every stick of it as well as all his clothes. You can come and look if you like, I still have a key.'

'Come on, then, there may be some clue that will tell us where he's gone or what his intentions are.'

Merrion's spirits sank as she watched them leave the room. It was far worse than she'd thought. Dai owned the property, he'd been left it by his mother, so he most certainly could turn them out if he wished to do so. Surely he wouldn't do that, she consoled herself. He must realise that he'd already done enough harm in sabotaging their business and letting Rhonda down after leading her on.

Evan's face was grim when he and Rhonda came back upstairs. 'We found this,' he said as he handed Merrion a document.

She took it from him, but it didn't make much sense to her. It appeared to be a legal agreement couched in terms she didn't understand. She looked questioningly at Evan.

'It's the draft of a contract. It looks as though Dai has already sold this property,' he told her.

Merrion looked at him in blank dismay. 'He can't have done. We're still living here!'

'I'm very much afraid that he has. From what it says here he's sold it with you as sitting tenants.'

Rhonda frowned. 'Does that mean the new owners can turn us out?'

'I'm not sure about that. I don't think they can, not as long as you pay the rent promptly,' Evan said cautiously. 'The fact that you haven't heard from them probably means that they are going to let you go on living here for the present. You should be all right for a while, providing, as I've said, you make sure you pay the rent on time.'

Merrion and Rhonda looked at each other in consternation. 'We've never paid any rent. Dai told us to leave it for a few months to see if we liked it here and although we've reminded him several times about it, he's always put it off.'

Evan frowned. 'Well, it says here that you are paying five pounds a week.'

'Five pounds! Duw Anwyl! We'd never be able to afford that sort of rent.'

'Rhonda's right. We'd never have undertaken to pay that sort of rent, not for one minute,' Merrion agreed.

'Well, if you haven't signed a lease or anything agreeing to that amount of rent, then you're probably all right.'

'Signed anything? Oh help!' Rhonda gasped, the colour ebbing from her face. 'Those papers I signed when I opened the shop . . . I seem to remember that there was some sort of tenancy agreement amongst them.'

'And you signed it?'

'Yes! I thought it was to do with the lease for the shop.'

Evan shook his head in despair. 'You really are going to need a solicitor to sort this mess out.'

'That's out of the question! A solicitor will cost money and we owe enough already!' Rhonda exclaimed emphatically.

'Well, not having one will cost you a damn sight more,' Evan warned.

'I think Evan is right,' Merrion agreed.

'First thing tomorrow morning, get something sorted out,' Evan advised. 'If you don't want to go to a solicitor, or feel you can't afford one,' he added quickly as he saw the look on Rhonda's face, 'then go to the police.'

'What good will that do?'

'They'll do all they can to track Dai down because what he's done is fraud.'

'If we go to the police, does that mean we won't need a solicitor?' Merrion asked.

'I honestly don't know,' Evan told her. 'I'm almost as much out of my depth as you two are.'

'What would you do then?' Rhonda snapped. 'After all, he was your friend.'

'I'd go to the police,' Evan told her firmly.

It took until mid-March to sort out their position. Almost three months of nerve-stretching worry and indecision that drained both Merrion and Rhonda and even affected Dilwyn and Nerys.

Merrion and Rhonda both managed to find work. The barmaid who had replaced Merrion at the Glendower Arms was leaving so she went back to her old job there. It meant confiding in Brenda about what had happened and fending off questions from customers curious to know why she was back working there again.

Rhonda, meanwhile, managed to persuade another stallholder in the Hayes market to sell her hats. This time, though, she insisted that they paid for them on delivery, explaining that it was the only way she could afford to buy materials to produce more hats.

The profit she made on them was a mere pittance because she was no longer able to use her original suppliers and so she had to buy most of her materials at the full retail price.

While the enquiries about Dai and his shady dealings went on they were still not paying any rent. Once things were settled they would have to do so, of course, and they had no idea how they would manage to make ends meet when that happened.

By mutual agreement Rhonda's wedding plans were no longer mentioned. The new clothes they'd promised to buy the girls and themselves had to be forgotten about. Finding enough money to buy food and fuel took all their combined earnings.

Dai wasn't traced and everyone assumed that he had left Cardiff, although where he had gone

was not clear. Evan thought that he had probably gone overseas when he discovered that
the law was after him and all his fraudulent
dealings had come to light.

The problem of being able to afford to pay
the rent never arose because the moment all the
legalities had been dealt with Merrion and
Rhonda were given three weeks' notice to
vacate their rooms in Loudon Square.

They were both devastated. 'Three weeks is
no time at all to find somewhere else to live,'
Rhonda said despairingly when they talked
about it to Evan.

'Perhaps I can help, then, there are some attic
rooms over the club where you can stay as a
temporary measure,' he told them gruffly.

'That's where you live, though, isn't it?'
Merrion protested.

'Yes, but my place is on the level below. The
only thing you will have to share with me is
the kitchen,' he told her stiffly.

'Surely you don't want all of us living above
you. There are four of us, you know, and the
girls aren't all that quiet and—'

'Take it or leave it,' he shrugged.

'Of course we'll take it. We've no option, now
have we?' Rhonda told him quickly.

'It's very kind of you, Evan, and we're most
grateful,' Merrion added quietly.

'That's settled then,' Rhonda exclaimed.
'Now, can you find someone to move our bits
and pieces?'

'Hold on, most of the furniture we're using here belongs to Dai,' Merrion reminded her.

'So what? He's taken everything else of ours, so surely he won't begrudge us this old stuff.'

'No, but the new owner might. He's probably been told that the place is furnished.'

'Bring what you need, I'm sure it will be all right,' Evan intervened. 'No one would blame you for doing that. I'll find someone with a van or lorry to come and give you a hand. Leave it to me.'

'You've been a wonderful friend to us, Evan,' Rhonda told him warmly. Standing on tiptoe she planted a kiss on his cheek.

'Anything to help two damsels in distress,' he said awkwardly. He smiled, but his eyes were on Merrion not Rhonda.

Merrion was very conscious of this, and knew that he was waiting for a reaction from her. Grateful though she was for all his help she didn't want to say anything that might give him the slightest hope that she held any feelings for him.

When things were going so wrong for them it was a great temptation to respond to his advances. He was physically attractive and she knew he would make a considerate and dependable husband. It would mean no more financial worries. Dilwyn liked him and Merrion was quite sure she'd welcome him as a permanent member of their family.

Yet she couldn't do it. He was too good a man to be deceived and much as she liked him, and was grateful for all his help, she didn't love him. There was room in her heart for only one man, the man who had haunted her dreams for the past eight years, and that man was Roddi Jenkins.

Both Merrion and Rhonda felt that the move to Bute Road was a retrograde step and they were thoroughly depressed as they left Loudon Square for the last time.

On their first visit to the rooms above the club, they were quite horrified to discover how neglected and dirty they appeared to be. They were up in the roof of the building and the ceilings slanted towards the small windows so that in places not even the children could stand upright.

As they looked around the place, disturbing dust, debris and spiders that had been there for goodness knows how long, they would have given almost anything to have been able to walk away, but they needed a roof over their heads.

The week before they were due to move in, Evan found a couple of out-of-work men to give the place a coat of fresh paint and Rhonda made up some curtains from cotton remnants that she managed to pick up quite cheaply at the market.

'Not that anyone could see in here even if

they wanted to,' she muttered as she sewed on the rings, ready to hang them up.

That was very true. There were three flights of stairs and the last set were narrow and winding. It had taken a great deal of effort to get the few bits and pieces of furniture that had belonged to them, and which they'd brought with them from Loudon Square, up to the four small rooms.

Even though they had very few personal possessions, it was a tight squeeze to get everything in. They made the largest of the rooms, which had a small iron fireplace in it, into a living room. They used two of the others as bedrooms. The remaining one, which was little more than a walk-in cupboard, they used to store all the millinery paraphernalia they'd brought with them from Loudon Square.

'At least it is going to be cosy,' Merrion said brightly, trying to make the best of things and in order to cut short Rhonda's diatribe of complaints.

The two girls thought it was a great adventure, but not so Rhonda. She continued to grumble incessantly, not only about how squashed they were in such limited space, but about the sort of district they were now living in.

'Sophia Terrace was a slum but this is even worse,' she protested angrily. 'Come over here and look out of this window, Merrion. It's broad daylight and yet there're girls outside soliciting sailors who look as though they've only just come ashore.'

'Well, that's because there's a Seamen's Mission only a few doors away,' Merrion pointed out. 'It's unfortunate that we are situated on this side of it and they all have to pass by here before they reach their lodgings.'

'Whatever you do, make sure that Nerys and Dilwyn don't hang around down in the street,' Rhonda warned. 'Perhaps one of us should meet them from school each afternoon and walk home with them.'

'Oh for goodness' sake, they're barely eight years old; they're not likely to notice what is going on or to come to any harm.'

'We can't be too careful, Merrion! I'm not only thinking about the street girls or the Seamen's Mission. There are some very weird-looking men who come here to Evan's Club.' She shuddered. 'I certainly wouldn't like to bump into any of them on a dark night.'

'You'd better not let Evan hear you saying anything like that or he might turn us out,' Merrion chuckled. 'Cheer up, we'll be able to move to a better address as soon as we clear off all our debts and get on our feet again.'

'That could be years away and in the meantime we have no choice but to live here,' Rhonda muttered gloomily.

'Yes, and we should be grateful to Evan for putting a roof over our heads.'

'He did it for you, not me. Why do you push him away all the time, Merrion?'

Merrion flushed. 'What do you mean? I don't.'

'Yes you do! You're as prickly as an old hedgehog every time he speaks to you. It wouldn't have surprised me if you'd turned down these rooms knowing that he's living in the same building.'

'I didn't, though, did I? So be grateful and make the best of them and stop moaning all the time.'

'He wants to marry you, Merrion, so why not say "yes"? Think how much more comfortable life could be.'

'Yours or mine?'

Rhonda shrugged. 'For all of us, I suppose. It's worth considering.'

Merrion shook her head. 'I have considered it and the answer is "no". Not now, or ever.'

'You must be mad, cariad.'

Merrion's lips tightened. 'Maybe.'

Rhonda shook her head in despair. 'You and your silly dreams.'

'Well, that's the way it is and I've no intention of changing my mind so can we stop talking about it?'

Rhonda shrugged. 'All right, as long as you don't mind me setting my cap at him.'

Chapter Thirty-Five

'Duw anwyl, Rhonda! What on earth has happened to you, cariad? Your face! What a terrible gash. How did you do that?'

Merrion dropped the outdoor coat she was about to put on and rushed to help as Rhonda, white-faced and shaking, stumbled into the living room.

Merrion could see that her coat was torn and fastened unevenly and that, concealed beneath it, Rhonda's arm was in a heavy plaster-cast supported by a sling.

'Oh, Rhonda! You've had an accident! Come and sit down, my lovely. Can I get you anything?'

'A cup of tea would be nice,' Rhonda gasped as she almost collapsed on to a chair. 'I can still taste the horrible medicine they made me take at the infirmary.'

'Infirmary!'

Tears streamed down Rhonda's cheeks as Merrion helped her off with her coat and then gently settled her more comfortably into an armchair.

'Come on, cariad, don't take on so,' Merrion murmured, handing her a handkerchief. 'Try and tell me what happened. Were you knocked down?' she asked anxiously.

Vivid memories of her own mother's fatal accident when she'd been run over by a tram shortly after they'd arrived in Cardiff flooded Merrion's mind and for a brief second her own eyes filled with tears.

'I wasn't knocked down, I was attacked,' Rhonda gulped. She shivered violently. 'It all happened so suddenly. I couldn't do anything about it.'

'Where was this?' Merrion frowned.

'In Bute Road . . .'

'Dammo di! In broad daylight? Who on earth would have the nerve to do something like that?'

'I think he was waiting to waylay me. It happened only minutes after I'd left the girls at the school gates. I was walking back towards the tram stop when he jumped on me from behind. He snatched at the suitcase I was carrying and when I wouldn't let go of it, he punched me in the face and then pushed me so hard that I fell. I put my hand out to try and save myself and that must have been how I broke my arm.'

'Duw anwyl! I can hardly credit it! And that's when you cut your face and tore your coat.'

'And ruined my dress, laddered my stockings, scuffed my shoes and my hat fell into the gutter,' she added with a slightly hysterical laugh.

'So what happened to your attacker?'

'The moment I crashed down and he heard me scream with pain he was gone like a bat out of hell.'

'And he left you lying there on the pavement. Duw! How wicked! Did no one try to help you, cariad?'

Rhonda gave a wan smile. 'Yes, I was lucky over that. There was a midshipman walking past and he stopped and helped me up and took me in a taxi-cab to the infirmary.' She sighed dreamily. 'He was really handsome and terribly kind. He insisted on them treating me right away and said he would wait until they'd seen to the gash on my face. He was still there waiting for me after they'd set my arm in a plaster. Then he ordered another taxi-cab and brought me home in it.'

'So where is he?'

'Gone, of course.'

'He waited at the infirmary and then brought you all the way back here and you didn't ask him in so that we could thank him!' Merrion said in a disapproving tone.

'Well, I thought I'd taken up enough of his time since he was on shore leave and had people to see. While we were at the infirmary he was talking all the time about his girlfriend. I gathered that he hadn't been back to this country for years and so he was really looking forward to seeing her again. I told him if he didn't manage to find her not to worry, he could always look me up again.'

'Oh, Rhonda, that was rather a rash thing to do, now wasn't it!'

'Not really, it was meant as a joke. The chance of him doing so is one in a thousand. All he was interested in was this Mary; she seemed to be the love of his life.'

'Well, I hope he finds her. He must be a wonderful sort of person to not only stop and make sure that you were all right but to take the time to see you safely home afterwards.'

Rhonda shivered. 'Yes, you're right. I don't know what would have happened if he hadn't come along at the moment he did. It was the most frightening thing that has ever happened to me, Merrion.'

'I can well believe that, but you are safe now,' Merrion comforted her as she studied the deep gash on Rhonda's face. 'I see that they had to put some stitches in,' she murmured.

Rhonda delved in her bag and found her powder compact and studied the cut carefully. 'Let's hope it doesn't leave a nasty scar,' she murmured anxiously, 'I'd hate that!'

'I'm sure they must know the right way to deal with these things,' Merrion consoled her.

'I'm sure they do, but it looks a little bit inflamed, even though they dabbed it with anti-septic,' Rhonda said irritably. 'I don't want to go back again. I'm too frightened to go outside the door again today. Put some ointment on it if you think it needs it.'

367

'I'll have another look at it when you've finished drinking your tea,' Merrion said.

'Patch me up for the moment and I'll go back again tomorrow if you think I must.'

'Yes, all right. Drink your tea and after that perhaps you should try and get some rest while the place is quiet.'

'Yes, once the girls come home from school I won't have a chance to do so until they go to bed.'

'Are we going to tell Dilywn and Nerys the truth about what's happened?'

'They'll see for themselves that I've hurt my face and broken my arm, but it's probably better not to tell them the details. It might scare them.'

'Or it might alert them to be on their guard when they're out in the street. I know it's a rough area around here, but I never thought anything like this would ever happen to me or any of us.'

'It probably never will again. He obviously believed that I had something of value in the bag.' She laughed disparagingly. 'I'd like to see his face when he opens it and finds it's a load of hats.'

'Did either you, or the chap who helped you, think to call the police?'

'Police! What's the point of doing that? The man scarpered the moment I fell down.'

'Well, if they found who attacked you, then they might be able to get your hats back.

Anyway, you should tell them so as to give them a chance to catch him and punish him.'

'Do you think they would bother trying to arrest him for stealing a few hats!'

'I wasn't only thinking about the hats, I was more concerned about what has happened to you. Look at the state you are in.'

'Oh leave it, Merrion. My head is thumping, my arm is aching and my face is stinging as if there were a dozen bees attacking me all at once.'

'Perhaps you should go to bed, then.'

'No, I'd never be able to settle comfortably with this arm. I'll stay here in the armchair and put my feet up on a stool.'

'If that's what you think is best. I'll fetch a blanket to wrap round you. Perhaps if you can sleep for an hour or so, you'll feel better. I'll just pop down to the pub and let Brenda know I won't be able to come in for a couple of days.'

'You can't do that, Merrion, you might lose your job and at the moment we need the money you earn more than ever. I won't be able to make any hats for weeks and weeks.'

'You won't be fit enough to collect the girls from school for a few days and I don't want them walking home on their own. I know they're old enough to do so, but at the moment . . .'

She didn't finish the sentence, but they both knew that their concern for the safety of Dilwyn and Nerys was uppermost in both their minds.

'Well, if you are sure that Brenda won't mind you taking some time off.'

'She'll understand when I explain it all to her. We ought to tell Evan about what has happened as well. If you can describe your attacker to him, he may even know who he is.'

'I can't describe him though, Merrion.'

'Not at all?'

'He came at me from behind and the next thing I knew I was on the ground in agony.'

'Do you think that sailor chap who helped you might be able to say what he looked like?'

'I really don't know. Possibly.'

Merrion sighed. 'If only we could ask him. Did he say where he was going? Where his girl-friend lived?'

Rhonda shook her head. 'I was in too much pain to bother to listen properly to what he was saying. He was nice, but it wasn't as if I was ever going to see him again, was it?'

'No, of course not. Well, in that case, you're probably right and it would be a waste of time going to the police.'

Evan was shocked by the news. He agreed with Merrion that Rhonda ought to tell the police, but he could understand that the way she was feeling it was too much of an effort to do so.

'I could always get one of the local cops to drop in when he's passing by. They know all the rogues in this area, by sight if not by name.'

'That won't help much because Rhonda didn't see his face clearly,' Merrion pointed out.

'What about his voice? Did he have a Cardiff accent? You haven't even said if he was white or coloured. You must have noticed something, Rhonda.'

Evan ran his hands through his hair, then leaned over and gently touched Rhonda's face with a forefinger. 'The bugger deserves to be caught and locked up for doing this to you and if I had my way, cariad, he would be. Let me know if there is anything I can do to help. I can keep an eye on you while Merrion's out at work, make you a cuppa, that sort of thing.'

'Thank you, Evan, that's very thoughtful of you.' She laughed uncertainly. 'Merrion says she will take a couple of days off, so that there's someone here to see that I don't do anything daft. She'll be here to collect the girls from school; we're a bit worried about them,' she added.

'I can understand you both feeling anxious, but Merrion needn't take time off work. I can collect them from school in the afternoon.'

'I should be well enough to do that myself in a couple of days,' Rhonda assured him.

'You need to take things easy, girl. You don't want to risk getting that arm bumped or the bones won't knit together as they should. I'm sure you don't want to go out with that gash on your face, either. I'll collect them for a week or two while you give your face a chance to heal up.'

Rhonda reached out and took his hand. 'Thank you, Evan, that's very kind of you.'

'I'll also alert the crowd that come here to the gym about what has happened so they'll be keeping an eye out for you and the two girls as well,' he promised. 'You can go back to work at the pub as soon as you like, you know, Merrion. I'll be here if Rhonda needs anything. I'll watch over her, I promise you.'

'Thank you, Evan, I'm very grateful. I'm sure she'll be all right in a few days' time, though, and be able to manage quite well.'

'I'm trying to prove to you that she is going to be quite safe while you're at work,' Evan explained.

'I know and I'm grateful. In fact, if it is all right with you, I'll go back tomorrow, but perhaps you could tell Brenda at the pub for me that I won't be in today.'

Dilwyn and Nerys listened in wide-eyed disbelief when they came out of school and Merrion explained everything to them. She tried to make light of it, but at the same time make them both aware of how worried she was about their safety. They both nodded solemnly when she told them that in future they were to wait at the school gates for either herself, Rhonda or Evan to collect them, and that on no account were they to walk down Bute Road on their own.

'Remember,' she finished, 'tomorrow it will be Evan who will be coming for you.'

They both promised they would wait for him and do whatever he asked when they got home.

'Can we practise making tea for my mam when we get in this afternoon?' Nerys asked.

When they reached home Evan greeted them with the news that there'd been a visitor for Rhonda.

'It was that sailor bloke, the one who helped her when she was attacked.'

'Really! Did you ask him if he could remember what the attacker looked like?'

'I didn't get a chance. Rhonda was so excited that he'd called that she almost pushed me out of the door,' Evan laughed.

'Well, I'd better go and see if I can jog his memory then,' Merrion smiled.

'Oh, there's no chance of you doing that, cariad, because he's gone already. He only stayed here for about ten minutes and then he was away. Rhonda said he'd only come in to make sure that she was all right.'

For the next few days the girls were as helpful as they could be. They tried to outdo each other in their eagerness to fetch and carry things for Rhonda.

'They'll soon get tired of waiting on you so make the most of it while you can,' Merrion laughed.

Evan was equally attentive. He insisted that

when Merrion went out she should let him know. He'd brought up an old ship's bell and he made Rhonda promise that she would ring it if there was anything needed and he'd come running.

Chapter Thirty-Six

'You're going out with him tomorrow for lunch and yet you don't even know his name?' Merrion exclaimed.

'That's right! Isn't it romantic? You'd like him, Merrion, you really would. He's quite tall, with dark hair, and he's rather good-looking. In fact, for a Good Samaritan, he's absolutely wonderful in every way.'

'So you keep telling me,' Merrion remarked wryly. 'You seem to have fallen for him in a big way and no mistake.'

'It's a tremendous surprise seeing him again. I never thought for one moment that he'd come and look me up again,' Rhonda babbled, her eyes bright with delight.

'Are you quite sure you're up to going out with him? You haven't even walked as far as the corner shop since the day of the attack.'

'Of course I am,' Rhonda interrupted confidently. 'I feel heaps better simply thinking about it. It will be a real tonic to get all dolled up to go out and it will do me no end of good.' She grinned confidently.

'Are you really sure? You are taking a tremendous risk and I don't want to see you upset.'

Rhonda frowned. 'What on earth do you mean?'

'Well, you've only met him twice before and we know nothing at all about him. Surely you know what sort of reputation sailors have.'

'I don't know how you can say something like that!' Rhonda protested. 'Not after the way he looked after me and took me to hospital and waited while they patched me up and then brought me home again.'

'No, I suppose you are right. It seems strange if he was simply coming to see if you were all right that he should ask you to go out with him and for lunch of all things! Do you think you are going to be able to manage a knife and fork with your arm in a sling?'

'Nothing strange about it at all. He's sailing later in the day and has to be back on his ship before six o'clock.'

'Mmm! So I suppose that will be the last you'll ever see of him?'

'I hope not! I want this to be the beginning of something, not the end.'

'I thought you said that he already had a girl-friend,' Merrion persisted.

'Well, it seems she has moved and he hasn't been able to find her. It's quite sad really, but he says now he thinks it is time to give up looking.'

'So he's simply cheering himself up by taking you out for a meal!'

'I don't know. I'd like to think there is more to it than that,' Rhonda said hopefully.

'Well, don't get too buoyed up. As I said to you before, sailors are well known for having a girl in every port they call at. They also have a reputation for breaking hearts, so watch yourself.'

'Because Dai Francis was an out-and-out scoundrel and cheated on us it doesn't mean that all men are like that,' Rhonda exclaimed tartly.

'I know, but I don't want you to end up being let down again, it causes too much heartbreak. What time is he collecting you?'

'I don't know exactly, I imagine it will be somewhere around midday.'

'So will I have a chance to meet him at last?'

'Probably not. You will have gone to work before he gets here and he will have left before you come home again,' Rhonda explained.

'Perhaps I should take the day off, you mightn't be back in time to collect the girls from school.' Merrion frowned.

'You know perfectly well that Evan will be collecting the girls.'

'So will he have a chance to meet this handsome sailor? Or do you think it might be safer if they don't get to know each other?'

'Are you teasing me, Merrion?'

'Of course I am!' Merrion hugged her. 'It's great to see that you are obviously feeling so much better that you can get so excited about this date.'

377

Rhonda flushed. 'It's not really a date. He happened to say that he was staying overnight at the Seamen's Mission in Bute Road because he sails tomorrow. When I asked him what time his ship left he said not until late in the day, so—'

'So you both decided that you might as well spend some time together before he had to go on board. I understand, I really do. I hope you have a nice time.'

Merrion was so curious about Rhonda's sailor that she delayed leaving the next morning with the express purpose of meeting him. She was sure that Brenda would understand if she was half an hour or so late. She knows I'm not likely to let her down, not when she's been good enough to give me my job back, Merrion told herself.

Rhonda was on edge. She changed her dress twice, discarded one pair of shoes for another, and kept titivating her hair and renewing her make-up, scowling at her reflection and bewailing the fact that no matter how much she tried she couldn't hide the scar on her face.

It was half past eleven before Evan called up the stairs to say there was someone asking for her and was he to send him up.

Merrion disappeared into her bedroom to give Rhonda a chance to greet him on her own. To her annoyance, by the time she came back out they'd already left.

She couldn't believe that Rhonda could have done such a thing. She raced down the stairs at breakneck speed, hoping to catch them.

'They've gone!' Evan laughed. 'Rhonda looked like the cat that got the cream. His visit has certainly cheered her up and no mistake.'

'Dammo di! Rhonda must have known I wanted to meet him,' Merrion exploded crossly.

'She's probably afraid to let you do that. She knows she doesn't stand a chance when you're around,' he told her, his gaze resting on her admiringly.

Her cheeks burning, Merrion turned away quickly. 'I must get to work, I'm late already,' she said, ignoring the message in his eyes.

When she explained why she was late Brenda was intrigued. 'Look, cariad,' she whispered, 'as soon as the midday rush is over you pop back home and make sure that you meet this chap. Be there when they get back, I'm as curious as you are to know more about him.'

'Are you sure, Brenda?'

'It's the only way to settle your mind that there's nothing to be worried about, now isn't it, cariad? You don't want Rhonda doing anything rash on the rebound from that Dai Francis, now do you?'

Merrion breathed a sigh of relief. 'Thanks, Brenda, I'll do that.'

'Don't hurry back. As long as you are here for nine o'clock, we can manage all right.'

'That's good of you, Brenda, are you quite sure you'll be able to manage?'

'Of course I am! You'll have to tell me all about him, mind,' she added with a broad smile.

Evan was surprised to see Merrion. 'They're upstairs, they've been back about five minutes,' he told her. 'I'm just off to pick up the girls.'

'Don't worry, I'll go and do it.'

'Are you sure that's a good idea? You don't want to miss him again.'

'I know, but now that I'm here I feel a bit awkward about butting in on them,' she admitted. 'I'll feel better about it if I have the girls with me, if you see what I mean.'

'You mean Rhonda won't be embarrassed because she'll be expecting them.'

'Something like that!'

The girls were taken aback to see Merrion and for a minute Nerys was almost in tears because she thought it meant that her mother had been hurt again.

'No, cariad,' Merrion assured her, pushing Nerys's auburn hair back from her face. 'Your mam is fine. In fact, she has a friend visiting her.'

'Friend?' Nerys's eyes widened. 'Who's that?'

'The kind man who helped her when she was attacked and who took her to the hospital.'

The girls exchanged looks, then they grabbed hold of Merrion's hands. One on each side of her, they made her walk as fast as she could.

'Slow down, both of you,' she pleaded breathlessly. 'What's all the hurry?'

'We want to get home so that we can see the visitor,' they told her excitedly.

They raced up the stairs ahead of her. As she followed them into the living room, Merrion stopped and stared in utter disbelief at the man wearing merchant navy uniform who stood up to greet them all.

For a moment she thought she was hallucinating. She clutched the edge of the table to steady herself. Her head was spinning. From somewhere far off she heard his voice and her heart raced. There was no mistake, it was the voice that had haunted her, awake as well as in her dreams, for so many long years.

'Merri? Merri, is it really you?'

'Roddi? Oh, Roddi!' As she stared up at the face that she'd last seen when she'd been sixteen, Merrion could only nod her head. It was as if her voice had vanished. Her throat was dry and her breath was coming in short gasps, almost as if she had been running for miles and miles.

He was older, but then, so was she. Even so she would have known him anywhere. She'd carried an image of that tall frame, those wonderful hazel eyes and that shock of dark auburn hair in her mind day and night for almost a decade.

Rhonda's face was a study, a picture of disbelief and chagrin. 'You two already know each other!' she gasped.

'Know each other!' He smiled broadly. 'This is like a miracle. This is my Merri whom I told you about the day we met. For years, every time I came ashore, I searched every town and village around Cwmglo, trying to find her.'

Merrion couldn't take her eyes away from him. Rhonda was right, he did look handsome in his smooth, dark, navy serge uniform. The glittering gold trim, and the blue insignia denoting his rank, gave him such an air of authority that she knew without asking that he was proud of what he had achieved.

'Are you telling me that this is your Roddi! The dream hero you've gone on and on about ever since the first day we met?' Rhonda said in a stunned voice.

'Yes, this is that very special man that you never believed existed except in my dreams. In my heart I've always known he would come back and find me and that we would be together again one day.'

'Duw!' Rhonda shook her head in disbelief. 'You're right. I never thought for one minute that he existed outside of your dreams,' she admitted.

'Well, now you know he does. What's more, I'll never be able to thank you enough for finding him for me,' Merrion said gratefully.

'You'd better tell me what has happened in all those missing years,' Roddi said eagerly. Then he stopped, his gaze going towards the two girls who were standing holding each other's hands and staring from one to the other of them with wide-eyed, unconcealed interest.

Roddi's eyes fixed on Nerys. Astonishment mingled with pride as he looked at Merrion. 'Merri, is this . . . is this our daughter?' he asked, his voice thick with emotion.

'No, no! Nerys is Rhonda's daughter!' She laughed uneasily. 'I never thought about it before, but her hair is very much like yours, isn't it?'

He nodded, looking rather confused.

'And this is my little sister, Dilwyn.' She held out a hand and drew the child towards them. 'If you remember, Roddi, she was born the night before the pit explosion happened, and a few days before we all had to leave Cwmglo.'

'So how are your mam and Madoc, then?'

'They're dead!' She sighed. 'Both of them were killed in a tram accident only a couple of months after we arrived in Cardiff.'

'I'm so sorry to hear that, Merri! That's terribly sad news. And what about your Uncle Huw? Did he come to Cardiff with you?'

Merrion laughed, a dry, bitter little noise. 'Yes, he did; like the rest of us he was afraid of what would happen if we stayed in Cwmglo once David Pennowen started threatening us. He left us high and dry though, a couple of weeks after Mam and Madoc were killed. He didn't relish the responsibility of looking after me and little Dilwyn.'

'Duw anwyl! So do I take it that you've not heard from him since?'

She smiled sadly. 'No, and I haven't heard from our Emlyn, either. Where is he?'

'He came with me,' Roddi confirmed. 'We were together for a while, but then we went our separate ways. We've run into each other a couple of times, though.'

'You've seen him!' Her face beamed. 'Oh, Roddi, that's wonderful. How is he?' she asked eagerly.

'Doing well, but missing his family. Like me, every time he comes into port he spends the whole of his shore leave looking for you all.'

'He's not on the same ship as you, though?' Her voice registered disappointment.

'No, but we keep in touch. I'll let him know I've found you and where you are living. Next time his ship docks here he'll come to see you, never fear.'

'It would be wonderful to see him,' Merrion sighed.

Roddi looked at his watch and his face clouded. 'Is that the time!' he exclaimed sharply. 'Duw! I must be on my way, I've cut it very fine. They'll be sailing without me if I don't hurry.'

'You will be coming back?' Merrion asked anxiously.

'Of course I will! As soon as ever I can.' His arms went round her and he hugged her close, his lips on her hair, her brow and finally her

384

mouth in a deep and passionate kiss. 'I'll be back, my darling, and we'll spend every minute of my next leave together.'

'And in the meantime you'll get in touch with Emlyn and let him know that you've found us at long last and that we're longing to see him again?'

'I most certainly will.' He released her and walked over to Rhonda and kissed her on the cheek. 'I'll never be able to thank you enough for reuniting us,' he told her gratefully.

As he walked towards the door, Merrion dashed after him, wanting one final embrace, but it was too late. He'd already bounded down the stairs.

She went over to the window that looked out on to Bute Road and watched as he strode away towards the Pier Head. She stayed there until he disappeared from sight, tears of happiness trickling down her cheeks.

Chapter Thirty-Seven

For several weeks after Merrion's reunion with Roddi, they all talked of nothing else. It was as if all their lives had been changed by him turning up in such an unexpected way.

For Merrion it was her most precious dream come true. Even though she'd always been sure that one day she and Roddi would be reunited, there were times in the days that followed when she found it hard to believe that she wasn't still dreaming and to convince herself that he had actually been there. The treasured recollection of his lips on hers and his strong arms holding her close to his lean body when he'd said farewell was something she dwelt on over and over again.

Rhonda was more than a little piqued that she had lost her handsome sailor, the hero who had come to her aid so gallantly when she'd been attacked.

'I really thought I had found the perfect lifetime companion,' she sighed. 'He had everything; looks, uniform and a devastating smile. Why did he have to be the man you've been dreaming about all these years!'

'Didn't you suspect that it might be him when

he said he'd been looking for his girlfriend every time he'd come ashore for all those years?'

'Not for a single moment,' she protested. 'He said her name was Mary, so I never dreamed that he meant Merrion.'

'He always shortened my name to Merri when we were kids,' Merrion explained.

'And you called him Roddi, so how was I to know it was him when he said his name was Roderick,' she stated flatly.

'And that didn't ring a bell and give you a clue?' Merrion smiled.

'He didn't tell me his name until we were at lunch. That day at the hospital I was far too upset to ask him, or even care what he was called.'

Evan looked extremely morose when he heard an account from Rhonda of all that had taken place. 'I bet you feel jilted as well, don't you?' she sighed.

'No, not at all,' he blustered. 'After all, Merrion and I are good friends, that's all.'

'Yes, but you would have liked to have been more than that,' Rhonda pointed out.

Evan shrugged. 'We all have dreams!'

'That's true, but Merrion's seem to be the only ones that have come true,' Rhonda said dispiritedly.

Nerys was in awe over what had happened. She fired questions non-stop at her mother, as well as at Merrion and even at Dilwyn.

'It's exactly like a fairytale, isn't it, Dilwyn?'

387

she breathed ecstatically. 'Your sister's boyfriend, who went away when you were only a few days old, suddenly appearing out of the blue like that. You must be so excited!'

Dilwyn looked disconcerted. 'I'm not sure. I don't know him properly, not yet.'

'Fair dos, but you must like him, Dilwyn. He's really handsome in his uniform!'

'True, but I still don't know what he's really like, now do I? We'd no sooner met than he had to leave.'

'I'd say he was gorgeous! I only wish he was my mam's boyfriend.'

'Yes, he's all right to look at,' Dilwyn agreed, 'but it doesn't mean he's a nice person.'

'How can you say that?' Nerys gasped in astonishment. 'He went to the rescue of my mam when she was attacked in Bute Road. He took her to the infirmary and even waited so that he could bring her home afterwards. Only a very nice person would have bothered to do that.'

'Yes, I suppose so,' Dilwyn admitted reluctantly. 'I'll feel more certain about how I feel when I've had the chance to get to know him a bit better.'

'You mean when he comes back again.'

'If he does. He didn't even tell us the name of the ship he was on.'

Nerys looked taken aback. 'I'm sure he must have told Merrion,' she protested.

'He didn't! She was ever so upset about it.'

388

'He must be coming back, though, Dilwyn, because he said he'd bring your brother Emlyn to see you next time he comes ashore.'

Dilwyn pulled a face. 'I don't know him either. Suppose he's horrible and I don't like him?'

'Merrion seemed pretty excited about your brother coming home. I heard her say to my mam that you'd be like a proper family again.'

'She's on cloud nine because her Roddi has come back after all this time,' Dilwyn pointed out. 'That's really what she's so excited about. She can't think of anything else. It's all she and your mam can talk about.' Dilwyn started to cry.

'What are you crying for, then?' Nerys frowned.

'Roddi's going to take Merrion away from me,' she gulped. 'If they get married, she won't have any time for me and I haven't got a mam like you have. Merrion's the only person who cares about me.'

Brenda was astounded by the news. She was pleased for Merrion's sake that Roddi had finally put in an appearance and she was intrigued by the story of how he had managed to accidentally find her after so many years.

'Duw anwyl, Merrion, I thought all that talk about this Roddi was your way of fending off unwanted attention from our customers, my lovely,' she pronounced. 'Does that mean you will be getting married and giving up your job, then?' she probed.

'It's much too early to decide anything like that, Brenda. We had less than an hour together, no time at all to talk about the future. Roddi had to dash off to get back on board his ship because it was sailing on the evening tide.'

'So where's he gone to this time, then?'

Merrion looked blank. 'He never said.'

'Ah well,' Brenda reasoned, 'you can soon check that out at one of the shipping offices, cariad. What's the name of the ship he's on?'

Again Merrion shook her head. 'Do you know, I don't know that either, only that it will be a long trip.'

Brenda pursed her lips and frowned. 'We could try and find out what boats left on last night's tide. Do you think that might help?'

Merrion shrugged uncertainly. 'Thanks, Brenda, but I think I prefer to wait until he comes back. He's promised to let my brother know that he's found us and is going to tell him to come and see us,' she added brightly.

'Your brother?'

'Yes, Emlyn, he's older than me. It's over eight years since I last saw him and he went off to sea,' Merrion explained. 'Roddi as well as all my family left Cwmglo at the same time, see. Roddi and Emlyn left right away, before the rest of us had found the rooms in Sophia Terrace, so neither of them knew where to find us when they came ashore again.'

'Duw anwyl!' Brenda's eyes widened in astonishment.

'Roddi said that they've both searched high and low for us every time they've been in port. We might never have found each other again if it hadn't been for Roddi going to Rhonda's help when she was attacked.'

'Daro! It's like something you read about, a dream come true and no mistake,' Brenda murmured shaking her head as if she found it difficult to take it all in.

After a while they stopped talking about it, although occasionally Dilwyn asked Merrion if she had any idea when Roddi would be coming back and whether or not he'd be bringing their brother Emlyn with him.

As the months passed Merrion began to think that perhaps it had all been a dream and that being reunited with Roddi had been a figment of her imagination. Whenever she had such doubts she reminded herself that Rhonda had been there to witness what happened.

It was a bleak Sunday in November when the dream that Merrion had held on to for so long finally turned into solid reality. They had just finished their midday meal and were sitting by the fire playing Snap when they heard heavy footsteps on the stairs.

When there was a knock on the door, they all looked at each other questioningly. They knew it wasn't Evan, because he simply called out and then opened the door and came in, and they didn't usually have any other visitors.

Rhonda went over and cautiously opened the door, wondering who it could be that Evan had let come up to see them.

'Who are you?' she demanded warily, staring at the stocky dark haired man who stood there.

Before he could answer someone standing behind him, whom she couldn't properly see on the dimly lit staircase, said, 'Hello, Rhonda, how are you? Is Merri in?'

As they stepped into the room, Merrion rushed forward then hesitated, not knowing which one to embrace first.

'Emlyn?' For a brief moment she stared at the solid young man uncertainly, then with a sob she flung her arms around him, hugging him close. 'Oh Emlyn, I never thought I'd see you again.'

'I've brought him back as I promised to do,' Roddi said as she released Emlyn and then threw her arms around his neck, kissing him warmly.

'Come on in, come in,' she urged. 'Emlyn, this is my friend Rhonda, and this is her little girl Nerys, and this,' she drew Dilwyn forward, 'this is your little sister who was only just born when you last saw her.'

They talked for hours; there were so many memories to be revived, so much news to be exchanged. Delighted though he was to be reunited with Merrion and Dilwyn, Emlyn was deeply saddened that his mother and little Madoc had met such a tragic end.

Twice during the long, exciting evening Rhonda made fresh pots of tea. The girls were falling asleep, but they refused to go to bed. They listened entranced as Roddi told them about all that had happened to him during the years he had been away at sea, and then Emlyn capped it with his own experiences.

It was well after eleven o'clock when Roddi said they must leave.

'I wish we could ask you both to stay here, but . . .'

'Don't worry about it, Merrion. I knew we wouldn't be able to do that so we took the precaution of booking beds at the Seamen's Mission before we came to see you. It's only a few steps away from here, but they shut their doors at midnight and we don't want to be locked out.'

'You'll both come back to see us again tomorrow, though?' Rhonda asked.

'Of course we will, and what's more we'll be here as early as you like,' Roddi promised.

'Why don't you come and have breakfast with us before the girls go to school?' Merrion invited.

The girls were very much in favour of this idea and tried hard to persuade Merrion and Rhonda to let them stay home from school, but Merrion and Rhonda were in unison declaring that was completely out of the question.

'Can Roddi and Emlyn walk us to school and come and collect us, then?' they chorused.

When a little later in the morning Rhonda said she had to go to the Hayes to deliver some hats, Emlyn suggested that he went with her so that Roddi could have a few hours alone with Merrion.

'We can pick up the girls from school on our way home,' Rhonda suggested.

'That's hours away, what on earth are you going to do until then?' Merrion frowned.

'Rhonda is going to take me around Cardiff and show me all the sights.' Emlyn grinned.

Roddi and Emlyn both had ten days ashore. By the end of that time Merrion felt as if she had never been separated from Roddi. They made countless plans for their future together and Merrion could hardly wait for them to be able to go ahead with them.

'I'll come to see you again early in the new year at the end of my next trip,' Emlyn told her. 'I doubt if it will coincide with Roddi's shore leave, though. My trips are much shorter than the ones he does. He's sometimes away for over a year at a time.'

'It will be lovely to see you again, but you don't have to come and visit us every trip, you know, not unless you really want to do so,' Merrion assured him. 'Now that I've seen you

394

again and I know that you are fit and well, I don't expect you to change your life, or desert your friends, simply to come and see me.'

'Don't worry about that, I'm definitely coming to see you all the next time I'm in port,' he told her with a twinkle in his dark eyes as he hugged and kissed them all goodbye.

Chapter Thirty-Eight

Emlyn's visits became a regular feature of their lives. He returned to Cardiff every ten weeks as regular as clockwork and always on a Friday. The moment his ship docked and he was no longer on duty he came to see them.

Dilwyn and Nerys marked off the days between his visits on a sheet of paper. On the Friday when he was due in port they hurried home from school and watched from the window until they saw him coming up Bute Road from the Pier Head, his kit bag over his shoulder, and then they'd rush down into the street to be the first to greet him.

In fact, Dilwyn and Nerys monopolised him. They planned in advance what they should do, where they would go. They even decided which pictures they wanted to go and see.

Emlyn always seemed to fall in with these arrangements quite happily, whether it was going to the park, taking them into town or to the cinema. 'It's a shame you can't come with us, you always seem to be working at that damn old pub,' he said consolingly as he and Rhonda and the girls set out on Friday evenings and again on Saturdays to enjoy themselves.

Merrion felt the same, but she said nothing. She knew she couldn't constantly be asking Brenda to let her have time off, especially when Saturdays was so busy, both at midday and in the evenings.

She consoled herself that at least the two girls were being taken out and were enjoying themselves. Rhonda always went along as well so that there was someone to help Emlyn look after them and Merrion felt rather guilty about this.

'It's good of you to give up so much of your time like this,' she told Rhonda gratefully as she combed Dilwyn's hair and helped to get her ready to go out with them. 'Are you sure you don't mind?'

'Don't worry, cariad, I enjoy the outings as much as they do,' Rhonda told her as she helped Nerys into her coat.

'If you are ever too busy to go along with them, then I'm sure Emlyn could manage to take them on his own,' Merrion persisted. 'They're used to him now and they all get on so well together that I'm sure they'd both behave themselves.'

'No, I wouldn't dream of it,' Rhonda assured her. 'In fact,' she added with a broad smile, 'I quite look forward to getting dressed up and going places with him.'

'I know what you mean,' Merrion sighed wistfully. 'I only wish Roddi did short trips like Emlyn does.'

'When Roddi does come home, though, he

will have three weeks' shore leave, not a couple of days,' Rhonda reminded her.

Merrion still worried that Emlyn was spending too much time with them. He must have friends he used to visit when he was ashore in the past yet he never seemed to go and see anyone else at all.

She knew it must be a novelty for him to have a family of his own to come and see, but she couldn't help noticing his deepening friend-ship with Rhonda and she began to wonder if that was the attraction.

As tactfully as possible she mentioned this to the girls one Sunday evening as they stood by the window waving him off. They looked at each other and began giggling.

'What is so funny?' she asked.

Still giggling and nudging each other they said that they didn't know why Emlyn came to see them so often but that they thought Rhonda could tell her. At almost the same moment she heard Rhonda's footsteps on the stairs and knew that she must have gone down to see Emlyn off at the door.

Rhonda's face as she came back into the room told its own story. Her eyes were dreamy, her lipstick smudged and her hair mussed up.

Merrion bit back the teasing words she had been on the point of saying about Rhonda flirting with Emlyn because she liked to have a man dancing attendance on her and taking her out and about. It was quite obvious that Rhonda and Emlyn were a lot more than merely good friends.

What worried Merrion was that Rhonda had been serious about Dai Francis, even to the point of planning to marry him. Afterwards, though, in next to no time, she had shown an interest in Evan and even in Roddi. She hoped that she wasn't taking a shine to Emlyn merely on the rebound because she certainly didn't want to see her brother hurt.

In the weeks until Emlyn's next visit, Merrion thought about the relationship between him and Rhonda from every angle. All the signs were there that Rhonda was serious about him, she told herself. The way Rhonda dressed up on the Friday when Emlyn was due back. The care she took with her appearance when they went out on the Friday and Saturday. Even the extra shopping she did, and the meals she prepared when Emlyn visited, all pointed to one thing, that Rhonda was definitely going out of her way to please him and to make an impression.

'What's so surprising about it?' Rhonda asked, smiling, when Merrion eventually questioned her about it.

'Well, I realised that the two of you got on very well. I also knew that you were seeing quite a lot of each other because you were both taking the girls out whenever Emlyn was here, but . . .'

'There are no "buts". We've fallen for each other and we both know it is serious and means everything to both of us,' Rhonda told her.

Merrion still didn't feel convinced. She wanted to hear it from Emlyn's own lips and she wanted it to be without any prompting from Rhonda.

The next time Emlyn came into port, and they all returned after their Friday evening out, Merrion waited until Dilwyn and Nerys were in bed and then, as she, Emlyn and Rhonda enjoyed a cup of cocoa, she made a point of telling him that she didn't expect him to spend every moment of his free time with them when he came ashore.

'Of course I want to come and see you now that I've found you,' he assured her forcibly. 'I enjoy taking my little sister out, what's so strange about that?'

'You mean you are doing it for Dilwyn's sake, to make up to her for all the years you've been apart?' Merrion questioned.

'Not altogether.' He grinned uncomfortably. 'Can't you guess the other reason?'

'Are you doing it because you want to see Rhonda?' Merrion asked bluntly.

'I thought you would have guessed long before now,' he said as he drained his cup and put it down on the table.

'You mean you never noticed until now that it was love at first sight between us?' Rhonda smiled as she reached out and took Emlyn's hand.

'Well, of course I realised that the two of you got on very well together,' Merrion admitted.

'We've fallen for each other,' Emlyn confirmed. Pushing back his chair he got up and put an arm around Rhonda's shoulders. 'I've never met anyone like her in my life before,' he added, his eyes lighting up as she smiled up at him.

'I'm delighted.' Merrion smiled. She stood up and went over and kissed Rhonda and then Emlyn on the cheek. Going to a cupboard she brought out a half-bottle of port and reached for some glasses.

'This calls for a toast to the future,' she said as she poured out the drinks. 'What does Nerys have to say about it?' she asked as she passed a glass to each of them.

Rhonda frowned. 'Well, we haven't told her yet, but she is very fond of Emlyn so I'm sure she'll be tickled pink to have him as a stepfather.'

'Stepfather!'

'Well, that's what he'll be when we get married, which is what we are planning to do the next time Emlyn has a long shore leave.'

Merrion shook her head in wonderment. 'Are you both sure about this?'

'Of course we are!'

'You've only known each other a few months – a few weeks, in fact, if you count up

401

the amount of time Emlyn has actually been ashore!'

'How long does it have to take?' Emlyn demanded. 'Do you want us to hang about and waste ten years of our life the same as you and Roddi have done?'

'Hold on, that's not fair,' Merrion said sharply. 'I haven't said anything yet, but we're hoping to get married next time Roddi comes on leave.'

'So when is that?' Emlyn demanded.

'In three or four months' time, I hope. I was going to tell you both as soon as we were sure of the date because we'll have to make arrangements about moving. I'm dreading having to tell Evan after all he's done for us, but there won't be room for all of us here.'

'There's no need for you to do anything about that, Merrion. If you want to stay on here, Rhonda will move out,' Emlyn said quickly. 'We've got our eye on a nice little shop with living space up over it in Salisbury Road. Now we know your plans we'll go ahead and Rhonda and Nerys can move in there almost right away.'

'Rhonda is going to open another hat shop?' Merrion asked in surprise. 'She hasn't mentioned anything to either Evan or me.'

'Yes, she certainly is, and this time it will all be in her own name, so there will be no one ruining it all for her.'

'Does that mean that you are going to stay in the Merchant Navy?'

'For the present. As long as it is only short trips like I'm doing now. Is Roddi going to stay at sea after you two get married?'

'Possibly not.' She bit her lip, not wanting to say any more at the moment. Like her, Roddi had dreams. He was tired of travelling the world; he wanted to settle in one place. His ambition was to run a pub in a small town where everyone knew everyone else. He wanted it to be the centre of a close-knit community. They had talked about it at length, and written to each other in such detail that Merrion could almost believe it was possible.

The only problem had been their reluctance to leave Rhonda and Nerys on their own. They'd even toyed with the idea of asking Rhonda to join them in the venture, although Roddi was rather reluctant about this as he wanted it to be just the two of them . . . and Dilwyn.

They had both agreed that Dilwyn would have a home with them for as long as she needed one, but they also dreamed of one day having a family of their own.

Now, or so it seemed, all their dreams were about to come true. First, there would be their weddings and then, after those, one by one, the rest of their dreams would be realised.

'I can hardly believe what you've just told me.' Merrion smiled as she looked from Emlyn to Rhonda and then back again. Emlyn had solved one of her major problems when he'd told her that Rhonda was planning to move, because that had been the main obstacle to the plans she and Roddi had. 'Tell me I'm not dreaming again!'

'No, you're not, so let's drink to all our dreams coming true,' Emlyn declared as he raised his glass.